P9-DBJ-829

Crossroads

CROSSROADS

Mary Morris

HOUGHTON MIFFLIN COMPANY
BOSTON
1983

Library of Congress Cataloging in Publication Data

Morris, Mary, date
  Crossroads.

  I. Title.
PS3563.O87445C7   1983   813'.54   82-15468
ISBN 0–395–33104–8

Printed in the United States of America

V 10 9 8 7 6 5 4 3 2 1

I would like to thank the National Endowment for the Arts, the Creative Artists Public Service Program (CAPS), the American Academy and Institute of Arts and Letters, the American Academy in Rome, and the John Simon Guggenheim Memorial Foundation for their generous support in the completion of this project.

I would also like to thank Sharon Dunn, Alice Fahs, and Ellen Posner for all their support and assistance.

for Johnny Morris,
Carol Wise, and Ro

In the middle of the journey of our life
I came to myself in a dark wood
where the straight way was lost.
          — DANTE, *The Inferno*, Canto 1

Crossroads

1

I NEVER FELL IN LOVE in my father's office, though I
wanted to and tried. I wanted to fall in love with one of the
boys in jersey shirts and polyester pants who worked out their
days designing parking lots and drove home on the freeway to
a ranchhouse in Chicago's northern suburbs. Instead I fell in
love in all the wrong places, in museums with bearded intellec-
tuals who'd share a painting with me, in buses and subways
with men who never got off at my stop, in the back seat of cars
with teen-age boys, on Caribbean islands with bored execu-
tives, in unreal and exotic places with men who'd flash briefly
through my life — but never in my father's office, where I
thought I belonged.

My father had begun an engineering firm on the south side
of Chicago after the war. He wanted to specialize in building
suspension bridges. His dream was to bridge the gap across the
Bering Strait and drive home to Russia in search of his ances-
tral past. It was a structural impossibility; the towers would
have to reach the ozone layer to support a fifty-six-mile suspension. The only bridge my father ever built was one made

of rope across a brook in a neighbor's yard. He eventually added five architects to his firm and settled for housing developments.

It was in his office that I decided to become a planner of cities. In the summers I used to run his switchboard, a chore that left me harried and confused. All those little lights to all those extensions reaching into the depths of the drafting room, making demands I'd never understand. When the phones weren't ringing in my father's office, I built cities I thought I might like to live in sometime. I made them out of discarded models and plans and drew them with colored pencils. At night I had city dreams. Huge, smoggy, gray buildings, a zillion people dashing around in an urban nightmare with big orange cranes set against the sky.

My father's office was a place of reason. It was not a place for irrational mood swings. I believed you could order people's lives. I thought if you gave them well-lit streets, nice houses, you'd make them happy. After my husband left me, I saw you couldn't.

Like many of my friends, I'd been sent east to college, for it is believed by Midwesterners with some sophistication that a serious education cannot be had west of Philadelphia. It was in the East, in graduate school, that I met and fell in love with a law student, Mark Lusterman, in a library and married him a few years later.

Mark and I married when we did in part because we thought it would keep him out of Vietnam. We'd planned to marry sooner or later anyway. Mark still got called up for his physical. His family doctor remembered Mark had fainted once after seeing a train wreck when he was three years old. The doctor wrote a letter saying Mark fainted under stress. When the sergeant yelled out, "All right, all you little fakers, let's see those phony notes from the doctor," and sixty boys in their Jockey shorts at a draft board in Brooklyn held up sixty letters, Mark fainted.

He didn't go to Vietnam and we were married for seven years. I thought I'd done the right thing by marrying Mark, but in time it was wrong. I knew it was wrong before he left me in February, the bleariest part of the month, and my only regret was that I hadn't left him first. Mark left me, classically, for another woman, named Lila Harris. A woman from my home town whom I'd once helped conjugate French verbs, never suspecting that a dozen years later and twelve hundred miles away from Chicago, she'd seduce my husband in the South Bronx. If my life with Mark was one of a simple, changeless passion, my life after he left me became equally simple — a rather straightforward and primitive desire for revenge.

After we married and moved to New York City, I took a job with the New York Center for Urban Advancement as their chief proposal writer and as a planner of special projects. I was their expert in roads. I could glance at a map of Manhattan and tell you where to put a stop sign. In college I studied journalism and urban studies. I wanted to go to wild, dangerous places and interview the people who lived in those places. I wound up in the slums of New York. Mark worked for Legal Action in the South Bronx, and sometimes when I had a project uptown we'd meet for lunch at a little Chinese-Cuban restaurant across from the district courthouse.

I was working in the South Bronx one Friday and thought I'd give Mark a call to see if he wanted to have lunch. He said sure but he was lunching with a colleague who was working on a big rape case with him. When I walked into the restaurant, the colleague jumped up and rushed to me, open-armed. "I don't believe it," Lila said. "I just don't believe it."

"Small world," I said. She looked great. Slim and healthy. Her misty gray eyes, her chestnut hair, always appealed to me. She'd become a vegetarian and did yoga every day after work. She'd never learned French. Instead Lila had done Berkeley's joint program in social work and law. When I went east, she went west. I'd always admired her spirit of adventure. Lila was working in prison reform, and her office was not far from the main office of the New York Center for Urban Advancement near the Battery.

"You mean you guys know one another?" Mark said. He looked half-pleased, half-perplexed.

We sat down. "We grew up together," I explained. Lila had been one of the Indian Tree crowd. She married a great guy named Robert in California — a businessman who could do imitations of all the Disney characters and who went to the hospitals to entertain the kids. He adored kids and he worshiped Lila.

I'm not sure when they started sleeping together. I'm sure it was already on their minds as we ate lunch but I don't think anything had happened. I like to think it was after Lila and I spent a day in the courthouse. She invited me to observe the rape case proceedings. She sat close beside me as we watched the trial. A tall, bony, young black woman had been raped by this huge dark man, and I could feel Lila tense up beside me when the young woman started to cry, recounting the details of the crime.

We confided in one another that day. Lila said she was getting bored with Robert. They'd been together so long. He was content doing financial consulting for major department stores while she feared she was getting ulcers from helping the disadvantaged. I told her how my marriage was in good shape, all things considered. I like to think they didn't begin sleeping together until she and Mark started working on the Savage Skulls case.

It was after the Savage Skulls began that Mark said he needed more space. I took him literally and started looking for a bigger apartment.

What he needed was breathing space, he told me one Sunday morning as I scanned the real estate ads. The concept was new to me. Time, I understood. When he needed time, there wasn't any quarrel. Often we didn't have time for one another, but I hadn't heard of space. "I just feel crowded, that's all." He sat in our large reading chair, newspaper open wide on his lap. He was still beautiful to me as the day I'd met him. His reddish hair remained full at the hairline; the gray-green eyes were still inexplicably sad.

I tried to remember how his youth had been squandered in dull, lifeless rooms in Brooklyn, how he hated demands because his mother had always demanded, never asked. Mrs. Lusterman, whom I could never bring myself to call Mom, was a golden, narrow woman with thick yellow hair who always wore tight yellow dresses and looked like a banana — of Polish Catholic descent. Her earlier traumas during the war were hidden, except in the constant motion of her hands. She seemed happiest beating eggs. His father was a distracted attorney, bored with it all. I only remember him saying hello and good-bye to me in all the years I knew him. Mark could also be spare with words.

"What do you want me to do?" I asked. He shook his head wearily, exasperated, and told me. "Don't cling to my every word. Don't wait for me to come home. Don't stay up until I go to sleep. Don't make plans for us until you ask me what my plans are."

I began doing exactly what he'd told me not to do. I hung on his every word. I looked for hidden meanings behind each action. I made breakfast dates for us at ungodly hours. I waited up. If he was late, I panicked. I couldn't bear the waiting. And I waited and waited.

I never used to care if he was a little late as long as he let me know. Suddenly I started to care enormously. One November night, just a few months before he left me, he called to say he wouldn't get home until around ten. "Can you bring me some moo shu pork from that place next door to the courthouse?" I asked him. They had the best moo shu pork in town.

"Sure, no problem."

He got home just before midnight with Chinese food from a

restaurant around the corner from our apartment in the West Sixties. "I didn't want it to get cold on the ride home," he explained.

Actually he'd been with Lila all evening and couldn't have bought the Chinese food at the place near the courthouse. I found out accidentally when Lila made a slip. Over lunch the following week she mentioned to me that Robert had been in Detroit for a while on business and that she and Mark had gotten a lot of work done the previous week when they worked at her apartment. "Which night was that?" I asked.

"Tuesday, I think." She paused. "Maybe Monday."

"Monday or Tuesday?"

"Tuesday." I could see her eyes dart as she tried to figure out if she'd made a mistake. She was pretty sure she'd made a mistake but she didn't know what it was. Mark had forgotten to give her his alibi for Tuesday night.

"So what's the story?" I said to him that evening. "Were you at the office or at Lila's?"

He paled as I'd seen him pale only once before, years ago in Cambridge when we were dating and he wanted to break up.

I begged him, "Tell me the truth but please don't leave me."

Mark threw up his arms. "It's impossible to talk to you about anything," he said. "All you do is imagine the worst. I didn't tell you I was working at Lila's Tuesday night because I knew you'd make a scene."

"I'm married to you," I said. "We've been together a long time. Tell me what's happening."

It was Robert who told me. He called me in the early evening, when he got back from Detroit, and sobbed into the phone. It took me a few moments to understand what he was saying, because the connection was bad and he was calling from somewhere on the street. At first I thought there'd been an accident. I heard words like "dead" and "hurt." Then I slowly pieced it together. Lila had left Robert. She told him she'd been in love with Mark for quite some time. "What am I going to do?" he sobbed to me. His life, his job, they meant nothing to him without her.

Mark was handling arraignments that night and he'd be at the courthouse most of the night. And I knew, as well as I knew anything, that he'd spend the rest of the night with Lila. I called the courthouse and had him paged. He arrived out of breath, and when he heard my voice, I could tell he was disappointed it wasn't Lila phoning. "What do you want?" he said, unable to conceal his annoyance. I told him what Robert had said. I wasn't going to fall apart like Robert. I wasn't going to cry or lose control. I just wanted him to tell me the truth calmly. "Just tell me," I said, "what is going on."

"Look, this has to wait."

"It can't wait. I'll come down there."

"O.K., I'll find someone to cover for me. Meet me at O'Neal's at ten-thirty."

At midnight I realized he wasn't going to show. I drank a lot of brandy, and everyone at the bar felt sorry for me because they knew I'd been stood up. The bartender gave me a drink on the house. "You look down in the dumps, kid. Waiting for some guy to show?"

I nodded. "My husband. He must have gotten held up in surgery."

"Oh, you married to a doctor?"

"A brain surgeon."

He was impressed. "I could use a little brain surgery myself. Find out what the hell I'm doing in this city." I paid my bill and walked over to Lila's.

She lived on a relatively safe block in the West Seventies, not far from where we lived. I went and stood under the streetlight and I rang and rang. All the lights were on in her apartment. I pounded on the buzzer in sharp staccatos. I was certain they were upstairs, peering down at me.

Nobody answered. Nobody came downstairs. I know the streets of Manhattan well. My specialty is roads. I know the

safe parts and the bad parts. I know the alleyways and the hot
spots. I decided to walk from Lila's in a series of geometric
patterns. I began with the square. I walked west to Broadway, then down ten blocks, across Columbus, then back. I
couldn't make a perfect square. I tried cutting corners to make
a circle, then a diamond, a triangle. Lila had been in my
geometry class sophomore year. The teacher was Miss Gower,
a spinster who only talked shapes. Her life was in two dimen-
sions, flat.

Lila wasn't very good in geometry, but she was worse in
French. In the locker room Lila used to undress not far from me
and we'd laugh about poor Miss Gower. Miss Gower never
laughed. She had nothing to laugh about. Lila had pale thin
legs with lots of hair around the groin. Very dark hair. One day
the hair was gone. She'd waxed the hair around her groin so
she could be in the swim show and nobody would see her pubic
hair. While I tried to find my way home geometrically along
Manhattan streets, I wondered if Lila still waxed her pubic
hair and I wondered if Mark rubbed up against it when he
made love to her.

Mark was home when I walked in, and he was distraught.
He didn't know what to do with his hands, his feet, so he made
nervous movements like his mother, tapping a finger on the
table, bouncing a foot up and down. He didn't know if he
wanted a drink or not. He didn't know why he hadn't met me at
O'Neal's. "But I've been seeing Lila for a while now," he managed to get out. "She reminds me of you in a lot of ways," he
muttered. "She's the way you were before we started having
problems."

"When was that?"

I sat across from him and tried to listen to what he had to
say. In grammar school all the teachers had seemed far away,
perched at the heads of the classes in their suits and dresses,
behind big desks. I'd always had a hard time listening, and
they seemed huge and distant. Now I leaned forward, trying to

hear what Mark had to say and he seemed so like those teachers and I felt so small and as if I could not hear. As if vast rows of students kept me from the wisdom that would enable me to understand airplanes or primitive man. "I've been seeing a lot of her. We're very close," he said softly.

He came and sat down beside me. "It doesn't mean I don't love you. Things are just complicated, that's all, but we'll work it out." He said he loved me as he always had and somehow we'd get back to the way we'd always been.

I can't say his leaving came as a complete surprise. It was his method that stunned and immobilized me for months and left me a zombie, not so much because my heart was broken as because it was betrayed. Mark had assured me he'd stopped seeing Lila and that he'd gone through a terrible period in his life, and if I'd just let him, he'd make it up to me. But then one day the following note was left on the kitchen table: "Dear Deborah" — Mark always used my complete name, as if we were involved in something very serious — "I suppose I should have waited and talked to you in person but somehow I'm a coward and couldn't bear to have you reaching out to me and begging me to stay. I'm sorry. It is, I believe, for the best, as I'm sure you'll agree in time. We'll talk soon, Mark."

Law school had taught him to be brief and to the point. These principles he applied to our marriage and to this final note to me. Though we'd been leaving one another in little ways for years, it came as a shock. He left me for another woman, who'd been my friend. I thought that in marrying Mark, I'd put order in my life, the order of my father's drafting room, the order of people who did things according to schedule and plan, but suddenly I was flung into the far reaches of an earlier chaos.

I held the note in my hand and read it perhaps twenty times. At first the words made no sense, but slowly the letters, the words, took shape in my mind. He was gone. It was that simple. Mark was correct. I would have reached out to him. I would have held him to me, like a desperate monkey in a flood, clinging to its tumbled tree. He had told me he'd stopped seeing her. But as I walked around our apartment, opening doors, drawers, peering into shelves, I saw that everything was half of what it had been and that he'd never stopped seeing her.

The first time Mark and I made love was in his dorm room when I was in graduate school. We'd met the previous afternoon in a library. Love has its arbitrariness, and libraries always made me lonely. He'd been staring at me from across a stack of tomes on contractual law. The next night we made love on his floor, and when we were done, he sat cross-legged, perfectly still, like Buddha. He didn't perspire, not a drop. Then he reached for a bag of chocolate chip cookies, ate one cookie from the bag, closed it. He offered to walk me home, because he had a midterm the next day. I should have known then, years ago, that a man who didn't sweat and could eat one chocolate chip cookie from a bag and close it, could leave a note on the kitchen table to say he was leaving.

For weeks I moved through the apartment like a wounded person. Sometimes I'd pick up the phone and try to call him, but I always hung up after one or two rings. Once, Mark picked up before I had a chance to hang up. I don't know how it happened, but I started to scream. I screamed at him until he hung up, and a few weeks later when I called back in the middle of the night to scream again, I learned from a recorded voice that Lila's number was now unpublished.

My friend and upstairs neighbor, Sally Young, kept encouraging me to go out and meet people. When I brought home the Lebanese doctor with the wild Afro and bulging eyes I met at a party, she joined us for drinks and was polite. But later she told me he looked like Omar Sharif being electrocuted. The trouble was, when I thought about it, Sally was right, and I felt more and more certain I had no judgment when it came to men.

My mother loved Mark as if he were her own, as if he were the brother I should have had, the one who did things right, not like my brother, Zap, who, if there was a wrong way to do something, would always find it. I tried not to fault my mother when, after I'd read her Mark's note over the phone, she said, "What'd you do to make him do such a thing?" What she wanted was more grandchildren, a tribe of grandchildren. The fact that my older sister, Renee, had three children and lived in Downers Grove didn't count. Renee had "fallen by the wayside" years ago, when a pair of her panties was found on a neighbor's rosebush. I was the one they'd pinned all their hopes on, like a tail on the donkey. "Maybe he'll come back," Mom said. "Maybe if you just give him time, he'll come back." I didn't bother making her see why I wouldn't want him to.

What I did want was to get back at Mark and Lila. It was that desire, that rage, that enabled me to get out of bed in the morning, wash my face, ride the subway to work. It was the knowledge that I'd find the way to hurt them that let me sit through meetings or work at the drawing board all day. I didn't know what form it would take or how I'd bring it off. I only knew I'd find a way to hurt them as they'd hurt me.

2

THREE MONTHS after Mark left, the City Council of New York decided it wasn't going to meet until the fall to vote on approval for the South Bronx Area Development Project, affectionately referred to in our office as "SAP," because it had entailed years of work and would never get built. That is, the City Council had planned it so that it wouldn't get built. I was in charge of the project and was still a builder of imaginary cities, the way I'd been years ago when I worked as the receptionist and switchboard operator in my father's office.

One night shortly after the City Council's vote, I was working late, and my boss, Mr. Wicker, walked into my office and surprised me. It was a warm night and I had taken to working later than the architects. It was almost eight o'clock when Bill Wicker knocked on the wooden molding of my open door. "Anybody home?"

I jumped slightly. My mind wasn't on work. "Oh, I wanted to finish up as much of this as I can."

He smiled. "Mind if I come in?" He walked in without waiting for an answer.

I pulled over a chair for him. "You're never here at this hour," I said.

"Well, you shouldn't be, either. You know, you aren't getting overtime from me. Besides, no one's going to vote on renovation for a few months now anyway. You can take it easy."

"I can still finish the report, though, can't I?"

He waved his hand as if fanning himself. "Oh, sure. Say, would you like to have a drink with me?" Bill Wicker was a civilized, elderly gentleman with daughters my age. Raising all those daughters, he told me once, had taught him patience and understanding. He commuted every day from Westport and never so much as yawned or had a silver hair out of place.

I cleared my throat. "I think I'd like to work. Is that all right?"

He nodded. "No problem. Just thought we could have a little talk. We can talk here, though, can't we?" He raised his legs, plunked them down hard on my desk, and crossed them. Mr. Wicker ran his hand through his straight hair, then flattened each hair back into place. "I want you to think about taking the summer off." He sucked in his cheeks. "With pay, of course."

"I don't want any time off."

He nodded. "I'm pretty sure you don't, but why don't you take it anyway?"

"Is something wrong with my work?"

He shook his head and looked stunned, as if I'd just said his fly was unzipped. "Cindy told me. And Frank. Well, they said you were down in the dumps over your marriage. You know, you can write that damn proposal anywhere. No need to sit in an office."

It's not easy to explain to someone who is offering you three months' vacation with pay to prepare a report for the City Council at your leisure that you don't want time off.

"Thanks," I said, "but I'd rather just stay here."

"Take it," he said firmly. Then added, a bit more gently, "How can you not want the summer free?"

How can you make someone see that what you want is to get up on schedule, ride and sweat on the subway in heat waves, sit under those fluorescent lights that make you sterile, instead of being on a beach, having fun? I didn't want fun. I wanted the grind. The routine. What's more awful to someone who has something to forget than free time?

Mr. Wicker ruffled my hair, then smoothed it down flat as he got up to leave. "Go to Europe. See the world."

After he left, I sat alone, staring down at New York Harbor, at a lone tug that passed in front of the Statue of Liberty. I thought how strange and foreign the East Coast of America seemed to me, and for the first time in years, I thought seriously about moving home. The East, I'd learned, was not the Midwest. The East never let me forget my humble roots, and I've never regretted those roots for a minute. In the end it has been the simple Midwestern clarity that has permitted me to understand some of what has occurred.

The New York Center for Urban Advancement, where I went to work every day, was located near the Battery. The building that housed it was one of a hundred buildings just like it and the corridor I walked down was the same as all the other corridors. And the offices themselves were sterile and undistinguished, not at all like my father's office. My father's office was located on the north side of Madison Street, just below the elevated tracks. The "El" churned by, snaking around Chicago's Loop and dropping grime like bird dung on pedestrians, through a nasty part of the city that looked like the old Chicago of the twenties.

The Chicago Bears had their office in the same building as my father. Often I found myself squashed between sprawling, athletic shoulders and fractured noses. Gangland slayings felt like real possibilities in front of the building where we worked.

The Bears were sometimes accompanied by even bigger men, mobsters, my father said. Real thumb-crushers and leg-breakers. Sometimes I had to ride the elevator to our floor when it was loaded down with Chicago Bears, and the elevator trembled under their weight.

But I used to love to play in the drafting room when I was a child. I loved the pencils, the pungent smell of the blueprint machine, the supply closet, all of which represented to me the rational adult world.

There were also pinups thumbtacked to the bulletin board, usually in the form of calendars. They seemed out of place among the tidy desks and carefully drawn plans. As I grew older and the months and years slipped by, the girls in the pictures changed with the times. They grew thinner, their poses less ludicrous, their faces more youthful, as if they attended junior college, until one day a Sierra Club calendar of redwoods appeared and a real woman, myself, Deborah Mills, was working on urban development projects in the drafting room.

Though I never fell in love in my father's office, Zap did one summer when I ran the switchboard — though I'm not really sure he fell in love so much as sealed his fate. He'd really been in love with Jennie Watson for years, and he was like one of those toys you punch and it keeps coming back. I walked into the drafting room one August evening and in the dim twilight saw my brother, clutching at the breasts of my oldest friend. I saw Jennie's spine arched over a drafting table. I saw Zap's hands slide up and down her ribs, and heard him rasp in a deep voice, "Please, please." I knew what it was then to desire someone desperately and to lose all sense of pride.

That evening I sat in my apartment, staring at the South Bronx project, which was sprawled on the desk along with a small pile of Mark's unpaid bills that had arrived that day in the mail. I stared at the Bronx battleground where Mark and I had spent Saturdays, envisioning little park benches where there was rubble. The bills were mostly for clothes. Some shirts he'd bought somewhere, shirts I'd never seen. I was trying to figure out if I should pay them or mail him the bills. Or walk over and hand-deliver.

In the end it's details that defeat us. The bills, not my doomed-to-fail urban planner's vision for the Bronx, were what I couldn't handle. It was the same when Mark left. I didn't cry when I found he was gone. I cried four days later, when I found a wet puppy shivering in the rain. I took the dog by its clutch collar and led it to the address on its tag. I rang the bell, and a tall, heavyset woman in black toreador pants stormed down the stairs, shouting at me. "What're you doing? Why did you ring that bell?" When she saw my face distort and saw her shivering hound, she began apologizing and even ran after me a little way as I dashed down the street. In the end, it was the dog and his screaming mistress who made me feel lost and destitute in the world, more than Mark and the note he'd left on the kitchen table.

The phone rang as I sat, immobilized by Mark's unpaid bills.

"Guess who this is?" a woman's voice said.

"It's Jennie." We'd lost track of one another over the years, after she married Tom, but I'd have known her voice anywhere. A few days before, Jennie Watson had received the directory from our high school reunion committee. My address listing was an old one, the first apartment Mark and I had shared in Manhattan, the one next door to the funeral home, where we'd had to push past mourners in order to get inside. Doom, it seemed, surrounded us. Our phone number had changed twice, but my parents' number was still good, and parents seem to be a kind of constant in the lives of overly transient offspring.

She was crestfallen. It was almost ten years since we'd

talked. "How'd you know it was me? Did your mother tell you?"

"We only spent half our lives together on the phone, remember?"

"Oh, God, do I remember. So, how are you?" I told her that my husband had just left me and I thought I was losing my job, but otherwise I was fine.

"Oh, that sounds great," she said. She was living on a farm in Thrace, New Jersey. I said I didn't know New Jersey had anything but chemical dumps. She reminded me it was the Garden State and that there were vast farmlands. "We got this one cheap." I was surprised she said "we." No one had imagined she and Tom would stay together, but now they had two children. All her sentences had "we" in them. They'd come east long after I had. Tom studied computer science at Columbia while Jennie went to Teachers College for her master's in biology. They'd planned to return to the Midwest after graduate school, but Tom was offered a well-paying job at Bell Labs and Jennie got a job teaching at Princeton Day.

With the insurance money from his father's death, Tom made a down payment on a hundred acres of farmland as an investment. "But now he's addicted. A real farmer. He works four days a week as a farmer. You know Tom." She laughed. "He always was a workaholic." I did know Tom and I didn't recall him ever working very hard. "What about you?" she asked.

"Are you ready for this?" She said she was ready, but when I told her Mark was living with Lila Harris, she was aghast. I told her I wasn't sure what I minded more. That they were together or that they had never had the nerve to come and just tell me. The conversation turned somber, so I decided to lighten the mood. "My boss has been planning exotic vacations for me. Yesterday he told me to go to Ireland. He thinks I'm Irish."

She paused for a second. "So you can visit us for a few days," she said. "We've got plenty of room. The kids are with my mother for the summer." She said it in such a way I understood that that was what I'd do.

3

A FAKE-WOOD-PANELED station wagon, with a drooling black dog, its head thrust out the window in the back, pulled up, and Jennie waved. I dropped the candy bar wrapper and peach pit from the food I'd brought with me into a trash can. They were ten minutes late and the bus had been a little early. I'd eaten the candy bar while I waited, then the peach. Waiting made me nervous.

Jennie, rushing toward me, still looked like a fox — that reddish-brown hair, the thin, pointed face, her long nose. She was still five-three and one hundred five pounds, and I felt huge beside her, as if my large bones could crush her frail bones. The opposite of course was true. She was one of the strongest women I'd ever met, and some boys couldn't beat her at arm wrestling. She shook my hand with the firmness of a man's shake. "So how was the trip?"

"It was good." It was bad. A nuclear disarmament demonstration en route to the United Nations had almost made me miss the bus. Someone who looked like Zap waved a "No Nukes" banner at me and would not let the cab drive on to the

Port Authority. Where had my brother been all these months when I needed him? The bus was hot and I had to sit near the motor. A Mormon woman sat beside me and showed me pictures of her eight children. I tried to envision this woman in a red leisure suit in bed. Then she interrogated me. "You married? Kids?"

Tom laughed as he swept me into his arms. My feet dangled in the air and I clutched his shoulder. He'd put on a little weight and lost some hair around the crown, but mostly he looked the same. He wore a blue T-shirt that said "I've Got Charisma," and held on to me a little longer than he should have. "You've changed," he said, scooping up my suitcase and heading toward the station wagon.

"Hey, what's that supposed to mean?" I rushed after him, but Jennie caught me by the arm.

"You know he says stupid things."

"I know, but you forget." I'd forgotten a lot, it seemed. I'd forgotten how Jennie was always a little formal when we hadn't seen one another for a while. I'd forgotten she was always a little late with some dumb excuse and that Tom said things without thinking. It had been almost ten years.

"Sorry we were late. Aretha Franklin got out at the last minute. That's the dog. We keep saying we're going to send her to obedience school." Jennie slipped her arm comfortably now through mine. Tom went on ahead. "God, it's good to see you."

"You look the same," I said to her. The first time I saw Jennie she was walking a raccoon on a leash down our street and she handed me the leash. "You walk him," she said. "He likes strangers." The raccoon's name was Calcoon; she'd found him sleeping in a garbage can. He'd taken to her immediately and later she told me Calcoon was the first thing she ever loved. I was the second. My brother was the third.

Our friendship, mine and Jennie's, was based on proximity. We walked the same route to school four times a day for years. Later, it would be based on conspiracy. She was my best friend long before Zap made the mistake of falling in love with her.

We both watched Tom as he walked ahead to put my things in the car. Everyone had been surprised when she married him and some had suspected she had to get married, but that wasn't so. There had been something large and rather stupid about Tom's body when we were teen-agers. Even though he had the first perfect back I ever saw, I felt certain he'd grow flabby with age. The jowly cheeks and soft paunch of a shoe salesman. But instead I could see, as he threw my bags into the back of the wagon, how the opposite had occurred. He'd turned solid, almost to the point of stiffening, and reminded me of a cousin of mine who had a rare disease that was turning her bones into stone.

"The farm's beautiful now, in June," Jennie said, leading me over to the car. "Except that Aretha Franklin's in heat. That's why we had to bring her with us in the first place. She's Cory's dog. We have no idea why he named her that. He was only five at the time. Cory and Melissa are with Mom for the summer. She likes them to come for a stretch since Dad died."

"He died?" Jennie's father was a man who always smiled, like Jimmy Carter. It drove everyone crazy. I wonder if he was buried smiling.

"Two years ago. I thought you knew. It was a blessing . . ."

I offered to sit in back but they wouldn't hear of it because the dog sat there, so we all squeezed into the front seat of the station wagon. I sat in the middle, between Tom in the driver's seat and Jennie by the window, my legs pressed against the stick shift. The seat of the car was old vinyl and torn in parts, so that a billowy cotton puffed out of the innards and I felt the springs below me. Jennie made some feeble apology about the old station wagon, saying how the Chevy wouldn't start. "Excuse me," Tom said as he reached down to put the car in gear and grabbed my knee. I pressed against Jennie.

Tom shifted gears again and this time struck against my leg. "Excuse me," I said, leaning farther away from him. I pushed against Jennie, who had her nose to the glass like the dog in the back, and I put my hand on her knee. She took my fingers and gave them a squeeze. "I just can't believe you're here."

"Me either." I moved away from Tom.

"How long can you stay?" he asked.

"Oh, I don't know . . . a week."

"As long as she likes," Jennie cut in.

"You can stay as long as you like." Tom said it in such a way I knew he couldn't mean it. He pushed his foot on the pedal.

"Slow down," Jennie said, her mouth wrinkled into a pout.

A few moments later Tom shouted "We're home!" as we turned down a driveway and all I could see were fields. I wasn't prepared for the fact that they owned all of this. In the distance I saw the barn, the house, the coops.

"Enough room for you?" Jennie said, as we got out of the car and walked across the lawn. The sprinklers were going and it made me think of a game we used to play. All the lawns had sprinklers when we were growing up. Some turned in many directions like dancers, and some had a lot of legs of water reaching out like spiders. There were the sprinklers that jerked around the way the spastic boy in school jerked around. Some went in smooth circles and some rose and fell. Some rose high like clocks and others exploded like fireworks. Some were hidden deep inside the ground and we could only see the water shooting out of the grass, as if from an underground well.

We'd catalogued all the different kinds, and the game was to run through the sprinklers, but each sprinkler was different and required a different approach. Some we'd back into slowly, shivering, our faces wrinkled, and others we'd dash through, and some we tried to crawl under. If we timed it right, we didn't get wet. That was part of the game. Stay dry. And then sometimes we just went in, hand in hand, Jennie and I, and there wasn't anything to do but take it like soldiers.

＊

Tom and Jennie thought I needed to meet new people, so the night after I arrived they threw a small cocktail party for me. It was one of those balmy June nights in which the moon carved out a niche for itself in a cloudless sky, and they set up card tables on the patio.

The Petersons, Ted and Roberta, arrived a little ahead of everyone else and were distressed at being early. "Should we leave and come back?" Ted offered. He kept tapping his watch and listening to it to make sure it was running. They wanted to sit on the porch until the others got there at seven-thirty sharp, but Jennie insisted they at least come out on the patio. Roberta wore a blue cotton skirt that was too short and a polyester shirt with bunny rabbits and a pack of Marlboros in her breast pocket. Ted was in shirt sleeves. He kept his hand on his wife's hip.

I followed Jennie into the kitchen to bring out some trays. "I hope this isn't going to be a disaster," she groaned, thrusting her hands deep into the back pockets, trying to pull her snug jeans off her pelvis a little. The doorbell rang. Ted and Roberta looked visibly relieved. Buzz Weidman and his girlfriend, Janice, lived together near Trenton, which was a big sacrifice for Janice, she told me right away, because she was in urban studies at Rutgers and hated the commute. Buzz, who did marketing for Bell Labs, had a big bald patch in the middle of his head, which he tried to cover up with a strand of frizzy brown hair, combed across the crown; it kept slipping out of place. He had done primal scream therapy, he told me shortly after Tom introduced us, which had taught him to go after what he wanted. Once he screamed for four hours, on and off.

Three more people arrived and one of them from the back was a dead ringer for Mark. He was the same height, with his hair cut straight along the back of his neck. For an instant I thought it was Mark. Everywhere you look, you see the person you love. On subways, in crowded theaters, I'd seen Mark a dozen times since I found the note he left me on the table in our kitchen. Sometimes I even went up to him, prepared to have it out, only to find myself face to face with a perfect stranger.

From the front Joe didn't look at all like Mark. He had dark eyes and freckles. He taught art at Silver Spring and a sculpture class at Princeton. His cousin, Irv, was in from San Francisco, where he worked for public broadcasting, and Irv's "high school sweetheart," Ilene, from East Orange, hung on his arm. We stood on the patio with drinks in our hands, talking about whether New York was dangerous or not. Tom said it was definitely dangerous and he'd never live there and he hated it when Jennie had to go to a lecture or something. Jennie frowned and seemed tense. "Tom thinks the whole city is Harlem." She passed a cheese platter. "You can go crazy out here, living in the sticks, if you don't go to the city once in a while."

Irv loved San Francisco except for the cold and the fog, which he claimed hung over his head like the plague and kept his spirits low. "Seal Point, you know, Seal Point. I've been there six times and I've never seen a seal. All I see is fog and hear seals barking. For all I know it's recordings of seals."

"Hey, Tom, the girls want some gin and tonics over here. Tom's a great guy," Buzz said. He patted me on the back. "C'mon, Tomasino, the girls are thirsty."

"I'll help you," I said and wandered back into the house with Tom. Buzz and Janice accompanied us into the den, where the bar was set up. It wasn't clear which girls wanted gin and tonics or how many were wanted, but Tom started making five. Janice had just bought a new car, a Nova, and it was a gas guzzler. "You New Yorkers don't have to worry about that sort of thing, do you?"

"What sort of thing?" Tom asked, handing me a gin and tonic I hadn't asked for.

"Cars," I said.

I went back out to the patio, where Jennie had bug bombs burning in red and green glasses to keep the biting insects away and a faint odor of DDT hung in the air. Ted and Roberta moved outside as well. She asked me how I afforded keeping my car in the city. "Oh, I don't have a car. We were just talking about cars."

Roberta said that the automobile was the state animal of New Jersey. Janice walked over. "You know," she said to me, "I heard that planners are working on a roller-skating map of Manhattan. You know, what streets to skate on. Manhattan's falling into its sewers and they're designing roller-skating maps." I told her I worked in slum renovation and didn't know about roller-skating maps. Joe wandered over with a little platter of cheese. When he smiled, his forehead wrinkled. He was tall and thick like a tree you could climb. Janice reached over and took some cheese and licked it. Her tongue was blue like a chow dog's. Joe munched on celery. "You girls talking shop?"

"Oh, not really," I said. "Just talking."

"I'm working on a series of paintings called *The City*."

"Oh, that sounds interesting."

Joe shrugged modestly. His straight hair fell to either side of his forehead and he kept brushing it away with a nervous hand. "You married?"

I laughed, amused at his directness. "Separated."

"I know. Jennie told me. I'm divorced." We both laughed, as if we were sharing a private joke. "Pretty awful, no?"

"The pits," I said.

"How long's it been?" He sipped his drink.

"Since February." It had been a long time since I tried to make conversation with a man I wanted to get to know, and I didn't know what to say next.

"Oh, now's the hardest time," Joe said. I felt at ease. "I've been on my own for four years now. I got custody. My wife was from Thailand. She went berserk in a supermarket in Arizona. I don't even know what she was doing in Arizona." He whipped out his wallet and showed me photographs of two dark-haired

but not very Oriental-looking children. "We were kids ourselves when we got married. Dumb mistake."

"Yeah, I know," I mumbled. Jennie waved at me from the
kitchen, thinking I needed rescuing but ostensibly to hand me
more food platters. "See you later," I said to Joe, but as I drew
away I experienced something I'd imagined lost to history, like
Pompeii or Hannibal's horse. I wasn't even aware of it as I'd
stood there talking with Joe, but as I walked away I felt myself
pulled back to him as if by some magnetic field, and that pull
left me lightheaded. Desire came creeping back as I scanned
the heads to see where Joe was going, desire that had lain
dormant since the winter, that had found its outlets mostly in
the swimming pool and in some dreary masturbation, ever
since that last night before he left, when Mark made wild,
inspired, hypocritical love to me.

"Having a good time?" Jennie asked.

"I was talking with Joe."

"Uh-huh, I saw." She arranged cheese puffs on a tray. "His
wife went crazy in Arizona. But he's got cute kids."

She handed me a tray of ham and cheese, and I carried it
back. Joe was in a corner, talking to Janice, who held him by
the sleeve, whispering into his ear. I tried to see the expression
in his eyes. I put the platter down and noticed a man I hadn't
seen before standing in a corner by the buffet. He held a Coke in
his hand and he looked crooked. At least he seemed crooked to
me, but perhaps I was looking at him at an angle, or perhaps
he couldn't make up his mind if he wanted to be there or not.
He smiled and it was a half-smile. His arms were half-folded
across his chest, the Coke was cocksided, his head was at a
slant.

I went back into the kitchen for another tray. "That's
Sean," Jennie said. She whispered without changing her facial
expression, the way people in spy movies do. "Don't take him
too seriously. I don't." But I could see where it might be difficult not to take him seriously. He stood alone in the corner

and it was clear he was simply bored with all of us. I put down a platter of egg salad sandwiches not far from where he stood, poured myself a glass of wine, and went back to join Joe.

As I passed, Tom caught me by the arm. "C'mon, you've gotta say hello to my friend. He's just back from the Coast. Yale graduate. Very smart." Tom pointed to his brain. Then he dragged me over to meet the man in the corner. "Sean, this is Jennie's friend from way back. Our friend, Debbie. You guys talk." Sean put down his Coke, rocked slightly on the balls of his feet, and extended a cold, damp hand. Now he was smiling. Or trying to smile.

We shook hands and his grip was firm. He apologized for his clammy palm; the Coke bottle had been very cold. He was big and he wore corduroy slacks and a blue shirt with rolled-up sleeves. His eyes were large and blue. They had an emptiness about them and his black beard made his eyes look bluer and emptier. "You from around here?" I asked, trying to sound the way I thought they might sound in that part of New Jersey.

He nodded. "My parents have a place up the road."

"Oh, you're a farmer?" He rolled his eyes and shook his head. "A teacher?"

He looked at me, bored. "I'm a stuntman."

"A what?"

"A stuntman, you know. I smash up cars and take punches for famous people."

"Oh," I said, "I've never met a stuntman." He did not appeal to me, and yet I knew that by objective standards he was an appealing man.

"Now you have." I expected him to yawn.

"It sounds interesting."

He sighed slightly. "It's not very interesting."

I'd heard his story before. He was on the way to make it big as a famous actor until someone found out he was a good athlete and now he was bitter. I looked at his arms. He had strong biceps with veins running through them. Thick, blue veins. Mark's arms were white and limp. They looked like a woman's arms, except for the hair. But underneath they were very strong and those limp arms managed sixty pushups a morning. Mark had deceiving arms. "Anything I might have seen you in?"

"Oh, I had a bit part in the Vietnam War."

I smiled. It was one of those odd and rare instances when I took an immediate and intense dislike to someone. When Joe waved at me from across the room, I was grateful for an excuse to walk away.

The guests left mostly in the same order they had arrived. Ted and Roberta had to drive the sitter home fairly early. Buzz and Janice kissed everyone on the cheek and said it was the best party they'd been to in decades. I watched as they put on their sweaters, jingled their keys. I walked outside and sat in one of the inner tubes on the old tree. As I rocked, the branch creaked.

Joe came outside to find me. "We'll be leaving soon." He swung his legs into the inner tube beside mine and we swung in opposite directions but with a kind of strange syncopation. Buzz and Janice waved at us from the porch. "Nice meeting you," Buzz called. "I'd like to see you again," Joe said. "Will you be here for a while?"

I felt complacent. "I'll be here this week."

"Good." He rose, smiling. "I'll give you a call."

He never did.

After everyone left, my eyes gazed in the direction where I thought New York City must be. A place that had been home to me and that I now faced with a kind of dread. It was the hour when shows were letting out, when the restaurants were getting crowded again. But here it was quiet and I felt safe. Even as a hand rested on the back of my neck, I knew nothing would happen to me out here.

"You should get some sleep," Jennie said.

"In a little while."

She asked me what I was looking for out there and I told her I didn't know but I thought I was looking toward Manhattan. She wrapped her arm around my shoulder. "Some planner you are. You're facing Pennsylvania." She turned me toward Manhattan, where she thought I wanted to be pointed. I shuddered. "Do you want to talk?"

I shrugged. "What's there to talk about?"

"Look," Jennie went on, "I'm not going to force you, but if you want to or need to talk, will you tell me?"

I told her I just missed him. There wasn't really much more to say. I couldn't say I wanted to get back at them. I couldn't even say that to myself. For a while we stood together, arms on each other's shoulders, facing a dark sky and a horizon, faintly illuminated, enough to let you know or at least suspect that America's most complex metropolis was just beyond these placid fields.

4

THE NEXT AFTERNOON the crooked man I didn't like at the party drove up to the house in a shiny red Datsun. As he got out of the car and waved at me, I realized I couldn't remember his name. "Where are they?" he shouted, and I pointed to the barn, where Tom and Jennie were renovating a room. He nodded and came over and sat down beside me on the porch. "Good," he said. "I really wanted to see you."

I'd been reading an architect's report for a possible design perspective on the SAP project, and he picked up one of those reports, flipping through like a gambler shuffling cards. "My name's Sean." He smiled. "Did you remember?"

"To tell you the truth, I didn't."

He nodded. "I don't blame you. If I were you, I'd have forgotten immediately." He ran his fingers through his thick, dark hair and, in the light of day, his face looked tired, his skin pale, as if he'd pulled an all-nighter, but he had wonderful eyes. I could see them clearly and now they seemed to sparkle, which they didn't do last night, even though he looked tired. "Well"

— he stretched back in the chair — "I came to apologize for being an ass last night."

I laughed. "Oh, there's nothing to apologize for."

He raised his hands, folded them in his lap, and leaned forward. "Yes, there is. I hate parties. I'm not very good at social gatherings. I was obnoxious. I'm not really a stuntman. That is, I'm a stuntman because I do stunts. I'm very athletic but it's not my goal and I don't plan on doing it forever." He paused. "I don't know why I'm telling you this."

"I don't either."

He scratched his head. "Should I stop?" I wasn't sure what he should do or what I wanted to hear.

Then he apologized for apologizing. "It's this thing I have. I always feel like I've acted inappropriately. I'm always saying I'm sorry." He said he always felt he had something to be sorry for.

I told him I didn't know what was worse. I'd been married to a man who never apologized to me except once in seven years in the note he left me on the kitchen table, saying he was leaving. "I don't know why I told you that," I added.

"Because you wanted to."

"No, I didn't." I was flustered and confused and somehow he'd gotten me to confide in him the details of the demise of my marriage.

"Well, I'm sorry if I made you say something you didn't want to say." He shook his head. "I'm apologizing again."

"I think lots of men have a hard time saying they're sorry. My father never does."

"Mine either." He smiled and lay back in the rocker, arms folded across his chest.

Sean had an open invitation for dinner that he'd never taken them up on, Jennie told me as we scraped carrots over the kitchen sink. Tom wore his Yankees cap and shouted in the other room as San Diego trounced Pittsburgh. Beer cans were lined up on the coffee table in front of Sean. Tom wished bursitis on any pitcher he didn't like; Sean popped open another beer and handed it to Tom.

Jennie hated it when Tom shouted about baseball, so she went into the den and stood in front of the television with her arms folded. "Are you going to get cleaned up for dinner or not?"

"I'm clean, I'm clean." But Jennie wouldn't move away from the television until he agreed to put on a shirt for dinner.

We went down in the basement, where she kept frozen food the way pirates keep buried treasure. She pulled a string, turning on an overhead bulb, and opened a trunk big enough to house a polar bear. Inside were packets of meat, poultry, fish, all neatly wrapped in plastic and labeled in Jennie's prize-winning handwriting. She dragged out half a cow she said would "do" for tomorrow. The next freezer was a vegetable garden hit with an unexpected frost. She came up with cauli-flower and string beans. Then there was a freezer for baked goods, an icebox for cold drinks. Rummaging in a deep freeze for a cheesecake, Jennie asked what I heard from my brother.

"Oh, he's fine, I guess."

"Oh," she said, trying not to sound surprised. "You aren't in touch with him?"

"He's somewhere in Europe. Sweden, I think. The last I heard he was in Sweden."

"What's he doing in Sweden?"

I'm not sure why I felt that Jennie was asking questions as if she knew the answers already, but it just seemed as if she was. "He's writing his memoirs and living with a woman. God knows." I brought Jennie up to date on my brother's recent history. How he'd done a year of veterinary school but then couldn't take it. How he'd managed to switch into Illinois med. "His teachers think he's some kind of a diagnostic whizz. For some reason when he asked for a year's leave they gave it to him. Who knows if he'll ever go back now."

Jennie slammed the freezer shut and I got goosebumps on

my arms from the chill. "I'm sure he'll go back. You know Zap. He's just rebellious."

She spoke as if she had some private source of information about my brother. I was sure he'd go back to medical school as well. I also knew that he hadn't been that rebellious until ten years before, when the woman he loved, Jennie Watson, went ahead and married Tom Rainwater.

Shouts came from the den when we got back upstairs. Jennie understood that someone was on third and she could probably start the vegetables. She patted butter on the mashed potatoes and plunged a fork into the chicken like a picador. Sean came into the kitchen. "Want some help? It's the bottom of the ninth, four to two."

Because I didn't like him very much, I looked away. My eyes landed on the bulletin board over the kitchen table. There were numbers in case of emergency, lists of things to do, and lottery tickets. I wondered if Jennie wanted to win a lottery. There was a faded picture of her parents, good Midwestern Republicans who wanted everything done in its proper way, the way Jennie did it all in her proper way. They were smiling in front of their summer house in Door County, Wisconsin. They'd never liked dissenters, premarital sex, interracial marriages, or members of the lower classes.

Jennie wasn't Jewish, which my parents didn't mind, but hers merely tolerated my presence in the Protestant household. They never explicitly said they didn't like me, but they never laid out the welcome mat either. Jennie's family fascinated me. The difference between our two houses was the difference of class, of race, of history. Her family lined up for everything — for the phone, for the bathroom, for meals. Mine pushed and shoved as if we were always waiting to see a rock star. In her house everyone did his or her own dishes, hung up his or her own clothes, the way I imagined they did on the *Mayflower*, while we spread our belongings out farther and farther, until Dad had to build additions to our house and soon these were filled to the brim, for my ancestors were ghetto people, then refugees, always on the go, escaping, who'd come on filthy ships and who'd never have enough room.

Whatever Jennie's parents thought of me, they couldn't tolerate Zap. They wouldn't put up with a Jew coming to look for their daughter, taking her off to play chess or see a French film. They wanted a guy who'd take her skiing and find his life's work side by side with the other male Watsons at Watson Electronics.

Tom hadn't fared much better when he started seeing Jennie. He was a coal miner's son and her parents forbade her to see him. When Jennie told her parents she was going to marry the boy they'd chased off their property two years before, they told her she could never see him again. She stopped eating. Her father had made his fortune in transistors and it seemed as if she wanted to become as pea-size as his inventions. Eventually Tom and Jennie eloped and were married in a meadow, where I was their maid of honor. They wrote for themselves one of those simple ceremonies in 1969: they promised to be faithful as long as they wanted to be faithful, and if they didn't want to be faithful anymore, they said, they'd talk about it.

When I called Zap to say Jennie was getting married, he said, "Give them my best." He sent some crystal goblets as a present, large and misshapen, the kind Dracula might serve, and proceeded to go crazy. He joined a motorcycle gang called the Unspeakables and left school. When he flunked his army physical because he was color blind, he threw a fit. "Go back to school," I offered as sisterly advice. "There're a lot of women in the world." Years later, when Mark left me after seven years of marriage, I'd see how stupid those words must have sounded to my brother.

I'm not sure when I first noticed that something was wrong between Tom and Jennie, but I think it was after they returned to the dinner table following the phone call.

We had just sat down to dinner when the phone rang, and

they both rushed in opposite directions to answer it. The call was from the children and once I heard Tom say, "Do you think you could let me get a word in?" Sean sat across the table from me, watching me with his blue eyes and looking bored. He didn't even bother making polite conversation while they were gone.

When they returned to the dining room, they glanced at one another with resentment they couldn't hide. I'd seen them give that same admonishing frown to one another at the cocktail party, when Jennie had said you could go crazy in the country. I hadn't thought much of it then. But I did now. "Just the kids." Jennie fluttered nervously. "Please, keep eating."

"Looks like your mother has everything under control." Tom spoke flatly and no one seemed sure if he intended that as a compliment or an insult.

Jennie sat at the head of the table, arms folded on the table edge as if she were about to conduct a symphony. "They asked if you're going to be in any more cowboy movies," she said, turning to Sean.

"Pass the chicken," Tom said.

"We'll go somewhere tonight." Jennie seemed to be thinking out loud. She hadn't waited for Sean's reply. "Tom, let's go out. Of course, there isn't much to do. We can go to a film at the mall but they only show gangster films." She repeated that there wasn't much to do in Thrace. Gangster films, bowling, a few Princeton bars forty minutes away, three taverns.

"Let's hit the Tall Grass," Tom put in.

"It's a dive," Jennie said. "I hate that place."

"No one says you have to go," he said, "if you don't want to."

We pulled into the parking lot beside some pickups, a few jeeps, old Fords, and one or two nice sports cars with dealers' stickers in the back windows. A blue neon sign flickered on and off and the name "The Tall Grass" illuminated the parking lot. It was, in fact, your conventional dive. We entered a smoke-filled room, lit only by several red light bulbs that hung naked from the ceiling. Dice were being tossed. Most of the men were fat, bellies swollen by beer. The women had puffy hairdos and wore short dresses. A few college kids played pool in the back; the sports cars in the parking lot probably belonged to them.

Above the bar was a picture of a mermaid, sadly out of place, far from the sea. She swam entrapped in tall grass, little green fishes gazing at her. Beside the mermaid was an old Playmate of the month, reminiscent of those calendars in my father's office, and she was impaled on a pair of deer antlers. A Budweiser lamp with a team of Clydesdales lit the bar. A poster next to the antlers read "1944: Rutgers 28, Princeton 0."

Jennie ignored us and pushed through the crowd toward a table in the back. We followed, first Tom, then I, then Sean. The juke box played something from the fifties by Danny and the Juniors. Then it switched to Freddy Fender singing "Rancho Grande." Jennie tapped her fingers on the table and held Tom's hand with her free hand.

"Martinis, right?" Tom said.

Sean ordered beer and I ordered white wine, but Tom and Jennie started drinking martinis. They drank two apiece quickly and started laughing. Everything seemed very funny to them. The red lights, Joe, the bartender, Sean's bad moods. Tom patted my hand. "You know what?"

"What?"

"I'm an Indian."

"You don't look like an Indian."

He ribbed Sean. "Tell her."

Sean waved his arms at Tom. "You're not an Indian. A wild Indian, maybe, but that's about it."

"I am too. Aren't I, Jen." Jennie shrugged. Her face was a little red. "Your parents think I'm an Indian, remember. They thought I looked like I had some other racial origins in my blood. They wanted an aristocrat in the family."

Jennie frowned and said Tom's family was French. His

mother claimed someone had married an Indian, which explained the name. But it was generations ago. Otherwise he was pure French. Tom ordered another drink but Jennie told the waitress to forget it. "You're getting drunk," she said to him.

When Jennie got up to go to the bathroom, someone stopped at our table and asked Sean if he hadn't seen him in a film he wasn't in. "Aren't you an actor?" the man asked. "They told me at the bar you were an actor."

"You're thinking of Robert De Niro. He was in that movie."

"Well, you sure look like him."

While I looked at Sean to decide if he looked like Robert De Niro (it was difficult to tell, with his beard), someone squeezed my hand under the table. I looked up and saw that it was Tom. I pulled my hand away and stared into his eyes to see if it was just a friendly squeeze, but his eyes were ambiguous, and I moved closer to Sean. The juke box was playing Johnny Mathis when Jennie returned to the table. Then it skipped twenty years to the BeeGees.

"Let's dance," Jennie said, running her finger up and down Tom's thigh.

"What's this thing about an Indian?" I asked Sean after they got up.

"Tom feels oppressed. Jennie's folks never could stand him. I think he got rich just to show them. The farmland alone must be worth a quarter of a million. He made good investments. But he'd never sell it. He loves it."

"And Jennie?"

Sean shrugged. "She's your friend. Why don't you ask her? I'm not around that much anyway."

"She seems happy. Isn't she?"

"I think she'd like to be in the city." Sean spun his glass in his hands and stared at the glass in the light. "It gets a little quiet around here."

Tom pulled me by the arm and was trying to get me to stand up. "Dance with me," he said. I didn't want to dance with anyone, and I certainly didn't want to dance with Tom. Jennie stood alone, bewildered, on the dance floor.

"We were just getting up to dance," Sean said, taking me by the arm.

"I asked first," Tom said.

"No, we were just getting up. Dance with Jennie." Sean looked in the direction where she stood. He took me by the elbow and I understood I was to dance with him for Jennie's sake. He maneuvered me over to where Jennie was standing. "Tom wanted us to join you," Sean said.

The band played "Michelle" and Sean wrapped his arms around me and pressed me tightly to his chest. I pulled away slightly. "You really should learn to relax," he said to me.

"I'm relaxed."

"I'd hate to see you when you're tense then." But he seemed pretty tense himself as he pulled me close and guided me in small steps across the floor, burrowing a passageway between couples. I didn't want to dance. Men lead in dancing, and I didn't want to be led.

Sean's body was different from Mark's body. Mark was shorter and his shoulders weren't so broad. He was small and compact like a tank; I fitted perfectly into that place along his shoulder, that slightly dented space where the arm joined the chest. I'd spent years curling into that space and going to sleep. Sean was bigger and beside him I felt smaller. His arms were longer than Mark's; they wrapped all the way around me. Sean stepped on my toe, grazed it, and I thought of Mark. We always danced well together and there weren't any mistakes.

We did other things well together. We loved to be in the kitchen, chopping vegetables side by side. We liked to walk with our feet in unison, imagining hypothetical futures for ourselves: a country we wanted to live in someday, a little business we wanted to open. It had all seemed so smooth and easy once, and now as I danced with a man whose feet grazed mine, I cursed Mark for going away.

5

I T WAS six in the morning, miles from where I thought anyone knew where I was, so when I opened Jennie's front door, I was stunned to see Zap standing there. He grinned at me, knapsack at his feet, through his dark mustache, resembling the person whose name he bore, the Mexican rebel. "What're you doing here?" were the first words out of my mouth.

A blond woman, the kind he always managed to find on his travels and who was always disposed to go with him, leaned against the porch railing and nodded at me. Zap scooped me up, and as I grabbed for my thin robe, he grabbed for me. "Boy, have I missed you," he said. He said it a dozen times until I believed him.

I'm the one who named my brother Zapata, though it was our mother who brought him a fake mustache from a giveaway twenty years before. Mom couldn't resist a bargain, an opening, a free sample. We had drawers full of little bars of new soap, marmalade in plastic boxes, first edition tampons.

She decided my brother, then Bernie, would make a great bandito, so for years I dragged him around with me on Halloween with his scratchy mustache, shoulder holster, and sombrero. He looked ridiculous and he hated being a bandito, because he was always in enough trouble without the costume. But then I saw Marlon Brando on TV and started calling Bernie Zapata. Bernie liked being a hero. The name stuck, later abbreviated to Zap.

His traveling companion was Anna, and he'd met her in a bowling alley in Stockholm. She offered me a rather sweaty, limp hand and I tried to imagine this fishlike body keeping my brother warm through the long Swedish winter. She was built like a weeping willow, with sturdy legs, wispy arms, and long, stringy yellow hair. She nodded in agreement to everything I said. Anna was the kind of person you have to strain to think of something to say, even if it's just "Hello" or "How was the trip?" I asked her how she was and she nodded and smiled at me. I wasn't even sure she could speak English.

"She's got friends near Pittsburgh," Zap said, speaking for her. "When I decided to come home, she came along, right, Anna?" She nodded. He whispered to me, as I walked out on the porch, "Nothing serious." He always had a woman but it was never serious.

Zap kept a hand firmly pressed to my shoulder as he led me over to where his motorcycle stood. "How'd you ever find me?"

He smiled. "Now how do you think?"

Anna went off to swing on one of the inner tubes on the old apple tree. He looked her way. "Mom told me." Anna wrapped her legs around the tube, held on to the rope, and started to swing. She shut her eyes and threw her head back. The motorcycle Zap had bought in Sweden stood in the driveway, an enormous beastlike black bike, wet with dew, which shimmered on its chrome. The sun, starting to break the horizon, a pale violet morning light, shone in the rearview mirror.

I walked barefoot across the grass, little pebbles jabbing into my heels and the balls of my feet. The grass was wet and the air cool, and under my bathrobe I didn't have a stitch on. Zap patted the bike on its seat like a horse; he sucked in his lips, the way he did when a woman captivated him. "You weren't in New York. I wish I'd had a set of keys to your apartment. We could've stayed there. I called Mom when I finally figured it out that I wasn't going to find you there."

"So I'll make you a set. How come you didn't call here before you arrived?"

He tweaked my nose. "What's the matter, sis, don't you like surprises?"

Tom had heard the motorcycle and was slowly making his way down the stairs in jeans and a ripped T-shirt. "Who the hell is that?" He bent down and peered from the landing. Zap laughed and waved. "Oh, my God, Zap. How'd you get here?" He barreled the rest of the way down the stairs, right arm extended. I stepped aside as they gripped one another in manly hugs. They hadn't seen each other in over eight years, though there hadn't been any hard feelings when Tom married Jennie. Zap once told me, "If I was hurt, it was by her. Not him."

I hadn't seen my brother myself in nearly a year and we hadn't talked since just after Mark left me. He'd gone to Europe when he left medical school and said he needed to put his head back together. Zap had been flip-flopping between professions for years. When he wanted to be a vet, our parents weren't pleased but they knew it beat standing on a street corner, drinking beer — something he'd done for years. When he switched to medicine, they were thrilled. He told them he was going to be a famous cancer research scientist and they believed him. They told all their friends.

When he left veterinary school, I was understanding. He wrote me a letter, explaining his disenchantment. Some of the animals he treated had died. It was true, he'd once saved a boa constrictor with gum trouble, but he'd also stood by helplessly as a collapsed giraffe languished in the St. Louis zoo. He knew, he wrote me then, that he just wasn't cut out to be an animal doctor.

When he left medical school, he didn't bother writing to me. Or to our parents. I think he knew what we'd say. He'd always been called a wayward genius and he probably didn't want to hear it again.

Tom and Zap walked over to the apple trees near the bird feeder. Anna joined them. He seemed taller to me, if that was possible. Perhaps he was leaner, older. His hair was thick, dark, not silky like our father's, and he'd never go bald.

Jennie opened the screen door and walked out. She was dressed in jeans and a flannel shirt. "Well, look who's here." She smiled and, with great composure, kissed my brother hello on the cheek.

"I'm just passing through but I had to see Debbie," he explained. "Mom said she thought it would be all right if I gave you guys a little surprise."

"We're surprised," Jennie said.

"Nice bike," Tom said, walking over to the motorcycle. He flung his leg over the side and sat in the seat, ran his hands over the chrome handles, adjusted the rearview mirror. If Tom felt uncomfortable about Zap's sudden arrival, he didn't show it. The metal of the bike was hot now in the July morning and he pulled his hand back when he touched the handles, as if the bike had bitten him. It was a black Arrow, one of the best of the Oriental models, better than Yamahas or Kawasakis in its road tests. Tom straddled the bike and lifted its front wheels off the ground, even though it weighed almost three hundred pounds.

"Hey, sis. How about if we go for a little spin." Zap walked toward Tom with his arm on my shoulder. Of course it was forbidden. We never were allowed on motorcycles, because our father once saw a girl's head sliced off when she fell from the back of one. We were barely allowed in cars. "Come on," Zap said. "You aren't going in your nighty, are you?"

"I guess not." I couldn't think of any excuses, so I went into my room and slipped out of my bathrobe. I dug for underwear, a pair of jeans, a T-shirt. I brushed my teeth but I couldn't get them clean. My clothes itched and nothing felt right against my skin. I found a jacket. From the window my brother looked like a Hell's Angel. When he dropped out of school the first time, Mom threatened to disown him. She said he could never stick to anything. My father called. "You talk to him," he begged me. "He listens to you." I was, in fact, the only one he listened to, and he wouldn't listen to me, either.

All my life I've protected my brother. Someone told Mom she couldn't get pregnant if she was nursing, so she nursed me and had him eleven months later. Our sister, Renee, was four years older and, though we were awed by someone who at first seemed incapable of doing anything wrong, she'd never be our friend. I feel as if my life began with Zap; I don't remember life without him. My first memory in this world is of my brother, staring at me from across the playpen as if he were trying to formulate something to say. We were more than brother and sister and at times it seemed we were more than friends.

Tom, Jennie, and Anna waved at us as we zipped along the driveway, a bumpy, cratered road pocked with holes dug by the dogs and Tom's pickup. We were moving. Tom, Jennie, and Anna shrank to the size of shrubs, then to nothing at all. Birds became bullets, the wind slapped like rushing water, shafts of wheat melted into a flat shelf of yellow. The clouds were out of time-lapse footage of a gathering storm; the sprawling farms receded. The isolated farmhouses were no longer so isolated, as distances became half of what they'd been. I wrapped my arms tighter around Zap, and the bike shifted into some new gear that seemed able to take us farther, higher. The bike groaned; pebbles shot out the back wheel. In the mirror I saw his face, his eyes squinting, lips sealed, as if he were performing some very private act.

We took the bends and twists of the bumpy road, meshed into the forks, and glided around curves. It was still a dawn light we moved through. The tiny vibrations began at the tips of my toes, eased their way through the balls of my feet, into my ankle bones, up my calves. It wasn't like being in a car, because you weren't in anything, and it wasn't like being on a horse, because you didn't vibrate like this on a horse. It was a little like love, closer to that, but I didn't want to think about that now.

It was amazing how things slipped away from you. Mark had slipped away just as all the houses and the trees were slipping away. It was almost six months, and in spite of myself, in spite of how much I wanted to hold on to him and not forget him, he was slipping away. Zap shifted again. Now we were soaring. We were children on an endless boat ride through the maze of the Fox River, our father navigating, telling us to mark seagulls "on right" and us laughing because we knew seagulls were bad markers and they flew away. Peeling oranges and letting the peels drop into the river, because in case Dad really was marking seagulls, like Hansel and Gretel we'd need orange peels to find our way home.

We passed a mall and Zap pulled the bike over and parked in front of a diner. We sat down in a booth and ordered. "I'm exhausted," I said.

"Me too."

"Are you going to stay long?" The waitress with lacquered yellow hair and a black skirt barely covering her wide, nearly perfect circle hips put down two cups of coffee with coffee sloshing around in the saucer. We put napkins down to soak it up.

"I'm just staying the day, maybe until tomorrow morning." He toyed with the wet napkin dissolving under his cup. "So talk fast . . . how've you been?"

How've I been? I wasn't certain how to answer that question. I did take someone's dog home and got hysterical when the owner wasn't immediately appreciative. I did call Mark and Lila's number until they had it changed to unpublished. I have been silently plotting revenge. My heroes of late had become John Wilkes Booth and Lee Harvey Oswald. "I'm O.K.," I said to my brother, starting to cry.

He reached across and held my fingers in his. "Guess that answers my question." Then he let go, smiled, and in a gesture I could recite from memory ran all five of his fingers through his black hair and twirled his mustache. Then he patted me on the cheek. The truth wasn't easy to admit. If he weren't my brother, he'd probably break my heart as well.

The waitress brought me a Kleenex, smiled at me with great empathy, and gave Zap a scowl. "Men ain't all there is in this world, honey." She walked away on those rotating hips.

"I'm innocent; don't shoot." Zap raised his hands.

"And you." I took his hands in mine. "How've you been?"

He shrugged. "I did a lot of soul-searching this winter. I'm going to give it one more try, if they'll have me."

"You're going to finish school?"

"Oh, you know, the family needs a doctor. If only to disprove all the hypochondriacs." While he spoke, he stared out the window, across the Delphia Mall, squinting as if he were trying to read something. I followed his gaze to a sign that read "The Home Safe Locksmith."

"What're you looking at? You want me to make you a set of keys for my apartment?"

He nodded. "I could use them." He looked back at me. "So what's next? Have you talked to Mark?"

I shook my head. "I know you never liked him. You don't

have to deny it. I know. Maybe you were right." I told him how Jennie and Tom had thrown a cocktail party for me and I'd met Joe, whom I liked but who'd never called me, and Sean, whom I didn't like and who came by to see me all the time. "That's the way it goes, isn't it?" He agreed with me that it was often the way it went. "Anyway, I'm not ready to meet anyone, or else everyone I meet is awful."

"Probably it's a little of both." He laughed.

I had my keys on me, so when we left the diner we went across to the Home Safe Locksmith. Zap bought a little key chain of a running shoe that had "Run for Your Life" inscribed on it. When the keys were finished, he put them on the chain.

"You can stay there whenever you want," I said.

"Thanks," he replied. "I'll do you a favor sometime." Then we got on the bike and sped back to the farm.

If I was ever jealous of Jennie, it was when Zap fell in love with her and when she led the high school marching band, twirling her baton in front of thousands of spectators who also envied her. Sometimes I silently prayed for her to miss, but her composure when she leaped on stage or into the middle of a football field was Zen-like, as if she didn't know anyone was watching her. Zap used to say he didn't fall in love with Jennie because she was head drum majorette, but in spite of it. He couldn't stand seeing her out there in front of all those people. "All those men are after you," he'd complain. And he was right.

It was as drum majorette that Jennie crossed the lawn with the breakfast tray, strutting and erect. Her confidence at times was appalling. A tray of steaming coffee with cinnamon sticks as stirrers. There was hot toast made from her own home-baked bread, jams made from the blueberries and wild strawberries she'd picked the summer before. Strips of bacon and fried eggs in a little pile.

Zap, now in a pair of cut-offs and a T-shirt that read

"Champs-Elysées," was planing wood with Tom in front of the barn. Anna and I played with the kittens. Everyone paused as the breakfast tray arrived. Tom looked at the tray and frowned. "It's almost noon."

Jennie shrugged and proceeded to serve from a tree stump. "No one's had breakfast yet." She passed a mug to Zap and their hands didn't even graze. Her hair was like autumn leaves and her face had the ruddy glow of a finely fermented wine.

Anna was back on the ground playing with the kittens when Sean drove up in his Datsun. The kittens had been born to a vagrant cat a few weeks before. "Good for the rats," Tom said as he planed wood. The kittens prowled in the shade, eyes intent on the ground like little Sherlock Holmeses searching for clues.

Sean walked right up to Zap and shook his hand. "You must be Deborah's brother. You look just like her."

"He does?" I doubted it.

"Around the eyes. So, you still fixing up the old rat's nest?" he said to Tom.

"Yeah, why don't you help?"

"Sure, I'll help." He poured himself a mug of coffee and made an egg sandwich. "I'm no carpenter; you know that, though. But it doesn't matter . . . I got a job."

"Falling off roofs?" Jennie asked.

Sean smiled. "Better than that. It's not definite yet, but looks like a real behind-the-camera job." He sat down and leaned back complacently against the tree stump. "I've been trying to lift your sister's spirits with my charms. Any tricks I should know?"

Zap smiled. "Ignore her. She comes around if you ignore her."

"Ah, I know the type."

"That's not true." I could see they were united against me.

I played with a white kitten that rested in my lap.

"So, are you going to tell us what kind of job you got?" I asked Sean.

"Not until it's definite. I'm superstitious. But it will change my life."

I tugged at Zap's sleeve. "Let's go for a walk. I want to go for a walk with you."

We headed down the hill toward the woods, past the pond. At the pond Zap picked up a rock and hurled it at the flock of wild geese. I'd never seen him do anything like that before. "What's wrong?"

"Nothing. Just thought they could use some exercise."

We kept walking but I knew something was wrong. "Where do you want to go?" he said.

"Around the farm."

He nodded, slipping his arm through mine, and we walked in silence.

Zap bent down and picked up a small insect that looked like a blade of grass. "Look at this," he said, "the perfect camou-flage." The insect, walking across his hand, looked pretty ner-vous, without the grass to hide in. He put it back down. "Must get crazy out here, without anywhere to go."

I bent down and looked at the bug. "You talking about Jennie?"

"She's not happy. It's obvious. She's like a stiff. Hardly talks. You know, I know her pretty well. She hasn't laughed since I got here."

"You only got here a few hours ago." The insect had disap-peared back into the grass, and we started walking again. I slipped my arm through his. "Maybe we weren't ever really friends. We were always so different."

Zap shook his head. Releasing my arm, he put his arm on my shoulder and I put my arm around his waist. He had the tight, smooth abdominal muscles of a swimmer and, even though he was slim, he was strong. "You weren't different. She's just unhappy."

"What're you going to do about it?"

He looked at me, surprised. "I don't know." He changed the subject. "Tell me about this guy Sean."

"He's awful."

"He doesn't seem awful."

I glanced at him. "You liked him?"

He nodded. "Yes, I liked him."

"Well, I don't like him."

"I don't see why not. He's got a nice smile and a good handshake. He certainly is good-looking."

"I hadn't noticed."

"You're in worse shape than I thought." He whistled through his teeth. "You don't even know a nice guy when you see one. So," his voice dropped low, "has Jennie said anything to you about me?"

"You just got here."

"I mean before. Did she ask about me?"

I shook my head. "She just asked if I'd heard from you."

He sighed, as if he'd expected to hear something spectacular after all these years. "I mean, what'd you think she'd say?"

"I don't know. I thought she might have said something about my letters."

"You mean you were corresponding?" I found myself growing irritated with him and with Jennie. Why hadn't she told me they had been writing? And he was acting as if he wanted to find out if I knew something I already knew. I snapped at him. "I didn't know it mattered so much to you. Then what'd you bother bringing Anna here for?"

"I wish you hadn't said that," he snapped back.

"It isn't serious with her."

"That doesn't mean I don't care."

We reached the stream at the edge of the woods and sat

down on two rocks, our feet dangling just above the water. We removed our shoes and socks and let our toes touch the water, which was freezing cold. "I just think you could be doing better for yourself."

"I always thought you could too. I mean, Anna's not a civil rights attorney or whatever Mark was, but she's not a son of a bitch either."

•"There were some very good things about Mark." I started kicking the water with my feet. "You just never liked him, that's all."

"I never liked what he did to you, that's for sure. It didn't have much to do with him. I thought he made you act in unnatural ways."

A school of fish swam beneath our feet and we watched them pass. It used to enrage me when Zap said bad things about Mark, but now I wanted to hear them. The fish kept our attention long enough that we could talk and not look directly at one another while we dealt with a delicate subject. "What ways?"

"Oh, you were always worried. Would Mark think this or that? You never seemed to know what he was going to do. You seemed to be hanging on a cliff for about seven years."

Zap started skipping stones. I climbed off my rock and waded over to his. I sat beside him. He wrapped his arm around me. "He made you doubt yourself. That's why I didn't like him. You never doubted yourself before you married him. Or maybe you married him because you doubted yourself and you thought he was so terrific."

"I was very young and you didn't know him well. He really is a very sensitive man, deep down."

"I couldn't dig that deep."

I kissed him on the cheek. "I haven't been very happy lately."

"I can imagine." He laughed. I'd written him long letters

about Mark and Lila. Lila to Zap was a vague childhood memory, someone he recalled from the dozen or so women whom I sometimes called my friends. But not one of our close crowd. Just a face that didn't mean much to him then. He knew Mark was living with her only five blocks away from our apartment. Zap tossed a stone and helped me up. "I just never liked him to begin with."

"Why did you come here?" I rose and dusted myself off.

"I came to see you. And I came to see Jennie." He shook his head. "She's not happy. Look, Debbie, I came to see both of you. But whatever it was between me and Jennie a long time ago, it hasn't gone away. I can't describe it."

I told him he didn't have to. I knew as well as anyone what he was talking about.

I knew he'd had her once, very briefly, on a mosquito-filled beach the summer before the alewives lay rotting on the sand. Technically he'd lost his virginity with her but she hadn't lost hers with him. He'd entered her and she told him to pull out, which he did before she could no longer call herself a virgin but not before he came inside of her, and Jennie spent one terror-stricken month, waiting to show signs of being pregnant and refusing to repeat the experience with Zap. He told me this one miserable night during the month when Jennie refused to try it again.

So he pulled out but he'd held on, living with the sense that he had something left to finish. His whole life had something incomplete about it. "I want to spend time with her," he repeated.

"So spend time with her."

"Do you think she wants to?"

I shrugged. "How should I know? We should get back."

"Look, I haven't seen anything better."

"Anyone," I corrected him.

He started walking. "I feel something when I'm with her."

I paused, with my hands in my pockets. "You know, I married the man I wanted to marry. That's the truth. I loved Mark and he was exactly what I wanted."

"What are you saying?"

"Sometimes we kid ourselves about what we feel."

He put his hands in his pockets. "I've had a long time to think about it."

"Too long, if you ask me. You don't even know her anymore." He was walking ahead of me back to the house. "So do what you want!" I shouted at him.

In the afternoon everyone who hadn't been on the motorcycle wanted to go for a ride. I sat on the porch, sipping iced tea, and watched as they left and returned. I wanted to work on my report but I was too shaken by the talk with Zap. So I just sat and watched as they came and went, and no one seemed to come back the same way they'd left.

Brave Sean returned a little shaky and said with a nervous laugh, "I'd rather drive cars off cliffs, I think. Your brother drives like a maniac." Tom, who'd left sullen and tense, came back smiling. Anna, who'd gone laughing, returned glum and I sensed there had been some discussion that upset her. And Jennie, who went last and was gone the longest — who left her usual orderly self — came back all disheveled, face dirty, hair out of place. "I'm going to take a shower," she said.

She returned a little later, wearing a pair of snug-fitting jeans and an Indian blouse with a bright red and blue print and no bra. She leaned on the railing of the porch, combing out her wet hair in the sun. "So who's ready for drinks? And sandwiches. I'll make some sandwiches."

"I'll help," Tom offered, rising from the rocker.

"No, dear, you sit. Let me do it." She motioned him back down and, as if she had special power in her fingers, he sat back down. She returned a few moments later with a tray of tall glasses, gin and vodka and tonic, sprigs of mint, limes. "Honey, can you tend bar?"

"So you think you'll go back to medical school?" Sean asked Zap.

"What?" Zap looked at Sean as if he'd never seen him before. "School? I think I'll go back."

"I kept dropping out of Yale. I finally finished."

"State schools are different." Zap spoke perfunctorily.

"Can't afford school anymore," Tom put in with unusual force. "I don't know how I'm going to send the kids." He was pouring drinks.

"I'm going to make sandwiches," Jennie said, jumping up again.

"I'll help," Zap said. I waited for her to tell him she didn't need any help but instead she waited for him at the screen door. The door banged shut. Anna glanced at the door when it banged. Tom was passing out drinks.

Sean engaged Anna in a conversation. Or at least he tried to. He began now with how she reminded him of Bibi Andersson with a little Liv Ullmann thrown in. He went on to discuss Bergman's notion of female fantasies in *Cries and Whispers*, the meaning of silence, his idea of the Swedish winter. He skipped on to talk about Bergman's tax evasion, his breakdown, on to deserters and Vietnam, to the Helsinki pact, to Kissinger, revolutions, treaties, disarmament, Swedish women. Tom rocked back and forth, sipping gin and sucking in his cheeks as if he were about to explode. Anna smiled and nodded but it seemed she had nothing to say.

"A lot of suicides in Sweden," Sean went on. "I hear it's the largest percentage in the world. They attribute it to the welfare state."

"Oh, really, I didn't know."

"Suicide's the most selfish thing you can do," Tom said rather mechanically.

"Well, in Sweden they're very selfish," Sean said.

"No, we aren't," Anna protested.

"I hear in Sweden a pack of cigarettes costs two dollars." Tom leaned toward me. "A beer costs five. Inflation is terrible. I'm not going to be able to send my kids to college at this rate."

He was leaning so close to me that I could feel his breath on my face.

"I think I'll help," I said. I got up and so did Tom. "Me too," he said, but I motioned him down with my hands the way Jennie had done.

I walked through the living room and the dining room and, for some reason, I was completely shocked when I saw them in the corner of the kitchen, Zap with his arms tightly around Jennie, and Jennie with her face buried in his chest. I don't know why it surprised me so much. I'd seen them kiss before when we were kids. I'd seen them kiss on the rides at Riverview, even on the parachute, where nobody wants to kiss. I'd seen them kiss on top of the bluff where we lived and on the Indian trails, under the old hunchback tree and in tons of parking lots. I'd hung around with them since we reached puberty, sometimes spying, sometimes tracking down their panting breath to save them from discovery.

I'm not sure what I felt when I walked into the kitchen and watched them. I know I felt surprised. Jennie's spine was pressed against the Formica counter, her hips thrust against Zap's, and his hands cupped her breasts. She kissed him on the neck and whispered indistinguishable words into his ear. It was dim in the kitchen but not so dim that I couldn't see Zap's hands, gliding along her ribs and trying to tear her blouse in two.

Later that evening Sean asked me if I wanted to go with him for a walk by the pond. I didn't want to go with him, but I also didn't want to be with anyone else. I've always had a difficult time saying no. As we walked, he told me he thought he'd gotten a job as an assistant director on a major motion picture. His agent would let him know in a few weeks. "An Arthur Hansom film, do you believe it?" He lit a joint and said how nice it was to come home to New Jersey once in a while. I'd never heard of Arthur Hansom at the time. "You aren't listening," he said to me finally. "What's on your mind?"

"Nothing, just thinking."

"I like your brother."

"He likes you."

We walked as far as the pier, then sat down. For a few moments we didn't talk. "This job," he said at last. "It would be a big deal."

"I'm glad."

He took his hand and put it under my chin. "May I kiss you?"

"That's the last thing I want you to do."

I expected some kind of a struggle. Instead he laughed. "What's the first thing?"

"I don't know."

"Usually I don't ask if I want to kiss someone. I just go ahead and do it. But you look like you needed to be asked."

"That's right," I said, getting up. I started back toward the house. Sean didn't move. "You coming or staying?"

"I think I'm staying."

They'd all gone upstairs by the time I got back. Zap had left me warm milk on the stove, with a note that said he'd see me in the morning but he was bushed. We always brought each other warm milk when we were kids. A fire smoldered in the living room even though it was a summer's night, but because it was cool outside the heat felt good.

I decided to work. I got my briefcase and propped my feet up on the coffee table. Inside my briefcase was a map of Manhattan with several plastic overlay sheets and colored crayon markers. There was another detail map of the Bronx and several aerial photographs of the specific area I was writing about. I would have to describe that area in minute detail.

I knew the maps like the back of my hand, but suddenly they seemed foreign to me. The blue spots marking available building space, the green spots for available landscape space, the red arrows for traffic circulation, and the brown slums, the black spots where neighborhoods had been destroyed — now they seemed like mountain ranges, like jungle habitats. Poor neighborhoods were tropical isles. Puerto Rico, Galápagos, Fiji. I was looking at a pirate's map. Certainly no place to live.

It needed rearranging. I knocked down skyscrapers, hauled in trees. I erased Eighth Avenue completely and put crosstown subways under Central Park, little red and yellow trolley cars moving above the ground. I gave everyone a view.

In the morning Zap and Anna were ready to head out. Anna kissed me on the cheek. Jennie squeezed Zap's hand as if she were offering her condolences. Zap took me aside. "I've got some things to work out. But I'll see you soon."

"Just give me a call before you arrive, all right?"

Tom and Jennie came out onto the porch to say good-bye. "Take care of my little sister, will you?"

Sean was there. "I don't think she needs much taking care of." Zap got on the bike and motioned me to come near him. As he hugged me, I whispered "Mind your own business" into his ear. Zap hit and accelerated, and Anna hopped on back. They put on their crash helmets and my brother winked at me. Then they took off down the dirt road and left behind them a trail of dust that took twenty minutes to settle.

6

I STAYED a couple of days longer than I'd planned, long enough for Tom and Jennie to drop their reserve and have a fight during the evening news. A husband had killed his wife after escaping from a mental hospital. Tom said, pointing to the television, "I bet she was fooling around. That's probably what made him crazy in the first place."

"What's that supposed to mean?" Jennie asked.

Tom said, "Nothing. Just what it says."

Jennie seemed to forget I was in the room. "Well, I know what it's supposed to mean and I think you've got a lot of nerve. You think I'm going to get involved with Zap, don't you? Or with somebody, with anybody. God knows who I could get involved with out here. Of course, it doesn't stop you, does it? It didn't stop you, did it?"

"Give me a break, will you?" Tom was shouting. "Zap came here to see you. You guys spent thirty minutes making four egg salad sandwiches. What am I supposed to be? An idiot?"

"You know, you're really driving me away."

Tom walked out of the room and Jennie asked me if I

wanted to go with her for a ride. When he came back, she said, "We're going out; I don't feel like discussing this now."

"Go wherever you want," he said. We left him staring blankly at the television.

I looked out the window as we drove and I watched as the trees zipped past, illuminated only by our headlights. Neither of us had noticed how fast she'd been driving. "You see, he's hàd a few affairs," Jennie was saying. "Nothing serious. Just once or twice, and he's told me about them. They always happen when things are bad between us."

A rabbit, startled and afraid, froze by the side of the road, then disappeared back into the woods. Jennie told me, "I found out a lot of things I never knew about Tom after I married him." But I understood Tom. He'd never felt good enough for Jennie. Her parents had convinced him of that and perhaps Jennie in her subtle ways had convinced him as well.

"You see," she went on, "the problem is . . ." She laughed softly. "I still love him. I just don't trust him. God knows, I've tried. You can't almost trust somebody. You either do or you don't." I knew that only too well. If Mark left Lila that same night and begged me to try again, it would never be the same. Actually, I wasn't sure.

"What are you going to do about Zap?" I asked quietly.

She frowned. "I'm not going to do anything. It would be wrong to do anything."

"I saw you . . ."

"I know you saw us. So we were holding one another. That doesn't mean we're going to take off together.

"It's just that he still thinks he's crazy about you."

She laughed. "Oh, your brother. He always wanted what he couldn't have." Then she grew serious again. "I don't want to hurt him. But, of course, I'm not leaving Tom. Or the children."

I sighed. "Nobody ever wants to hurt anybody."

I hadn't noticed that she was pulling over to the side of the road. "Did you see that kid?" she asked.

I shook my head. "What kid?" I hadn't seen anything.

"He was back there, hitching. He'll never get a ride on this road."

I was annoyed that our talk was being cut short. "Are you crazy? Isn't that dangerous?"

But she had her heart set on picking up a hitchhiker. She shifted into reverse. "There are two of us and one of him."

The argument didn't hold up for me. "I don't care. We were going to get a drink."

I turned and saw a blond-haired boy rushing toward the car, a look of gratitude on his face. "We'll get a drink after we drop him on the main road," Jennie said, rolling down her window. "How far you going?"

The boy looked to be about eighteen and he kept pushing his long hair off his face. He wore an orange and black Princeton T-shirt and a pair of bleached-out jeans. He had a nice smile, so I assumed he wouldn't drag us off into the bushes somewhere.

Bobby Jones introduced himself to us and jumped into the front seat beside me while I leaned forward so that he could climb into the back. He was going to a party outside of Cranford and if we could get him to the highway, that would be "just super."

"You would have been on that road all night," Jennie said.

"I would've missed the party if you girls hadn't stopped."

I was taken aback at the word "girls." Both Jennie and I were old enough, technically, if I did a quick calculation, to be this boy's mother. "Do you go to Princeton?" I pointed to his T-shirt.

"I'm here on a swimming scholarship. I broke their butterfly record last year."

We were pressed tightly into the car and I could feel his arm muscles against mine. I pictured him as a butterfly, a yellow swallowtail, beautiful, elusive, transient, touching down on a soft petal, then moving on. "You look like a swimmer," I said.

"You girls just cruising?"

Jennie switched on the radio. The BeeGees were singing "Stayin' Alive" and Bobby Jones started bouncing his left leg up and down. "We're going drinking," Jennie said.

"Well, it's going to be a great party. Why don't you come?"

"I told my boyfriend I'd be over." Jennie started to speak with Bobby Jones's relaxed, laid-back inflection.

"So give 'im a call."

Jennie glanced at me and winked. "Well, we could give you a ride to where you're going, but I don't think I'll go to the party. We've gotta get back."

"It's a long drive. I'll jump in the back."

I didn't want him to jump in the back. "The dog sleeps in the back," I said.

"I sure don't want to smell like a dog tonight." He fluffed his golden hair. He looked Nordic, Aryan, the opposite of men I'd known, completely uncomplicated. "You girls go to school?"

We gave him our names, so he stopped calling us "girls." Jennie used her maiden name. I'd never changed mine. "I go to Rutgers," Jennie said. "Debbie's a junior at Barnard."

"They got a nice pool at Columbia." He turned to me. "What're you studying?"

"She's going to be an architect." Jennie spoke for me, knowing I had a hard time lying.

"I'm not sure," I put in. "Maybe journalism. Journalism and urban planning."

"Sounds pretty heavy to me." It seemed he had trouble absorbing the heaviness of my professional choices. He returned to the pool. "You swim in it?"

"All the time." Jennie had started the game and I knew that for half an hour or so I could pretend.

"You swim distance or speed?"

Distance sounded as if it would entail less discussion, so I said I swam fifty laps three times a week and he nodded, impressed and silenced. What I liked about lying to him was that Jennie and I were conspiring again, the way we had when we were kids. And if Bobby Jones was dumb enough to believe we were college students cruising in our father's car, if he wanted to ignore the fact that we were wives, mothers, divorcees, so be it.

He leaned against me and looked toward Jennie. "You go to Rutgers?"

"I'm studying art. I'm a ceramicist." He didn't understand the word. "A potter. I make pots."

"Guess I got a ride with some very talented ladies." And he took a flask from his back pocket. "Can you make bread with pots?" He handed Jennie the flask.

It took her a moment to translate that sentence into English. "Sure, people buy dishes, don't they?" She took a swig, grimaced, and passed it to me.

"Wish I had some smoke, but those guys back there, my friends, they cleaned me out. I'll get some more at the party. Why don't we go? C'mon. Call your boyfriend. Tell 'im you've got a flat tire, but make sure he doesn't come and get you." As I passed him the flask, his fingers slid over mine. Then he took his left arm and put it across the back of the seat, and when I put my head back, it rested on his arm.

Jennie cut into the next Mobil station. "Got a dime?" she asked me. We got out of the car and I followed Jennie to the pay phone. "Fill 'er up," she called to the gas station attendant.

"We're not seriously going to that party, are we?"

"I could use a party." She picked up the receiver to dial.

"But we've told him all these ridiculous lies."

"If he goes to Princeton, I'm a Rhodes Scholar. He's just trying to impress us."

"You think he's lying?" But she motioned for me to be quiet and closed the door to the phone booth, shutting me out. I caught bits of what she said. That I wanted to see a film in Princeton; did he mind?

The station attendant finished putting gas into the car by the time Jennie was off the phone. She'd convinced Tom I was depressed by their fight and needed a film to cheer me up. In the car, Bobby Jones watched us, flask in hand, and he waved for us to come along. Jennie signaled for him to wait. "Let's find a newspaper." She handed the attendant her credit card and asked if he had one. He pointed to the office, where we found yesterday's covered with grease. "O.K., did you see *Star Wars*?" I nodded. "Fine. We'll tell him we saw *Empire Strikes Back*. I hear it's more of the same."

This time Bobby Jones slid over and he sat in the middle, between us. He handed me the flask as I slipped in beside him. His arms were broad and I was wedged between his swimmer's arms, his butterfly wings, and the window. "You girls paid with a credit card, huh? Not bad." He laughed as Jennie started the motor and I tried to figure how old you had to be to pay with a credit card.

The party was in the garage of someone whose parents lived somewhere half the year and somewhere else the other half. We parked a good two blocks away, even though Bobby kept saying, "You can park closer." But if the police raided, we didn't want them to get our auto registration. The house, Bobby told us as we walked into the garage, was "off limits" without special permission of the host. "You know," he said, saying the obvious, "if you'd like a little privacy."

Everyone knew Bobby. He was slapping hands with all kinds of people and kept saying, "Gimme five, brother." He made a general announcement that he'd brought "a couple of chicks along." "This is Deborah," he said, pointing to Jennie. "And this is Jennifer," pointing to me.

"It's the other way around," I said.

He corrected the announcement. "I'm bad with names. Let's get a drink," and he took me by the arm. We were greeted by a black man named Victor, who wore coveralls and seemed gay and was serving some kind of brownish punch. And by

Rupert, our host, who wore white jeans and red suspenders but no shirt. His chest was covered with thick, black hair. They called Rupert's girlfriend, whose real name was Natalie, Chiquita Banana, and I never found out why. Natalie, who told me to call her Chiquita because everyone else did, took me aside. "You here with Bobby?"

"Well, he brought us to the party."

"So that means you're with him." She wore a black T-shirt and no bra and she chewed a wad of gum in the side of her cheek. She was a freshman at Douglass and told me that almost everyone at this party went to Rutgers. "Oh, good," I said. "Jennie should feel right at home." I was growing more comfortable with misrepresenting ourselves, but I wondered if our clothes were correct. We wore jeans, T-shirts, sandals, but we both had bras. But it wasn't just the clothes. I knew that, in no way, was I still able to resemble Chiquita.

"I go to school in New York."

"It's dangerous. I hate that city."

"You get used to it."

"Have fun with Bobby." She grinned at me, envious, I thought. Then she disappeared into the crowd.

I found Jennie talking with Victor and helping him pour hard punch. "Watch out," Victor said, handing me a cup and straightening his earring. "It's a real sleeper. Bottles of hard stuff."

The punch was in an old bathtub and there was plenty of it.

"We can't stay late," I whispered to Jennie.

"Would you relax and have some fun?"

Rupert had fixed up the garage for the party. It was clear that he came from some wealth. The garage was equipped with a quadraphonic system, complete with tape deck, headsets, a million records, and a tuner that looked like an EKG. Sound floated around me and seemed to come from all directions. I sipped my punch until I found I was having trouble standing, so I sat down on one of the three mattresses on the floor.

Couples lay in each other's arms. A bleary-eyed boy passed me a joint and I took a toke. This isn't a good idea, a small voice somewhere in the middle of my pituitary gland said. The girl who'd been lying in the arms of the bleary-eyed boy, a tiny, red-headed child, got up and walked away and began kissing a rather tall, gawky boy who leaned against a wall. They walked outside. The Village People sang "YMCA." Then Kansas sang "Dust in the Wind," making me feel mortal, vulnerable. After that, I didn't recognize the music, and the bleary-eyed boy sat stupefied and looking lonely in the corner. I asked him what the music was and he knew all the groups. They had space-age names. Flying Saucer, Satellite Returns, Lunar Module, Jet Stream. Pink Floyd sang "Dark Side of the Moon," which put the bleary-eyed boy into a trance until the red-haired girl returned and, no questions asked, the boy took her back.

Other couples drifted in and out of each other's arms with equal facility and I felt like an anthropologist, trying to understand how these primitives bonded. "Hey, how'ya doing?" Bobby flopped down on the mattress beside me, squeezing my left biceps.

"I'm a little sleepy."

"Oh, that's the punch." He took a joint out of the air, it seemed, puffed it, and passed it back into the air.

"What's in it?"

"It's easier to tell you what's not in it."

"Oh, great." I leaned my head back against his arm. It took me a few moments to realize he was rubbing my arm with his index finger in a gentle circular motion whose intent could not be mistaken. After a few complete elliptical orbits, he whispered, "Wanta see the house?"

"Maybe we could just go for a walk?"

"Naw, too many mosquitoes. You'll get eaten alive." He was pulling me to my feet with a jerking stroke, as if he were raising a flag.

"I need some fresh air."

"We'll open a window." But I was adamant and finally he agreed to take a walk. "Let me get a little ice for this drink first, O.K.?"

We passed Jennie. "I'm going for a walk," I mumbled. She said something about when we were leaving but I didn't quite catch it and she didn't repeat it. The ice, it turned out, was in the kitchen of the house. Bobby fumbled in the freezer. I wouldn't go beyond the kitchen, I told myself. The house had become in my mind some dark force of evil and corruption, some den of iniquity. Bobby hit the ice tray on the Formica and ice fell onto the counter. He plunked a few cubes into our glasses. The kitchen lights were bright and I didn't want to look at him and be betrayed by a few white hairs, a wrinkle on my brow.

When he started to lead me toward the living room, I protested. "Look, you wanta go for a walk? The door's that way." For some reason that made sense to me, so I followed, but when we got into the living room, which was very dark with only the light of the street light, he paused. "Boy, am I tired. Let's sit for a minute. I wanta talk to you." Why is darkness sensual? I asked myself. Why is it we never want to make love in a kitchen under fluorescent lights?

But no one was going to make love here. I'd made that decision as we sat down on the sofa, and once I make a decision, I stick to it. The living room seemed like a good compromise, except after a few moments I felt uncomfortable there. The walls were covered with bad art, Jersey kitsch, and all the lamps had plastic slipcovers. The furniture was covered with white sheets, as if someone had recently died and the rooms weren't to be used again.

I sat beside Bobby, twirling my glass in my hands and feeling very much the awkward age he thought I was. "I like you," he said. I kept turning the glass, faster and faster like a globe, and Mark's mother with her endless motion of hands came to mind. I stopped. "Let's go upstairs," he said.

I didn't want to go but I found myself walking, climbing the stairs. We entered Rupert's parents' room, which had the biggest king-size fake brass bed I'd ever seen and yellow wall-to-wall carpeting. The whole house, I suddenly realized, was done in yellow wall-to-wall carpeting. I thought to myself, I can't make love with yellow carpeting everywhere. And suddenly it was the carpeting and not the arms of an eighteen-year-old boy I couldn't bear.

The bedroom had the whole family photographed above the bed in various stages of development and ecstasy. Baby pictures, wedding pictures, graduation, a football victory, a million shots of the family dog, usually with a blunt object between its teeth. We lay down beneath them, and Bobby began to move across my body in a perfunctory and predictable fashion. It made sense that this rather pure, simple boy would be the one to shatter Mark's hold in a rather simple, meaningless act. No real man could do it, so I submitted and began to breathe deeply, the way I do when I go to the dentist.

He dug his tongue into my mouth about as far as a tongue could go and squeezed my breasts. "Take this off." He tugged at my green T-shirt. His clothes, mine, were pulled off. Shoes fell like bombs. Two bewildered goldfish in a nearby bowl watched, wide-eyed but apathetic. Then he assumed what must have been his posture for a racing dive and proceeded to plunge. "I don't have any birth control with me," I said, suddenly brought back to my senses. "Don't worry," he gasped. "I'll pull out." Which is what he did, seconds later, spilling himself over the fake quilted spread, which matched the color of the indifferent goldfish. "Jesus," he moaned, gritting his teeth, and I looked at him with the somewhat mesmerized expression of a person watching a television program for the hell of it.

"You were great." He sighed, rolling over, embedding his sperm into a round stain on the polyester spread, and I fell asleep beside him, more as a result of the punch than of his prowess.

When I woke, someone was calling my name. I looked out, and in the driveway I saw Jennie, confused, calling me as if she'd lost a puppy. I shook Bobby as I left. "Gotta go," I said. "Do you know what time it is?"

"Don't go, babe." He tried to pull me back down but I pulled away. "When can I see you?"

"In a week or so."

"O.K., gimme your address." I told him where I lived and gave him the phone number of American Airlines, confident he wouldn't remember a thing.

The air was cool and fresh as Jennie and I walked to the car. "I'm afraid you'll disapprove of me," I offered as an apology.

"I've never disapproved of you in my life. So you went to bed with him, so what? Probably did you good."

"I think it was the punch."

Jennie put an arm around my shoulder. "I think it was the body." We reached the car. She was also a little drunk, and Victor had gotten weird with her. That was when she'd begun looking for me. "Is that the first time?"

"First time." I crawled into the front seat.

"How was it?"

"Awful."

I turned on the radio. It was "Oldies but Goodies." As Jennie drove, I wrote letters to Mark, informing him of my new involvement with Robert Jones. "Dear Mark, I hope this letter finds you well. I've been seeing someone for a while now, a younger man, not as smart as you but certainly more potent, and I think it would be best if we finalized things between us . . ." That didn't seem strong enough. "Dear Mark, I hope you and Lila are well. I'm living with someone as well. Rob coaches swimming at Princeton, where he is finishing his graduate work in international affairs. We are incredibly happy . . ."

Jennie was speeding. "You should slow down," I said.

"It's really late. I didn't know it was this late." Her face seemed compressed into her eyes, her eyes squinting sharp on the road.

"I'll talk to Tom. Don't worry."

"I'm not worried." She wasn't convincing.

The streetlights on the road rushed past me, and the road was bright, reflecting the lights. I thought about my body. How it felt raw and exposed, barely satisfied, and only half awake. The lights on the road, all evenly spaced, held me.

7

I'D BEEN BACK in Manhattan only a week when Sean called. He was going to be in New York for interviews and asked if he could see me Wednesday night. I probably would have said no if the apartment hadn't smelled like Mark and felt like Mark when I returned. There were tennis racquets, dishes we'd bought together, and other reminders. My sense of rage and injustice came back. Mark was living only a few blocks away with Lila, and I still wanted to hurt them as they'd hurt me. I tried to stay busy. I spent time with my upstairs neighbor, Sally, who worked for *Women's Wear*, and with other friends, but still I couldn't forget. So when Sean asked me to go out with him, I said yes.

I had just stepped out of the shower when the doorbell rang. Glancing at the clock as I wrapped myself in a robe, I saw he was an hour early. I hate people who are early, so I buzzed him in and prepared myself to tell him I wouldn't go out with him. When I looked through the peephole, I saw Bobby Jones standing in the hallway.

I opened the door hesitantly. "Hi." He beamed. "Remember me?"

More than I cared to. "How'd you find me?"

"You gave me your address and some crazy phone number, remember? What'd you think? I'd forget you?"

He waltzed into the living room, moving with an athlete's gait, that strange swagger in which the torso doesn't budge. "Is this your grandfather?" He was pointing to a photograph my father had taken of Albert Einstein.

"No," I said flatly. "That's Albert Einstein."

"Far out." He looked at my head, wrapped in a towel, my bathrobe, as if noticing them for the first time. "Did I catch you at a bad moment?"

"I'm expecting company at six."

"Oh, you've got time."

Time for what, I thought. At the rate he made love, there was plenty of time. But Bobby was intent on scrutinizing the apartment. "You live here with your folks?"

I tried to recall what stories Jennie and I had told him that night, but I couldn't remember. Liars need good memories. "I used to live here with this guy but he split. So now a friend lives here with me but she's not around much."

Bobby wasn't a complete fool. He glanced at the bleached-wood Scandinavian furniture, at the African wall hanging, the director's chairs, the potted plants. This was no college girl's place. Where were the beer cans, the papers piled high, the Indian-print bedspreads flung across everything you sat on? "You got any stash?" he asked, after a pause. Mark had walked out with the small funeral urn we'd picked up in Greece and I hadn't bothered to replace it.

"How about some Johnny Walker?"

"Sure," he said, flopping down on the sofa. He was disappointed but consenting. I wondered if he was old enough to drink, as I poured two shots of Scotch and handed it to him.

"I'm just going to comb out my hair." Bobby found the stereo and was content. He put on an old Stones album and lay back again into the sofa. I pulled on a skirt and blouse and ran a comb through my long auburn hair, which I then twisted into a knot.

Bobby sat up and opened his eyes when I walked into the living room. "Hey, babe, you look great. Come here."

"Look, I have to tell you something. My friend just made up that whole story. I'm not in college. I'm not in graduate school. When you were learning how to tie your shoelaces, I was graduating from college. I think I'm old enough to date your father."

"You mean you're over thirty?" He seemed despondent.

I nodded.

"I don't care. We can have a good time, can't we? I like the idea of an older woman." I'd never been the older woman before.

"I have to get ready to go out," I said.

He nodded. Then asked me somewhat sheepishly, "Who's Albert Einstein?"

I was in the middle of explaining the theory of relativity and Einstein's perception of space and time when the doorbell rang, and Bobby looked at me, a little stunned.

"Is that your date already?" I nodded solemnly. "Is there another way out of here?"

I felt saddened, as if I had tampered with someone's innocence the way someone had tampered with mine. "The front door will be all right," I replied.

Sean passed Bobby Jones on the stairs, glanced at him with a somewhat suspicious look, and walked into my apartment. Bobby Jones winked at me as he left. "Who's the kid?" Sean asked as he walked in. He smiled and there seemed to be something different about him, which I attributed to his clothes. He wore a blue and white striped shirt, a blue blazer, and white corduroys, and seemed more grown up to me than he had when I saw him at Jennie's.

"Oh, just someone. I'd better change."

"You look all right."

"But you're dressed up." I pointed to the liquor cabinet and he poured himself a drink.

"Contributing to the delinquency of a minor?" he called as I walked into the bedroom.

"I think it's the other way around. Where're we going?"

"To a sneak preview."

I don't remember much about the sneak preview except that Clint Eastwood starred and Sean took a fall off a roof. "That" — he pointed to the screen as a body tumbled down — "was me." It was shortly after he fell that Sean took my hand. I'm not sure I remember him taking it but I do remember looking down and seeing his hand wrapped around mine. Sean looked to see what I was looking at. He whispered to me, "I'm just holding your hand. Is that all right?"

"I guess it's all right. Are you going to fall again?"

"A little later."

"Do you get paid much for doing this?"

"More than you can imagine."

Someone shushed us. I sat staring blankly at the screen for the remainder of the film, uncomfortably conscious of my hand resting in his, waiting for Sean to fall off the roof again.

Friday was the kind of night when you can see the air oscillating in front of you, when everything seems to be moving at the wrong speed. Sean picked me up at seven sharp, which is what he said he'd do when he phoned me that afternoon at my office to say he'd be in the city a few more days. I had decided, since I was back in New York, that I'd go in to work a couple of days a week and Bill Wicker said it was fine with him.

Sally was visiting when Sean picked me up. I was in the bathroom, so she got the door. She called to me, "There's some gorgeous guy here to see you." It was Sally's humor but she made Sean uncomfortable immediately. When I looked at him, standing in the doorway, I saw, however, that Sally had perhaps made an accurate observation. Over dinner, he seemed restless. "Your friend, is she always so blunt?" I apologized for Sally, saying she was a journalist and generally said what was on her mind.

After dinner Sean wanted to walk to Times Square and maybe catch a show. He had no idea what show, what kind of show, he wanted to see. We bought a paper that felt wet to the touch and wilted in our hands. "You want to walk to Times Square in this heat?" But he insisted. Most of the films I'd seen he hadn't, and vice versa. "Here we are," he complained, "in the middle of Fun City and we can't find anything to do." We decided to stroll. He rolled up his shirt sleeves before we'd gone two blocks, and I put up my hair. "Why don't we decide what we want to do and take a cab?" I suggested.

"Why don't we just walk and find something?"

"I think we should go somewhere air-conditioned."

It was the kind of night when every smell is stronger than anything you've ever smelled before, the kind of weather people have in mind when they warn travelers, "Don't visit New York in July." So I was with a madman who wanted to walk throught the grimiest parts of the city in a July heat wave. Mark would have known where we were going and we'd have taken a cab. It would have been planned before we walked out the door. We were both great planners. Most people who visited our apartment noticed that all our books were in alphabetical order.

"Look" — Sean took me by the elbow — "when was the last time you walked to Times Square?"

"They have a subway that takes you right there. It's very efficient. Isn't that easier?"

But Sean won. He didn't want to be indoors. It was the war that had made him hate being inside. As we walked, he told me about his "bit part" in Vietnam. He had dropped out of Yale at the height of the war and the army made him a deal. He didn't have to take off to Canada and he didn't have to bribe some poor doctor. He just had to run the radio station for servicemen in Saigon. He'd never seen real action. But he spent nine months inside a radio station, reading off lists of dead and MIAs and POWs in between the Stones and Roberta Flack, and the greatest effect it had on him was that he'd lost the ability to be indoors for long.

He loved to window shop. "I'm a consumer," he said as we passed a head shop. "Everything I see, I want to buy."

"I always buy things I don't really want."

He shook his head as we paused in front of an antique store. There was a walnut chest in the window he said he liked. He knew it was walnut because of the grain and the color. "I like walnut and oak best," he said. "What do you like?"

"Formica." I was a little annoyed.

He laughed and said that sometimes he found me very funny.

"You know, if you've never just walked to Times Square for the hell of it, it'll do you good," he said, as he started walking. At Lincoln Center we bought some ice cream cones at an outdoor Italian café on Broadway. "Why will it do me good?" I didn't see anything good about spending the evening walking around Manhattan when the humidity was 94 percent and the temperature about the same. "It's very hot. Why don't we just sit in front of Lincoln Center and watch everyone go to the opera?"

"You're an urban planner. And you don't experience the city. It doesn't make sense."

"I don't need to experience anything. I look at maps. They tell me what I need to know. I look at charts; they tell me how many people live somewhere, walk somewhere, how many cars go by in an hour, and so on. Then I write elaborate grant proposals for millions of dollars based on those facts." I was being glib and stubborn. In truth, a large part of my time was spent examining neighborhoods and writing rather emotional reports about urban conditions.

"In other words, you wouldn't go to Times Square unless you had tickets for a show?"

"That's about right."

"Well, a change will be good for you." I wasn't sure I liked being told what would be good for me, but lately I wasn't necessarily the best judge anyway. Sean wanted to see the night life up close. He wanted to feel the pulse of the city, get its filth all over his shirt, his neck, his hands. "I always know when I've been to Manhattan," he said. "My shirt gets dirty in half an hour."

Two transvestites and a bag lady passed us. The neighborhood was starting to change. Street people appeared, the emaciated kind who took drugs. Panhandlers. People with no place to go. And no one to go to. We passed a peepshow and Sean stopped. "Have you ever been inside one of these?"

I shrugged my shoulders. "It really doesn't interest me."

"Have you ever been inside?"

"Let's go somewhere nice, O.K.?"

"We'll go somewhere nice but I'd just like to see what it looks like inside one of these places."

"I think," I said, "that this is one of those things in life I can live without."

But he was already handing a few dollars for admission to the shriveled lady with no teeth and very little hair, and we walked into a room filled with little booths, the kind you take four pictures in for a quarter. Some of the booths had their curtains closed and I could see pairs of shiny shoes that businessmen wear. I decided I was in no immediate danger. We picked a booth, closed the curtain, and dropped a quarter into the slot. "Do you do this often?" I asked Sean.

"Every chance I get." We both peered into the movieola as the film began. It was an eight-millimeter, home-type movie that seemed to have some kind of plot. A woman is devastatingly drawn to another man's male lover. The man seems to be her husband or fiancé. While the men are willing to fondle and tantalize the woman, they end up making love to one another, though the picture fades before they actually get into anything too complicated.

As we left our booth, we saw a small group of men, very middle-class, homebody types, in jackets, heading into what was called "the theater." The word "Theater" was written in very elegant pink letters with lots of swirls, each letter outlined in black. "Must be some kind of vaudeville act," Sean said.

"The theater" consisted of about twenty booths, all in a circle, each with a curtain at the entrance and a black window in front, facing the stage. We entered a booth, closed the curtain, and put another quarter into another slot. The black window began to rise and we heard music coming from the other side of the window.

When the window was up, I saw two women, in G-strings and with spangles on their nipples, writhing on the stage and clawing their way toward the windows that were open. Pairs of little eyes peered from their windows and the eyes seemed to grow glassy as the dancing grew more frenzied, and for a few moments I found myself transfixed by the shimmying breasts and gyrating hips. The women seemed to have some kind of oil on their skin, and when one of the women sat back on her heels, swaying in a circular motion in front of our window, she looked like a snake in heat as she crawled in the direction of our window.

"All right," Sean said, catching me by the elbow as I hailed a cab. "I made a mistake. It was a big mistake. I'm sorry. I didn't know it would upset you." Regular Broadway theater was getting out and there weren't any cabs to be had.

"I'd just like to go home. Is that all right?"

He held me firmly by the elbow. "I made a mistake. I've made a lot of mistakes. I didn't mean to upset you. I'm an actor; I make movies. I didn't think going in there would cause this crisis."

"You're apologizing again," I told him. "There isn't anything to apologize for. I'd just like to go home."

Sean held me tightly, but when I stared at where his fingers had wrapped themselves around my arm, he loosened his grip. "I didn't take you to a peepshow to upset you. I didn't take you there to make you feel bad or because I thought it would be good for our souls or so you could stage a protest on Seventh Avenue or walk away from me or so we could have a disagreement about my inappropriate behavior or so you can decide all men are impossible. I took you there as a goof. For the hell of it." I was staring at a piece of gum, flattened on the sidewalk, as I told him I didn't think it was "a goof" to watch people humiliate themselves.

Sean stared at the same piece of gum I had my eyes fixed on. It was a brownish wad that had gotten walked on for a long time. For decades, maybe, and it was in the shape of an eyeball with a dent in the middle, where someone had put a cleat, and it seemed to be staring back at us. A miserable, brown eyeball, a wad of gum, permanently embedded in the sidewalk of Broadway. Chewing gum comes from Chicago, where I come from, and at that moment I wished more than anything that I were home. That I'd never left home.

He raised his voice. "Sometimes I think you like to have a bad time and take everything so seriously. I think disagreeing and being very serious makes you feel nice and safe. Do you want to know something? Everyone is scared. Everyone is just as scared and afraid as you are. Everyone. And I haven't been with a woman in a long time, so why don't we just say that we're all scared and we all make mistakes and start the evening over."

A small crowd had formed, ready to absorb any tragedy that came their way in New York, and watched us argue. Sean shooed them away with some determination. I looked around Broadway. All the cabs were filled. "I'm sorry," I said. "I just don't see what the big deal was. Walk to Times Square. Watch some sad people make a display of themselves."

He rubbed his forehead. "I really am doing it all wrong, aren't I? I just haven't been with a woman in a while."

My hand reached up. "You know," I began, "you can drop out of fine universities and risk your life doing stupid stunts, waiting to make it big somewhere, and make all kinds of profound statements about how other people should live their lives and what they should do and what they need, but in the end I don't see where your life is any great model for how we should live. You know what you are?" I went on. "You're a watcher. You look at people and make judgments. You sit back and watch and criticize. No one means anything to you. Nothing means anything to you. That's why you'll never be a great actor or director or whatever you want to be. How can you understand someone else if you can't even understand yourself?"

"Did it ever occur to you," he said, "that you push people away from you?"

What was I doing in this mess? I glanced around me and looked at a sign across the street. It was one of a man, the size of a building, continuously smoking, an endless flow of vapor, day after day, year after year, pouring from his mouth. Like some steamy oracle, some deadly pronouncement, he ruled over us. I looked back down at the wad of gum and knew I was being watched on all sides, and those writhing breasts at the entrance to the peepshow seemed to be observing this as well.

The light above me was green and a sign read WALK, so I walked. I crossed Broadway and left Sean standing in front of the peepshow. I was aware of traffic that came to a halt, of screeching brakes, and then of people pushing past me. I crossed to Forty-second Street and headed down the steps into the subway. Pimps and hookers in their pink satin heels were doing business on the stairs. Puerto Rican boys, radios blasting, raced down. Theatergoers used the railing, walking arm in arm.

I went with them all. There was a big procession of us, heading to the token booth. I went down with the Chinese and the Japanese, the blacks and the Chicanos, the tourists and the permanent residents. The rich and the poor. The native New Yorkers. I went down with the cops and the criminals, the runaways and misfits and members of the Racquet Club and the illegal aliens and the professors and the *Times* reporters and the single people and the divorced and widowed people and old people and frigid and impotent people and those who looked like they'd had too much sex altogether and those who looked like they hadn't had it in years. I walked among the workaholics, the alcoholics, the coffee drinkers, the pill poppers, the weight watchers and Turkish bath users, the chain smokers, the people who'd stopped being chain smokers, the people who'd been hypnotized, terrorized, mesmerized, analyzed, declawed, defanged, who'd improved themselves, exercised themselves, rid themselves of any germ of self-destruction. They were coming home from night school; they were going out to mug somebody. Everyone was going to improve themselves somehow. Everyone was going to take the same goddamn express train I was going to take.

Sean was right about one thing. I had only been thinking about myself for a while. But who was he to try and take my mind off it? As I entered the subway, my future suddenly seemed in doubt. The token taker hollered at me as I pulled out a twenty. I fumbled for a five while people standing in line behind me sighed impatiently and someone asked me to move out of the way.

I decided to get lost, to lose myself underground. I decided to ask the pimp in the pink suit if he could use an extra hand. I walked toward him and he started to smile. All his teeth had been filed to gold points and he had a dozen gold chains around his neck. He was tall and shiny on top, like the Chrysler Building. The pimp smiled as I walked toward him through the tunnel and he seemed to be leading me deeper and deeper inside and I was lost somewhere in the bottom of the city I knew by heart on a drawing board.

Sean was standing in the same place where I'd left him, staring at the brown wad of gum stuck into the sidewalk, and he glanced up when he saw me coming, a look of sadness in his eyes. My hand was raised in a clenched fist. He was a stuntman, after all. He could take a punch for me. I don't think I would have hit him, but he caught my arm and held my wrist lightly between his fingers. "I'm really sorry," he said.

"So am I," I replied.

I don't know how long we held one another, but it seemed like a long time, long enough for the tourists from New Jersey, those shell-shocked housewives from the Oranges and their husbands in green leisure suits, to stop and stare at us, as if we were the show they'd paid those exorbitant bridge tolls to see. After a while, we walked slowly. "Look, what do you want to do?" Sean asked me.

"I think I want to go home."

He agreed to take me home, but only after I agreed to see him again the next night.

That was the night we ran into Mark and Lila. We had gone down to MacDougal Street for Indian food and were on our way to the Lone Star when I saw them walking toward us. It was too bad, because Sean and I had been having a fairly good time that evening. He'd done an imitation of a Hindi accent in the restaurant and folded his napkin into a mouse so that it frightened the woman seated next to him. We were laughing as we strolled up Fifth Avenue and my arm rested in his.

I squeezed Sean's elbow gently. "Listen," I mumbled, "I'm not sure what I should do, but my husband and the woman he lives with are walking toward us."

Sean looked up discreetly. There were a lot of people on the street but somehow he knew who I meant immediately. "Do you want to avoid them or do you want to say hello?"

I looked up, expecting they would have disappeared, turned off down the block, or, rather like phantoms I'd just conjured, vaporized and floated away in the air. They could not have had any real substance; they seemed more to be figments of some perverse side of my imagination. At times I have thought we invent the world with our minds, that the weather, the people, what we do with the people, can all be controlled with some simple act of will and that if you will evil, you will have it, and if you will good, you will have that.

I knew I wanted to avoid them but I refused to just cross over. The age of gladiators, of knights and great heroes, is long gone and the great battles are now being fought quietly at home or in the heart, but they also require enormous courage. I said, "I think we have to say hello."

"Then just keep walking." Sean folded his free hand over my fingers. "And act like you're crazy about me."

Mark and Lila had seen us as well and they seemed to be having a similar conversation. They were reaching the same conclusion. They kept coming toward us. If Sean hadn't been with me, I think I could have killed her. I'd spent months fearing this encounter, terrified to walk into the Museum of Natural History, to ride the 104, not knowing what I'd do when at last I ran into them, as I knew I would. I think I could have killed her not only because she was with Mark, but because I'd helped her conjugate French verbs back in high school, when she could hardly spell her own name, and it seemed to me that people with that kind of history owe one another, if nothing else, an apology.

They stopped first and acted surprised. "Well," Mark said, "small world." He pecked me on the cheek. Lila was silent, morose, though forcing a smile. I could tell I'd ruined her evening. It was difficult to know if they were happy. Lila looked a little yellow to me, as if she were recovering from a disease.

Everyone was uncomfortable, so Sean picked up the ball and carried it marvelously. "We were just going to hear some music. You folks going to dinner?" They were going to eat "something." They'd just seen a double feature at the Waverly. Mark looked as if he needed to eat. He seemed thin to me in his khaki pants, and Sean seemed strong beside him in his jeans and workshirt.

Mark sneezed into a handkerchief with *ML* monogrammed on it. He liked having his initials on his belongings, as if he needed to be reminded of who he was. Lila said "God bless you" twice. She seemed a bit uneasy, the way Helen must have felt when she realized what she'd done to Troy.

"Got your allergies early this year," I said. Lila flashed my way, as if I weren't supposed to know that my own husband had hay fever. But I looked back at her. I wanted her to know that I knew about more than his hay fever. I knew about the two little moles at the base of his spine, the scar below his nipple where he'd been stabbed in a street fight with a pocket knife; I could find his circumcision scar in the dark. I knew him as well as I knew Manhattan. I knew his body as well as I knew anything.

"How's the Bronx project going?" Mark sneezed.

Lila said "God bless you" again.

"The council keeps pushing us back. I've written all the reports."

"You write terrific reports," Mark said. Lila was displeased. She didn't like it when someone else was praised. She had her thick hair pulled back with a red ribbon. She used to

wear it that way when we were teen-agers, and all the boys
pulled the ribbon. Once I thought she was cheating off my
paper during a French exam. I moved my arm away so that she
could see. I always wanted to cheat off her paper during Euro-
pean history exams. Lila knew the dates of all the big battles.

I looked at Lila with all the objectivity and scrutiny of a
judge about to hand down a terrible verdict. I looked at her
jaundiced features, her chestnut hair, her thin legs. She was
transparent and tough as a spider's web and with about as
much substance. I memorized her, the way a spy memorizes
his instructions before setting them on fire.

"Where do you work?" Lila asked Sean.

"In film."

"You look like an actor." She smiled.

"Thanks," Sean replied, uncertain if it was really a
compliment.

"So, how've you been?" I asked Mark. I didn't care so much
to know the answer as I cared to detain them more, in the face
of Lila's discomfort and desire to move on.

"Busy, busy, busy. The wheels of progress turn slowly."
Had he always spoken in clichés? I tried to remember. He used
to always repeat himself for emphasis. Once he repeated himself so many times in court "for emphasis" that the judge
finally said, "Mr. Lusterman, I believe you've made your
point."

"We've got a big rape case in the office now," Mark con-
tinued, seeming to free-associate. "Lila refused to defend the
guy. She took one look at him and said, 'That's a rapist if I ever
saw one.' You should see this guy. Nobody wants to defend
him."

"Isn't he entitled to a defense?" Sean said. "Isn't that what
you guys do?"

"Where'd you go to law school?" Mark asked.

"He went to Yale," I broke in. Mark had done his under-
graduate work at Queens College and had always been

jealous of those who had Ivy League educations.

Sean squeezed my fingers, trying to divert a fight. "I didn't go to law school. I know a great little Indian restaurant, if you guys are hungry." They weren't particularly hungry.

"It was nice running into you." Lila turned to me.

"Wait." I'm not sure what I was going to say, because Sean tugged me and led me away, but I know I was prepared to insult her. He put his arm around me and we went on down Fifth Avenue. For a few moments we walked in silence. "I want to go home," I finally managed to say.

"You always want to go home."

"This time I mean it."

But Sean bought the *Voice* and decided we had to go to the Village Gate, which was in the opposite direction, because Howlin' Wolf was playing the eleven o'clock set. I didn't want to go but he led me, and I followed numbly, not caring very much where I went. We found a table in the back of the smoke-filled room. I felt as if it were happening for the first time. As if Mark had just left me and it was happening again.

"I just want to go home," I said.

"In a little bit." Between sets Sean said, "Do you want to talk now or do you want to just forget it?"

"I want to forget it."

"You don't want to talk?"

I shook my head. I never wanted to talk again.

"You know, you're completely transparent. It's so obvious what you're feeling." I didn't know that. "Interesting thing about polar bears. They have no facial expressions. That's what makes them so dangerous. You never know if they're going to attack. You're different. You can't hide a thing."

I was getting involved in the analogy. "Does that mean I'm not dangerous?"

He paused for a moment. "No, it just means you're different from a polar bear."

Someone came up and asked him if he was Robert De Niro.

"Robert De Niro doesn't have a beard," Sean said.

"You do look like him." I examined Sean's face. That was when I decided I would go to bed with him. Or rather, that I should go to bed with him. I could not, after all, continue being faithful to a man who no longer loved me, except for an occasional encounter with a hitchhiker half my age.

Sean turned back to me. "Why do you let other people run your life?"

I didn't answer. I didn't see how anybody was running my life. "I don't know what you mean."

"I mean you're letting them make you miserable."

I shrugged my shoulders, not really seeing that there was any alternative. "I suppose you've got control over your life."

"I have some control." He asked the bartender for the bill. "I'm controlling myself right now." From what he would not say. "I mean, I can understand you'd be upset after running into them, but why don't you just call her up and tell her what you think?"

My fingers clenched the bar. "I wouldn't give her the satisfaction."

"Satisfaction? What is this? The Middle Ages? If you're upset, get it off your chest."

I stared into my drink. The ice cube had melted with a hollow spot in the center and I stuck my finger in. "You don't understand." I turned the ice cube with my finger in the hollow spot.

Sean sighed. "Maybe they fell in love, maybe they were just right for one another. I don't even think you really want him back. But keeping it inside like this can only drive you nuts."

"I've known that woman since I was a little girl. She used to eat peanut butter sandwiches that my mother made for her at my house. You just don't go and do what she did."

"So tell her that. If you haven't talked to her about it . . ."

"You just don't understand. You don't get it, do you?" The bartender looked our way. "I hate her. Do you understand that?" The bartender motioned for me to keep it down. People at the bar were staring at us. "I hate her. I hate her."

In the cab I sat far away from him, my arms folded over my chest. "O.K.," he said as the cab sped up Sixth Avenue. "I can see why you hate her, but you're only hurting yourself."

But I didn't understand that. My rage had suddenly become a precious point of honor to me. If I was hurting myself, it was only as the kamikaze pilot hurts himself in completion of the mission and destruction of the enemy.

When we got back to my place, Sean took off his shoes and made himself comfortable. I curled up beside him. "Listen," he said, "I know you're upset, so I'll sleep here on the couch, all right?" I shook my head. "Oh, you want me to leave?" I shook my head again. "You want me to sleep with you?" I nodded. Sean got up and poured himself a cognac. "See that outside? That's morning. I think we should just get some sleep."

"I don't understand."

He came back with the cognac. "Listen, somewhere along the way I got to be a realist. If I touch a table" — he touched the table—"I want to feel the wood. If I touch a lamp, I want to feel the heat of the lamp. And if I touch a woman, I want to feel that woman."

I had no idea what he was talking about.

"What I'm saying is, I don't want to make love to you when you're thinking of someone else."

I'd never heard anything more ridiculous. "Is that very important?"

He laughed. "Not usually, but I'm afraid I care about you."

Sean unbuttoned his shirt, and when he was down to his T-shirt, I saw a large gash, as if something had bitten into the side of his arm. I leaned forward and touched it. It was a smooth, cratered hole in his shoulder, running down the biceps, and he'd gotten it in an explosion while doing stunts for a war film a few years back. "That's when I decided to do some serious work behind the camera," he told me, fluffing a pillow.

Five blocks away Mark slept in Lila's arms, and that was the worst pain I'd ever known. Women don't usually go to war or to sea, and most of our adventures are of the heart. We all fought our own wars and Sean had almost fought in a few real ones. All the wounds I'd ever known were inside and had a kind of unreality about them. And suddenly the internal wounds seemed insignificant to me, the way all the people you've had crushes on are gone in the face of someone you can really love.

He tucked me into my bed and kissed me on the forehead. I tried to pull him down. "No, not tonight. I don't want it to be tonight." But we were both exhausted, so he flopped down on the bed next to me and fell fast asleep.

It was almost morning, and the birds were just starting to sing. Five blocks away Mark slept with Lila, and I hadn't stopped wanting him back with me. The sky was a translucent blue, the color it turns just before they turn out the street lamps, but it seemed so very dark to me. I was thinking about Mark and Lila lying in bed together and I couldn't break away and the world was so very dark and empty as I tried to arouse Sean and have him make me forget. But Sean wouldn't be aroused.

The first night Mark and I lived together in our Cambridge apartment, we stayed up half the night. We cleaned the whole apartment, and when we were done cleaning, he pulled my shirt out of my pants. He lifted the shirt and unbuttoned a few buttons that exposed my belly. He touched the dark line that divides me, the one that descends from my navel to my groin. He followed the line up and down, then landed on my navel. He said because I love you, I know something about you. I know you have a light right here in the middle, a pilot light, and you can't let it go out. You must never let the light go out.

8

S EAN wasn't my type. I was fairly certain of that right away. He liked to get stoned and go to a film in the evening, but Mark liked to slave away in a tie and shirt sleeves, trying to save the poor. Sean had as much in common with Mark as Hollywood had with the Bronx, but I decided to see him, if only to keep my mind off other things. We saw one another frequently but we didn't become lovers, and I knew we'd gone through the kind of ambivalence men and women go through before they settle into becoming friends.

I knew I would never fall in love with him. You can always tell when you're going to fall in love with someone, and I could tell that Sean wasn't the kind of man I'd fall in love with. He was too uncomplicated and easygoing for me to fall in love with. He took things too much in stride. I wasn't even sure a person could fall in love in the city. I knew it was difficult to stay in love in the city. But to fall in love you have to stand still, and how do you stand still in a city where nothing stands still?

One night after dinner, Sean wanted to go down by the

Hudson to see the sunset. "What for?" I asked. "A New York sunset is just pollution."

Sean smiled his crooked half-smile. His blue eyes, almost turquoise against his blue shirt, tried to figure out what I wanted. "All right. We'll do whatever you want."

I didn't know what I wanted to do, so we went down to the river. Sean lent me his copy of the *Voice*, which I sat on while he sat on the grass. He had met with Arthur Hansom that afternoon and was excited about his new job as an assistant director. "You know, I'll probably be going to L.A. soon." The sunset looked boring to me. A rather mottled shade of orange. "I've got to take care of locations, casting, all kinds of details. And then maybe I'll get a chance to direct."

"Oh, I didn't know you wanted to direct." He wore pale blue socks and jeans, and as he rested, leaning back on his arms, his pants rose up in such a way that I could see the skin between his socks and his pants.

"Everyone wants to direct, unless you really want to act. I want to make something that's all mine." For some reason I couldn't take my eyes off the small patch of very white leg. It made me uncomfortable to think of this large, handsome man with such a white, skinny, hairless leg, the kind of leg you'd expect to see on a polio victim, a withered useless limb.

It was at that moment, as I stared at the white leg, that the rat ran by us, or rather around us. It started from a tree not far from Sean and I saw it in the corner of my eye. It was your average brown, filthy New York City rat, and I thought I saw its white tooth, one huge, white, pointed tooth, as it raced by. I jumped up, screaming, "Oh my God, did you see that? It ran right by us."

Sean, who had also seen it, jumped up too, not because of the rat but because of me. "It's gone," he said.

"Ugh, it makes me sick. I knew we shouldn't have come down here. Mark and I never came down here."

Sean looked at me rather somberly. "Well, I'm not Mark. Come on, let's go somewhere else."

I glanced down, afraid that I'd see the rat at Sean's foot, staring up at his pale white leg, but I was relieved to see that both the rat and Sean's flesh were out of sight. When we got back to Broadway, Sean said, "Come on. I want to take you somewhere."

"Where?"

Sean took me by the arm and led me toward Columbus. "It's a surprise. Don't you like surprises?" He smiled, almost to himself. "No more horses, no more smashing cars. And I'm solvent again." When we came to Baskin-Robbins, Sean stopped. "I'm treating you to ice cream."

"That's the surprise?"

"O.K., so I'll take you to the Four Seasons when I get my first paycheck, deal?"

I said it was a deal.

"What kind of ice cream do you want?"

I thought for a moment. "Maybe I should pay for this. You just got the job."

"Look, you aren't under any obligation. What flavor?"

I pondered the options. "Chocolate," I said definitely, after a moment of silence.

He waited. "What kind of chocolate? They've got a dozen kinds of chocolate in there. Marshmallow Magic, Rocky Road, Fudge Ripple . . ."

I raised my hands. "I don't care. Anything chocolate."

He put his hands obstinately on his hips. "What d'you mean, you don't care? You have to make up your mind. What d'you want?"

"Really, it doesn't matter." He was getting on my nerves.

"Of course it matters. What you want always matters."

Mark never asked me about ice cream. He asked me about what I thought of the latest Supreme Court decision or the volunteer army or the budget for the new administration, but if I said chocolate, he'd never say what kind of chocolate. He'd say that in the grand scheme those decisions were unimportant.

"It matters?"

"Of course it matters. What you want is what you feel. You want a sweater because you feel cold. You want a mint julep because you feel hot and sticky . . ."

I'd read somewhere that the lovelorn should eat chocolate because chocolate has an enzyme that you release when you're in love. I thought very hard. Marshmallow Magic sounded too illusory, and I'd had my fill of the bittersweet. I wanted something with strength and texture, yet at the same time gentle and smooth. "Jamoca Almond Fudge."

"Is that all?" I nodded and he smiled encouragingly. "Wait here." He went inside, took a number, flashed it to me, and signaled that there were three ahead of us. In a few moments he returned with two cones. His was yellow.

"What'd you get?" We strolled toward Central Park.

"Banana Republic." I made a face. "Here, try it." We lapped quickly at the cones, which in the summer heat were already beginning to run in little rivulets.

We exchanged cones but I didn't like the Banana Republic at all. "I like the name, though."

"Yeah." His tongue worked quickly around the cone. "Makes me think of torrid, dangerous places that aren't New Jersey. The only flavor I won't try is Bubble Gum." He fumbled for napkins that were in his pocket. We reached the parkside and sat down on a bench.

"What about Peanut Butter and Jelly?"

He pulled out the napkins. Taking my cone again, he gave it a few licks, bandaged it, and handed it back to me. "Oh, I tried it once, but I was in California. I didn't know what I was doing."

When we'd finished our cones and wiped our hands, he said, "Ready?"

I said, "Ready." But we didn't go anywhere.

We sat, staring ahead of us at the traffic zipping uptown, at the landmark buildings across the street set against the darkening sky. Neither of us made a motion toward leaving. When he reached across the bench and pulled me toward him, I was already reaching for him. He pulled me to him, took my chin in his hand, and I was already sliding into his arms. And when he raised my chin and kissed me, my mouth was already turning toward his mouth. I was aware of how sticky our hands, our lips, were from the ice cream. Of how sweaty we were from the heat. Our teeth accidentally banged together when our mouths first met. We tried it again. Our noses met. A hair from his mustache tickled the lining of my nose. Our overbites didn't quite mesh. It wasn't a perfect kiss, but it was a kiss, and I kissed him back for a long time.

Afterward he held me. His beard rubbed my cheeks. Our sticky fingers intertwined. His heart beat too fast and he couldn't hide the fact that it was something he'd wanted for a while. "We should go," he said. We both agreed we should go, but we just sat there.

Two Hispanics passed us, smoking a joint. They whistled and caressed one another in ridiculous ways, mocking us. "Let's go back to my place," I said.

We walked to my apartment in silence, our feet shuffling along in stride. I didn't know what I wanted to do. I didn't know what was the right thing to do. I didn't know what I felt or what I wanted to feel. But I knew too many months had passed since Mark left me and that it was time to begin to go on.

We'd hardly said a word as we walked back to my apartment and we didn't say anything when we got inside. I flicked on the overhead light and Sean flicked it off behind me. When I turned toward him, he placed his palm under my chin. "Ever since I met you," he said, "I've wanted to make you relax." He kissed me on the lips.

Gently he unbuttoned my shirt. "I better go to the bathroom," I whispered. But Sean shook his head. He told me I wouldn't need any birth control, not right now. "I just want to make you relax. That's all I want to do right now."

So we went into my room and I lay back on the bed. Sean took off his shirt. "Now just relax," he said again. He stroked my hair, my cheek, as I nestled into the pillow. "I want you to forget about everything," he told me as he kissed my eyes, my neck, my mouth. He took off my shirt and let his hand slide over my breasts, my legs. "I just want you to be comfortable," he whispered. He unbuttoned my pants and rubbed my belly. He kissed my breasts gently and then his lips moved down to my belly. I closed my eyes.

For the first time in months I forgot where I was. He told me to relax as he kissed my stomach, my thighs. So I relaxed until I thought I was falling asleep. Until it seemed my body grew heavy like a stone and I didn't know if I was moving or being moved. I relaxed until I thought I was made of lead, and then, when I knew I couldn't relax anymore, I began to feel lighter and lighter. I felt so light that my hand, gripping Sean's shoulder, flew up to my mouth to stifle a cry. I was light and floating. I took a deep breath of air. I was like some anaerobic form of life that floated up from the bottom of the sea and didn't die. I felt myself emerge, feeling lightheaded as a mutant strain.

I must have dozed off for a few moments. When I woke, I found Sean resting but awake at my side. Then I got up, went into the bathroom, and found my diaphragm. It seemed dusty to me from disuse, like some old relic you'd come across in your grandmother's attic. When I got back in bed, I leaned on my elbow beside Sean. I began kissing him gently on the mouth as he dozed; my hand reached down, caressing him. "I'm not satisfied yet," I told him. Sean pulled me down toward him. We made love furiously and then, when we were finished, when we were really spent, Sean cradled my head in his hands.

"Now," he said softly, "you should be able to sleep."

But while he slept, I didn't sleep. Not at first. I lay still, my head cradled against his shoulder, thinking how I was in a strange state of peace. The kind of peace that does not need to sleep. I lay there fully awake, thinking about my amorous history.

The nature of desire has always been a mystery to me. In high school I dated big, stupid football players. The kind you had to brush up on your hand signals before you could go out with them. I had nothing to say to these Neolithic creatures and yet I desired them. I wasn't completely inexperienced when I met Mark. I'd made my first pathetic sexual attempts in the boiler room of the *Leonardo Da Vinci,* en route to spending my junior year abroad studying Roman piazzas, with a deck-hand who smelled like salami and wanted to paint frescoes like Michelangelo. He also had a penchant for oral sex, and so we crossed the Atlantic, lapping at one another while the engines churned away.

And then I finally lost my virginity in an MIT dorm with a college boyfriend named Ralph Rothman. Neither of us had ever had sexual intercourse before, not all the way, and our first attempt failed because Ralph put Vicks VapoRub on his penis as a lubricant and he came to bed smelling of eucalyptus; within moments he was writhing in pain. Our second attempt, a few days after Ralph healed, was an improvement, only because it was less dramatic.

With Mark sex wasn't really something you did with your body. You had to use your mind, your eyes, your words. Sometimes he seemed to like seeing me more than he liked touching me. In the midst of the most complex problems of contractual law, he'd ask me to remove all my clothes above the waist. And I'd sit, trying to solve urban-housing dilemmas, worried about low-income units, while Mark wrote briefs, pausing to examine my breasts. Occasionally he'd walk over, touch them, then go back to his books. In some way he sealed me to him.

We overslept the next morning, and woke when the phone rang. I knew it must be Mr. Wicker or his secretary, calling to see why I was late. "Oh, God," I muttered to Sean as I reached for the phone, "it must be my office."

It was Mark. He said he had to see me, that it was important. "You don't sound happy to hear from me," he said. I told him his timing had always seemed strange. Sean sat up, kissed me on the shoulder, and headed for the shower.

"I want to see you," Mark said again. I told him that if it was about a divorce, I would get in touch with my lawyer. "No," he said flatly, "it's not about a divorce. I just want to see you."

That evening we met at seven o'clock at the Echo Inn, a small bar in Little Italy. I'd prepared myself mentally to wait for Mark. To my knowledge and recollection he had never been on time to meet anyone. He always used to send flowers on my birthday and on our anniversary because he knew at least flowers would arrive on time. But at seven o'clock sharp, Mark was waiting for me.

He sat in the booth in the back of the dimly lit bar, his jacket removed, tie undone, a shirt collar slightly frayed. He started to get up to kiss me on the cheek, but I motioned for him to keep his seat. Still he maneuvered a kiss before I had a chance to sit down.

Mark liked the blouse I wore. I liked his tie. He liked my hair. "You look great. You really do." He reached across for one of my hands but I pulled away.

The waitress hovered near our table. Mark signaled her impatiently. "Just a minute, folks." She disappeared with an armful of dirty dishes.

"I spent some time in the country this summer with Jennie Rainwater. Funny you never met her."

"Oh, remember, you lost track of her." He twirled his drink in his hand. He had ordered something before I'd gotten there. "You know who I ran into? Peter Kramer, remember? That guy who lived near us when we were downtown next to the funeral home. He asked about you." The waitress came over. "You want a vodka tonic, right? Two vodka tonics."

"Wasn't Peter that guy who was always in love with foreign correspondents and they were always getting shipped all over the world?"

Mark laughed. "I only remember the one who worked for NBC who got sent to Iraq."

"God, I'm sure there were others." We were quiet for a moment. "What'd you want to see me about?"

He stiffened. "I just thought we should talk, that's all. I haven't seen you for a long time."

"Talk about what?" I was having trouble deciding if my coldness was an act or authentic.

"That guy I saw you with. Are you dating or what?"

"I really don't think that concerns you anymore."

He leaned back against the cushion, pressing his head against the wall. "I'd just like to know what you're doing. I've been thinking about you a lot lately." He scratched his head, and dandruff flakes fell on his shoulder. Had he always had dandruff? For some reason I'd never noticed this before. "I was thinking . . ." He seemed to be talking to the judge. He stared up and spoke methodically. "Maybe we should give it another go."

"I was thinking we should file for a divorce." I smiled at him, the way you smile when you run into someone you used to know and you're happy to run into them but you can't for the life of you remember their name. "I just think it's time."

He leaned forward on his hands. "You know, these have been bad times, but what about the good times? What about Bermuda? What about when you broke your wrist and I took care of you? What about that summer in Maine?"

"I'm not the one who left."

He cleared his throat. "Look, I'm confused. We got married when we were very young. I'd hardly been on my own at all. I think I'd like to see you." He paused. "I want to see you again."

"Mark, this is ridiculous . . ."

He stared into his glass. "I'm trying to talk to you."

I sighed. "I know that. I understand that. I even appreciate that. But don't you think your timing is a little funny? Have you tried to talk to me at all since you left? When I needed to talk, you wouldn't even come to the phone."

He turned his drink in perfect circles. "I couldn't talk then. You drove me away. You were so introspective, you were too dependent on me. I mean, maybe I can be cold and distant, but you were always on my back."

The waitress brought us a little bowl of peanuts and I began eating them, one at a time. "I think it would have been much more productive if you'd said something at the time."

He shook his hand at me, a courtroom gesture I've always hated. "It's just your damn ego that's involved."

"You're damn right it's my ego."

"I want to see you again." He reached across the table for my hands.

"No." I was adamant when I spoke but I was filled with silent doubt. He was my husband. He was the man I married at twenty-four and I thought that lying in bed with him on a Saturday morning was about the best thing that I'd ever known. We owned things in common. His money was my money and my money was his. This wasn't some fly-by-night affair. This was what I'd committed myself to. But what had I committed myself to, I wondered. To a man who never sweated in bed, who could eat one chocolate chip cookie and close the bag; to a man who could leave a note on the kitchen table and depart. To a man with, as far as I could tell, nearly perfect control.

Mark held my hands tightly in his. "Look, can't we just see one another? Just until we figure this out?"

I was still looking for a way to hurt him and Lila, but not at the expense of hurting myself. If he'd done this to me and now he was doing it to Lila, I was fairly certain he'd do it to me again. "All right" — I squeezed his hands — "I'll see you." His face brightened. "If you leave Lila."

He frowned and shook his whole torso. "You don't understand. I'm confused. I'm not sure what's best. I need . . . well, I need to see both of you, just until I'm clearer."

I had the sobering memory of a kiss on my lips from the night before, and even if I hadn't had that memory, I'd been told lies by this man. I had to look at him very intently to remind myself that no matter what I'd done to hurt him or what had happened between us or how I felt about him, he was not a man to be trusted.

"I'm afraid," I whispered, "that's not possible."

Then, angry, still half in love with him, but knowing there was no going back, I looked away.

When Sean left for Los Angeles at the end of September, I was relieved, and plunged into work. Two of my smaller projects had received funding: a traffic-pattern alteration in the Bowery and a commercial revitalization project on the Lower East Side. Neither was as big as SAP, but they were enough to keep me busy. I was at my desk from early in the morning until after dark. From the back of the office, I could see the place where the East River met the Hudson, and I could spend hours staring at the confluence, at the point where two huge bodies of water merged. It was always turbulent at the point of confluence.

Sean phoned me about once a week from California. On our last call, he sensed I was distracted, so he told me when he would be back and said I should call him when I felt like it. It was almost a week after he said he would be getting back that I called him at his parents' place in New Jersey. "Can you come to New York?" I asked when he reached the phone.

"Tonight?"

I thought for a moment. "No, tomorrow night."

When I met him the next night on the corner of Mott and Canal, he looked bored as he rocked on the balls of his feet. I was late and he was a little annoyed, but I was glad to see him. "What took you so long?"

"The subway was mobbed."

"No, to call me. You waited a long time."

"I don't know." I slipped my hand through his arm.

"I don't either." He kissed me lightly on the cheek.

"I've been very busy."

"So have I."

We walked slowly, looking for a restaurant, though neither of us seemed very anxious to eat. "Why'd you call?" he asked me at last.

"I don't know. I guess I wanted to see you." It had been almost a month that we hadn't seen one another. "Look at that intersection." I pointed to where the Holland Tunnel fed into Chinatown. "It should have been redirected years ago."

"Where should we eat?"

"I don't care."

Sean sighed. "If you don't care, why'd you call me to have dinner with you?"

"I didn't call you for dinner."

"So why did you call?" He was growing impatient with me.

I took a deep breath. "I called because I wanted to go to bed with you."

Every weekend for the next three weeks in a row, Sean came into the city. We spent the whole weekend together. On Wednesdays he often had meetings, and we'd spend that night together when he was in the city. He'd arrive from the meetings a little flushed, excited. He'd talk a blue streak all night about the film industry and how crazy everyone was. On the fourth weekend, Sean called to say he'd been invited upstate to visit some old friends. "They're great. You'll love them."

He picked me up from work on Friday and kissed me as I climbed into the car. "Bring your long johns?"

"Is it going to be cold?"

"Get in." He pulled me to him. "I'll keep you warm."

Sean cut over west and headed straight uptown. "We're going to miss rush hour if I've got anything to say about it." He took Riverside to the Henry Hudson Parkway, and we were off. From the parkway to the thruway. The thruway to Albany. "I can make it there in four hours flat," he proclaimed and proceeded to do just that.

I watched him drive as we sped madly along. He drove with precision. He drove the way some men think. He moved with cold logic, straight to the point. There was something direct and honest in the way he drove and if he'd been my type, I would have fallen in love with him for that. "So," I said, trying to make conversation, "tell me about Sandy and Earl."

"They're great," he said. "You'll love them."

"I know. You said that, but what's great about them?"

"Oh, you'll see. They're swell people."

"How do you mean 'swell'? I mean, what're they like?"

He made a *tsk* sound. "I don't know. You'll see."

It was the word "swell" that first made me think something was wrong. Nobody says "swell" anymore. "So how was your week?"

"Oh, fine. Not much happened."

I settled into the cushy bucket seat and watched, his hand resting not on my knee, as it usually did, but on the little green plastic ball of the gearshift. His fingers caressed the ball, which glowed an almost Day Glo green; his hand massaged it like a breast. "Nothing happened?"

He shook his head and turned on the radio. I leaned against the window and he motioned for me to lock my door. His hand gripped the green plastic ball.

"Is something wrong?"

He shrugged. "I just want to concentrate on the road, O.K.?" There wasn't much to concentrate on, actually. It was a pretty straight and even stretch of highway, without much traffic. All he had to do was point the car in front of us and talk to me.

"Sure, that's O.K." Something was wrong. I couldn't pin-point it. I started retracing our steps. Had I said something stupid? Something insensitive? Had I not shown sufficient interest in his job as assistant director? Or perhaps I was just expecting him to behave the way Mark behaved. With Mark, silence was synonymous with anger. "I got a new assignment. Seems they want to alter traffic patterns down in the Bowery."

"Oh, yeah?" He pulled off the road. "Let's stop somewhere. I'm hungry."

"You're not interested in my new assignment?"

"I just want to get a bite of something."

I tried to explain that my new assignment had to do with more than just traffic problems. It had to do with population distribution, with sociology, with urban design, with pollution, with politics. It was no use. He wasn't listening. He was looking for a Howard Johnson's. The window felt cold against the back of my hand and I knew winter was coming. I could feel it in the glass. The sky was very clear and the few clouds overhead were white, but I knew that ahead of us, up north, winter was coming. My first Christmas without Mark. I hated being cold. I moved away from the window, closer to Sean, and let my hand fall on his thigh. "How did you meet them?"

He sighed, as if he were about to make a huge effort. "Let's see. I met Sandy when I was doing soaps out in L.A."

"I didn't know you did soaps."

"I don't like soaps. The money's good but I hated doing them. I had to play this stupid gynecologist. Sandy was casting director. We got to be friends. She quit after she met Earl. He's a photographer and he teaches. They've got this great thing going. Now she runs a little theater outside of Saratoga."

"Sounds nice."

"It's very nice."

The last three weekends I'd spent with Sean he had talked nonstop. He talked about everything. About the film, about my work, about what he liked for breakfast. Maybe it was driving that made him quiet. I looked at the road. There were trees, and hills that were starting to rise into mountains. The trees, the road, the leaves starting to turn, they all reminded me of those weekend jaunts Mark and I used to take out of Cambridge. The older you get, the more things remind you of other things. Everything reminded my father of home. Every lake was Lake Michigan. "Trees," he said about the redwood forest; "we've got big trees right in Wisconsin."

We pulled into a pancake house outside Albany. Sean ordered strawberry pancakes. I ordered a bowl of clam chowder. The chowder tasted fishy. The strawberries ran off his pancakes like blood. He ran his fork with a bit of pancake on it around his plate in circles as if he were going to paint a picture. I sighed and ate slowly. This wasn't quite what I'd had in mind. So he was moody. Lots of men were moody. Lots of people were moody. A cup of coffee loosened him up. He described the little brook that ran behind the farmhouse. The two apple trees. A dog named Sophia. He sipped his coffee and told me about the way the leaves up north turn a special shade of scarlet. Like those cornpuffs in the box of Trix. Did I remember Trix? Those round balls of mauve and russet and orange?

He reached across the table for my hand and dipped his sleeve in the syrup and strawberry sauce in his plate. "Damn." He frowned and seemed at a loss for what to do.

"Here," I said. I moistened a napkin in my ice water and gently wiped his sleeve. He smiled and kissed every finger on my hand. But when we got back in the car, he drove in silence. "How much farther is it?"

"We'll get there eventually," he answered.

"What do you want to do this weekend?" My hand rested on his hand, which rested on the Day Glo green gearshift.

"I don't know. We'll do something."

It seemed I'd spent most of my life trying to understand men. My father, Zap, Mark, and now Sean. Women, I've always understood, more or less. What moves us, I think, is the desire to fill spaces, to destroy emptiness. The womb, the heart, the shelf. But men seem to be running away from emptiness. They drive fast, they go places. The sky was darkening as we passed through Albany, heading on Route 87 toward Saratoga.

What was I doing here, I asked myself. Why did I have to bother to start again? It is always at this time of day that I get maudlin. Sometimes I think these memories of dusk are going to kill me, and it is this time of day that always brings me back to my family.

My father hated going out of his way. He dreaded getting lost. Every Sunday we drove the thirty miles to see my grandparents, and when we drove home it was always dusk. He hated driving at dusk and he always took exactly the same stretch of road. Sometimes when we drove back from my grandparents', my mother would say, "I feel like something sweet. Why don't we take the kids for ice cream."

"Ice cream?" he'd shout with cries as distant and piercing to me in the back seat as if he'd just driven off a cliff. "Ice cream!" he'd yell. "You must be out of your mind. I'm not driving fifty miles out of my way for ice cream. We've got ice cream at home. We've got a freezer full of ice cream. We've got ice cream nobody eats. You want me to get into all that traffic in Kenilworth? You want to take Sheridan when it's pitch black and they haven't got a goddamn light on the highway? You heard the weather report. You know it's going to pour. I'm not going to get trapped on Sheridan Road in a storm because you want ice cream."

My mother would always move close to the window. "Sorry I asked," she'd reply, and sometimes, "Pardon me for living."

"Ice cream. It's practically winter and you want to get ice cream."

And then we drove the rest of the way in silence. It took me twenty years to understand that my father wasn't angry about ice cream at all. He wasn't angry because we had a freezer full of ice cream. What he was angry at was some minor offense someone had committed in the course of the day, the kind of thing he could never get angry at. If he poured me a glass of orange juice and I didn't say thank you. If he asked Zap to play golf but Zap wanted to play tennis. If he'd gotten the car washed and nobody noticed. He was a man plagued with an inability to get angry at the thing that was really upsetting him.

My father never actually did anything with us. Instead he'd drive us to the movies, drive us to ride horses, drive us to a school play. And he'd either wait in the car for two hours until we were finished or he'd come back. But it was difficult to get him to come inside. And if he drove us somewhere and you forgot to say thank you, he waited until you made the fatal error of leaving on a closet light or forgetting to put the butter away. "Who do you think pays the goddamn bills around here? You have to be such a goddamn slob. Let me let you in on a secret. If you're lazy now, you'll be lazy all your life." When she could, Mom would whisper to us, "Did you say thank you when he picked you up from swimming?"

I've spent a lot of time trying to understand the men in my life. And dusk seems the time of day when it is most difficult for me to understand. It is the time when the light seems most uncertain. And as I drove with Sean, silent beside me, intent on the road, I thought how it was the time of day when my father came home from work. There was always a blue-black sky behind him as he stood in the doorway, a little bewildered as if he'd come to the wrong house.

I am told I was the one who waited for him. I waited until he stood in the doorway and then I rushed to get his slippers. I never said a word, but silently I untied his shoes and helped him into his slippers. My father was always exhausted when he came home. He'd take two ice cubes in a highball glass and pour himself a Scotch. Then he'd sit down with his paper and watch the news. Usually he fell asleep in the chair and I'd watch him. A kind of torment would come over his face, as if the news stories that had put him to sleep had entered his dreamy thoughts.

But my first memory of dusk isn't of my father coming home tired and falling asleep in a chair, his face contorted with the news of the day. It's from a time before he was so tired. He was looking out the window, hands thrust in his pockets, and suddenly he turned to us. "Come on," he said. We were already in our pajamas, Renee, Zap, and myself. He grabbed the blankets, scooped us up, stuck us in the back seat of the car.

He drove as if he were escaping from the Gestapo. Renee was angry because she'd missed the end of "Uncle Johnnie Coons," and Zap was already half-asleep, but I was wide awake as he pulled into a field somewhere and dragged us out of the car. "There," he said, pointing to the sky. He lifted us up and put us on top of the car. "What do you think of that?" We didn't know what to think. We didn't know what we were supposed to be looking at. He folded his arms across his chest. "That's the finest sunset you're ever going to see . . ." The three of us gazed at the orange and scarlet horizon. "So remember it."

When we walked in, Sandy kissed Sean on the lips for what seemed like a long time. Sean laughed nervously and pushed her away a little, pretending to be admiring the work they'd done on the house. "Hey, you exposed the beams."

"You have no idea how difficult that was," Earl said deadpan. Sandy swooped down on Sean again. She squeezed him as if testing to see if the fruit was ripe. Then she squeezed my arm.

Earl was somber and thin, yet a little flabby at the waist, like someone on the verge of deteriorating into middle age. When he smiled, the only thing that happened to his face was that his lips curled upward. "We're glad you made it," Earl said, making me fairly certain he wasn't very glad.

"It's just impossible to pin you down." Sandy was exuberant. "And you must be . . ." She squeezed my fingers, trying to remember my name.

"Debbie," Sean said.

"Sean told us all about you on the phone. You're an architect, right?"

"I'm an urban planner."

"You guys must be starving."

"We ate on the road." Sean was trying to be polite.

"Oh." Sandy looked uncomfortably at Earl.

"But we can eat something," I offered.

"She made a feast." Earl could have been saying, "She has cancer."

Everybody seemed to me incredibly awkward. Sandy kept squeezing us. Earl spoke in monotones. He walked across the kitchen as if being dragged by an invisible dog. First they gave us the tour of every nook and cranny of the house. The storage room, the wood-burning stove, the antique wallpaper, the bay window. "We bought it for five. The roof was burned off," Earl informed us.

"Now it's worth at least forty," Sandy broke in. "Thanks to all the work Earl put in."

"We couldn't have afforded it otherwise."

Sandy squeezed Sean's arm as we toured. She seemed to need to squeeze things, as if she were blind and had to make sure they were there. At one point the men disappeared somewhere into a closet to look at pipes. Sandy pulled me aside, her fingers digging into my arm. "He never brings women around. Must be serious this time," she whispered into my ear.

Sean overheard. He rolled his eyes at Sandy. "Sandra, let's not get all dramatic. How about some drinks?"

In the middle of dinner, Sandy reached over and held Sean's hand. Earl grimaced. Then she threw her head back and laughed. "I'm just so glad you're here."

That was when I knew Sean and Sandy had been lovers. The minute I figured it out, everything fell into place. Sandy's clutching at him, Earl's somber tolerance. After dinner we crawled into bed. We slept in an old brass bed in the carriage house under Earl's grandmother's crazy quilt, and Sean began making love to me with the wonderful precision I was growing used to. He probed and turned and dipped. He brought me up and down and he paused and made me wait until I couldn't wait any longer. The quilt was warm and we tossed it off. It was a hundred years old and belonged in the museum. And all I could think about was that Sean and Sandy had been lovers.

What did it matter what had happened with him and another woman, probably years ago? I tried to tell myself it didn't matter, but what mattered was that he hadn't said anything to me. I felt very close to him after we made love, so I asked, "Were you quiet in the car on the way up because you and Sandy used to be lovers and you were thinking maybe this visit wasn't such a good idea?"

Sean lifted his head off my chest, where he was resting. "Is it important?"

I explained that it wasn't important that they had been lovers. It was important that he hadn't told me and that he'd been moody in the car all the way up. "Why didn't you just say we were going to see an old girlfriend? At least I'd understand why Sandy is almost hysterical and Earl looks like he swallowed a frog."

"Oh, they're always like that . . . But O.K., we were lovers five years ago for a couple of months. It wasn't much of a thing. I was back from Vietnam and was trying to get over someone who'd dumped me while I was overseas." He kissed me on the cheek. "Is that O.K.?"

I shook my head. "I think you should have told me."

"I really didn't think it would matter. You're being oversensitive."

The carriage house hadn't been winterized as yet and I was beginning to feel a chill. I reached for the crazy quilt. "Maybe I am, but I think you're wrong. You don't understand. I've been hurt by just that sort of thing."

Sean sat up. "What sort of thing? It was a long time ago. You don't even care about me very much anyway."

"I care about you," I said, unsure of how I meant that.

Sean shrugged, "Well, I care about you, too, but I really didn't think something that happened years ago would make the slightest difference. And you know what else? A lot of people have been hurt. People get hurt all the time in ways you can't even imagine. I'm not Mark. I'd never hurt you the way he did. And be glad you aren't that woman, whatever her name is. Instead of being hurt you should be relieved."

Now I was sitting up. "I think about that woman a lot. I still want to get back at her."

"So why don't you call her up and tell her to go to hell? But don't concoct that I'm going to do the same thing to you. I should have told you that I'd been with Sandy five years ago, and I thought about telling you, but then I thought it wouldn't matter very much."

"You think I should call Lila up and tell her to go to hell?"

"I think you should get it off your chest."

"I can't tell you how much I despise her . . . "

"Deborah, you know what? Everyone has a past too. Even me. Lots of people have had things happen to them."

We both sat cross-legged on the bed. "What's happened to you?"

"Oh, not much. My mother took off when I was three and

came back when I was ten. That might not have been so terrible if my father hadn't told us she was dead. Anyway, I flunked out of Yale . . . I'm skipping a few years. I went overseas and wrote to this girl back home. I was ready to marry her. She was sleeping with a friend of mine the whole time but writing me these terrific letters. She didn't tell me until I got home that she was going to marry the guy. Anything else you want to know?"

I shook my head. I wasn't in love with him, so what should it matter what had happened with him and another woman years ago? He was right. It didn't matter, but something mattered as I rolled over and went to sleep. I dreamed of Mark. I dreamed of him as graphically, as poignantly, as I had since our parting. He is naked, in the dream, and erect by a riverbank and he is calling to me. Oh, God, Deborah, I've been such a jerk. I didn't know what I was doing. Come to me, please. I can't stand being without you anymore. I am naked as I make my way toward him. I cross the river and he is there, waiting for me, lying down beside railroad tracks that go nowhere. Gently I lower myself down on top of him.

I woke up, surprised and perplexed to find myself with Sean. "Can a woman have a wet dream?" I asked him. Taking this as encouragement, Sean made love to me again. Afterward, he reached down and pulled Earl's grandmother's quilt over us. I studied the pattern of the patchwork. The patches of the crazy quilt were in all colors, sizes, and shapes. An endless piecing together of mismatched scraps, and I thought what vision you need to be able to do that.

"Bet you guys needed your long johns last night," Earl greeted us in the morning. He wore striped pajamas and was grinding coffee by hand.

"Oh, Sean wouldn't let her freeze." Sandy smiled, squeezing Sean's arm. Then she squeezed me.

The next afternoon, as we were getting ready to leave, I

helped Sandy cook a batch of chocolate chip cookies. "You know," she said, "he really likes you. I can tell. I know him well and I know he likes you."

I was beginning to like her; there was something sympathetic about her frenzy. "Anything I should know about him?"

"Oh . . ." She took cookies off the sheets with a spatula. "There is one thing. He goes away when he's hurt."

I committed that to memory. When we were ready to leave, Sandy gave us the entire batch of cookies. She kissed me good-bye and I found myself squeezing her. In the car home I fell asleep and Sean ate all the cookies but two, which he saved for me. "How could you eat all those cookies?" I asked him when I woke up. We weren't far from my apartment. When we got there, both of us noticed the light on right away. "Did you leave a light on?" Sean asked me. I shook my head, and when I put my key in the door I knew it wasn't locked. Sean and I looked at each other, perplexed, as Zap opened the door.

9

I WAS SURPRISED to find Zap there, but I was even more
surprised to find Jennie. My brother always shows up when
you least expect him, but Jennie has always been very
predictable.

Zap trembled as he opened the door. "I used the key," he
began with apologies. "I hope that's O.K. I tried to phone. I
didn't scare you, did I?"

I shook my head. "What's up?"

He shook hands with Sean. "Nothing. How you doing?"

"Fine," Sean said, "just fine."

Neither of us knew Jennie was there until we heard a toilet
flush and turned around as she walked out of the bathroom.
There was an incandescence about her as she came down the
corridor. It was as if she had an aura, like Sean's plastic shift,
only this was a kind of white Day Glo, the type that radiates
from Halloween skeletons. I knew that I'd seen her radiate that
way years ago, when I walked into a steamy drafting room in
my father's office and saw Jennie with Zap; Jennie's body
seemed to invent the light.

Sean seemed to be almost as stunned at seeing Jennie as

Jennie was at seeing Sean. "What're you doing here?"

"I got myself a baby sitter and came in to look at graduate programs in biology."

"Yeah, I bet. I need a beer." And he stomped into the kitchen.

"What are you doing?" I asked.

Zap stared at the ground. "Can we go for a walk?"

"I don't want to go for a walk. I just got back from a long weekend. What are you doing?"

"Zap asked me to meet him," Jennie answered. "And I wanted to get away. It's no big deal."

Zap looked as if he were suffering from permanent jet lag. His hair was frizzled, his beard stubby. "She wanted to get away."

"Did you tell Tom?"

She grew nervous and began rubbing her eyes. "No, no, I told him I was coming to see you and look at schools."

"I don't think I like this . . ."

"Look," Zap said, "would you please take a walk with me?"

It was dark as we strolled, both of us with our arms folded across our chests, toward Central Park. When we reached Central Park West, we walked along the parkside on the brick sidewalk and I was aware of how unsmooth the brick was beneath my feet.

"You can't just do this," I said. "You don't seem to understand. There are others involved."

"I'm not doing this alone," he protested. "Jennie wanted to come and I don't even know what's going to happen."

"I don't think I can tolerate this in my house." And suddenly I felt a terrible rage grow in me, as if I were being invaded by thieves. "What'd you do with Anna?"

"Anna's in Pennsylvania. That's over with. But if you can't tolerate this in your house, all right, we'll go to a motel. We'll check into the Plaza. But I want to spend a little time with her and she wants to spend time with me."

"When are you going to grow up? You can't always have everything you want."

Now he was shouting. "I'm almost thirty-one. I want something concrete in my life."

"I'll get you a cement mixer."

"I'll go to a hotel." He kicked a stone. "I'll get right out of your life."

I raised my hand, prepared to strike my brother, and he looked at me with a strange look I'd never seen. "You were always the favorite." He lowered his voice. "It was always Debbie this and Debbie that and why can't you be more like Debbie."

I stopped. "Are you crazy? That was Renee. You don't know what you're talking about. I was the one who was like you, remember? Peas in a pod?"

"Well, you aren't like me anymore."

Zap had always been rebellious. Even before he was born, three doctors with stethoscopes resting on our mother's womb shook their heads at one another, and my mother was certain she carried a dead child. The doctors reassured her. Not dead; just misplaced. They resorted to an x ray and found the baby upside down with his right hand raised high above his head in a posture one doctor prophetically noted resembled the Statue of Liberty.

By the time we got back to the apartment, we weren't speaking. I've thrown alarm clocks and forks at my brother in moments of adolescent rage, and he's been known to clobber me for general stupidity, but this anger was different to us. We had nothing more to say.

Sean was nursing a beer in the kitchen and reading the back of a cereal box. Jennie leafed through a copy of *Progressive Architecture* in the living room. I wasn't absolutely certain that either knew the other was in the house.

She smiled at me, then grimaced, pointing toward the kitchen. I went into the kitchen, where Sean had just eaten a bowl of Rice Krispies. "No nutritional value," I said.

"Tom's my friend. What am I supposed to tell him?"

I patted him on the shoulder. "Do you want to go to bed?"

"Look, this is serious. What am I supposed to tell Tom? He's my friend." He crushed the beer can with his hand and tossed it into the wastebasket across the room, missed, and cursed under his breath.

I really didn't know what he should tell Tom, but we both wanted to get out of the house. Even though it was late, we decided to see a film. We went to see a disaster of a disaster film in the neighborhood, something about a volcano, and all Sean did was criticize the special effects, cross and uncross his legs a dozen times, refuse to eat popcorn, and when he held my hand, he tapped his finger on my fingers.

When we got home, they'd gone to bed. Or at least they had disappeared into the spare room. Sean and I crawled into bed. He pulled me close to him and asked me if he could stay with me for a while. "You mean live here?"

"Just until I find a place . . ."

We drifted onto separate pillows. "It's just that . . . I don't know. Sure, you can stay here while you look for a place but I need more time . . ." I heard dry leaves swirled on the street outside. I'd never really thought it could be winter again. "It's just that I keep thinking . . ."

"About Mark?"

I sighed. "That's right. I keep thinking maybe I should see him. Oh, I don't know."

"Don't worry about it." Sean rolled over to the other side of the bed. "I'll have a place in twenty-four hours."

The Trim Time Health Club is located in the basement of an office building. Specifically, it is located on the third-level basement in one of the darkest, most mildewed, drain-clogged dungeons ever to go by the name of health club. It has the honor of being rated by *The New York Times* as the worst health club in the city. I've been a member for the past three years.

It's a kind of health club for derelicts. Huge women with breasts that droop to their waists like the ears of a floppy dog emerge from cloudy vapor and disappear somewhere into the dressing room. Identical black twins, who look as if they've been cut from the same cookie cutter, move in unison. Ballerinas and homosexuals float by in the pool on red kickboards. A miniature madwoman in her seventies does a pas de deux to silent music in front of the mirrors of the equipment room.

Jennie and I undressed discreetly in the main locker area with the other women, women with snakes tattooed on their spines, women with scars on their breasts and bellies, women who hid themselves in a corner so that the rest of us couldn't see, women who stood nude in the two public phone booths, making calls with anxious faces. Jennie and I slipped out of our clothes, careful not to look at one another. I'd always admired her shapely yet firm body, and I could tell from the corner of my eye that she hadn't lost it.

We shuffled down the stairs in our clogs. At the Trim Time, you don't want to walk around barefoot for fear of slipping in the slime or contracting some vile growth between your toes. We jumped into the pool just as someone sailed over our heads. "Jesus!" Jennie exclaimed, watching the man usurp our lane. "You've gotta be quick around here," I replied, trying to keep her gaze away from the dead cockroach that was floating past us in the wash drain.

We'd gone about ten lengths when we both paused to notice a little, rather terrified-looking man standing in a corner in a pink bathing cap, jerking back and forth, his hand groping for something in front of him as if he were trying to catch a fish. But whatever its flaws, there are no fish in the pool at the Trim Time Health Club.

"Look at that," Jennie said, a little perplexed and intrigued. "That's disgusting. Do you think he's dangerous?"

Is a masturbating man dangerous? Only if he's doing it in public, I guess. I was fairly certain he wasn't dangerous, but I thought perhaps I should inform the guard, who weighed in at about two-eighty. Her name was Agnes, and when I told her that a man was playing with himself in the pool, she frowned, put down her copy of *Mademoiselle*, rose on her elephantine legs, and peered down at the man. "This is a pool, buddy, not a peepshow."

The man raised his hands, trembling, looking terribly apologetic. He said he couldn't find the tie to his swimsuit.

I slipped back into the pool beside Jennie. "God," I said, "I don't know why I did that."

"You never can tell." She tried to console me.

"He was harmless."

I felt depressed and the water suddenly felt cold and filled with chemicals. My skin broke out in bumps. I looked in the direction of the man, who had ceased to jerk but was standing perfectly still, dejected, facing the corner of the pool, and he looked at me and stuck out his tongue. Jennie stuck her tongue back at him, defending me. "He's nuts," she said.

What does it mean when our private acts are suddenly made public? Or when a private act is inadvertently observed? The bathroom door is left unlocked and we are caught on the toilet. Or touching ourselves. Or touching someone we shouldn't be touching. There seems to be no end to the secrets we need to keep.

In the steam room I lost Jennie in a thick, white mist; all I could observe was a vague, ghostly form. I was pretty certain I could get her to talk to me in the sauna as soon as the twins and the other women left, but we stopped to get a drink of water on our way from the steam room and she screamed because she almost stepped on a Japanese water beetle that lay dying on its back near the drain. She was a little revolted by the time we got to the sauna.

The twins and the two other women were in the sauna

when we got there. One of the women was very fat and had
wrapped herself in a wintergreen plastic trash can liner. She
was a glob of sweat. The twins were dancers with perfect,
taut black bodies, and everything one did the other repeated.
The fourth woman was black and had white cream all over
her face. She looked like a frosted cake. The twins got up,
stretched, touched their toes three times, and left. The masseuse came in to get the fat lady in the trash can liner. The lady
with the cream on her face stood up after a while and said she
was going to faint. She staggered out.

Jennie assured me that had she seen my health club, she
never would have felt uptight about taking me to the Tall
Grass. I told her Mark wanted me to join the New York Health
and Racquet and that I told him I didn't think a civil rights
attorney needs gilt mirrors with rotating strobes in order to
stay in shape. But Mark liked the nautilus machine and the
coed sauna, so he went ahead and joined Health and Racquet
and I joined Trim Time and maybe that was when our problems first were made visible.

I rubbed baby oil on Jennie's back. She let her head float as
I massaged her neck muscles. "Let me do you," she said, turning around after a while. She began at the base of my neck,
working into the muscles of my spine. I let my eyes close, then
opened them quickly, thinking for a moment that I saw the face
of the little masturbating man, staring at us scornfully, about
to go and tell the masseuse what we were doing.

"You know," Jennie said, "there are some things you just
can't share with a man."

"I know. Is there anything you can't share with a woman?"

Jennie laughed. "Just one as far as I can tell, but you can
probably do that for yourself."

"Probably." I laughed.

We sat naked now, facing one another, sweat in beads on
our torsos and legs, with the glow of athletes about us, as if we
were training for some important match.

I extended a leg, trying to put my head to my knee. "What do you think you're going to do?"

"About Zap?" Jennie was also trying to put her head on her knee, and I was stunned to find that our former drum majorette was as stiff as I. "I'm not leaving Tom, if that's what you mean."

I nodded. That was what I'd meant.

It was one of those clear, cold nights that happen rarely in Manhattan, the kind of night they use in the fake sets for Fred Astaire when stars are light bulbs, mimicking the tall buildings, and Fred and Ginger waltz across some nonexistent footbridge in Central Park when no one in his or her right mind would be in the park. Those nights are almost magical and the streets can whisper as if they're calling your name.

I thought I heard mine being called as Jennie stopped in front of a folk art store on Columbus to admire a little vase she thought she'd like for her living room. It was a pale, earthenware vase, done in brown and blue. "Look." She smiled happily.

"Jen, what happened last night?"

Both of us kept looking at the vase. "Nothing happened, I'm afraid. It's difficult to talk about . . . I couldn't . . ." Her voice trailed off and she kept her eyes fixed on the little vase. I raised my eyes, looking into our faces reflected in the glass. We were many years older than when I first saw Jennie walking a raccoon on a leash, and I almost expected to see two strangers on the brink of old age, but instead I saw nothing in our faces that wasn't completely familiar to me.

Jennie was starting to loosen up as we turned down my street. A homosexual couple in purple body shirts walked by us, hand in hand, and Jennie commented how times had changed. "Who would have thought I'd have a fling with your brother?"

"Oh, it's a fling?"

She laughed. "I'm not sure it's even turning into that. I'm

not very good at this sort of thing, I'm afraid. Maybe I'm too uptight. He just had this thing in his head about me. Anyway, it was lousy. Or at least I was lousy. And I told him, well, I let him know I was going back to Tom. He didn't put up much of a fuss."

We both felt relieved and lightheaded as we walked up the steps to my apartment. We were laughing as we walked into my living room. We stopped laughing when we came into the kitchen and Sean motioned for us to be quiet because he was on the phone with Tom. "It's for you," he said, passing the phone to Jennie, and he and I left the room.

Zap sat in an armchair in the spare room, reading an old magazine. Sean knocked on the door. "I think you better go to a movie," he said. "Tom's coming over."

Tom arrived almost an hour later. He looked awkward and strange, like the country mouse visiting the city mouse. "Well, hello," he said. He looked around. "So this is where you live?" I nodded and I could tell from the way he said it that he didn't like my place.

"Would you like something to drink?"

"I think I'd like to talk to Jennie for a few minutes first." Sean and I went into the kitchen and gave Tom and Jennie the living room to talk in. For some reason I had expected to hear shouting, but it was very quiet in the living room. I washed the dishes in the sink while Sean read a film magazine. It was almost an hour before Jennie came into the kitchen and said, "Tom's leaving. He wants to talk to you before he goes."

I pointed to myself. "Me?" She nodded.

Tom sat alone on the sofa, a beer can in his hand, looking more thoughtful than I'd ever seen him look. He stood up as I walked in the room. Then he sat back down and motioned for me to sit beside him on the sofa. He reached across and squeezed my hand. "I know Zap went out to a movie, so I don't want to stay here much longer. Jennie told me what happened.

She told me . . . everything. But I already had decided that I'd forgive her no matter what. I've been impossible. I've been terrible all year. I mean, I guess I should be angry, but for some reason I'm not. We're going to try and work it out again. I told her to stay here tonight and talk to Zap."

"Are you crazy?"

He shook his head. "She's not going to sleep with him again. I believe her. I have to believe her. I'll lose her if I don't believe her. God, I feel like hell."

He called to Jennie that he was leaving, and she came into the living room. "Are you sure you'll be all right?"

He nodded. "I'll be home when you get there tomorrow." They started to kiss, so I walked into the kitchen.

Sean sat alone at the table and looked up at me as I walked in. "That's the hardest thing Tom ever had to do," Sean said.

To my surprise Zap wasn't very upset when Jennie announced that she was going back to the farm the next day. I was sitting with her when she told him that Tom had come over and she was going back. During the day she had registered for her class. "Hey, look," Zap said, "I'm sure it's for the best. In fact, I know it is." He offered to sleep on the couch, and Jennie accepted his offer. Later that evening, while Jennie was taking a bath, Zap sat on the sofa, strumming his guitar. I sat down beside him and asked how he felt.

Jennie, Zap told me as we sat on the sofa, was as cold as a freezer and dry as a desert and he'd waited twelve years for a thrill that had probably never existed in the first place. Now he could get on with his life. Like a morphine addict going cold turkey, he shook as he told me that for all practical purposes nothing had happened between them. "It's funny," he said, putting down the guitar. "I don't really want her anymore." I rose to go to bed and asked if I could get him anything. He shook his head and put his hands on my waist, pulling me to him. "You were always my kind of woman," he mumbled, "and I was always your kind of man."

I stood there for a few moments, uneasy, uncertain of what to do next. Then I took my brother's hands off me and walked away.

When Jennie was leaving the next day, I handed her the little vase she'd admired in the window of the folk art store on Columbus Avenue. When she opened the box, she started to cry. "God, I feel like I've messed everything up. I never should have come here."

I gave her a hug. "You haven't messed anything up."

"Are you sure? I'm afraid that everything has changed."

"Nothing has changed," I assured her, pretty certain that everything had. "If you need me, you know I'm here."

She said she knew and I watched as she got into her station wagon, which looked so incongruous on West Sixty-eighth Street in New York. She started the motor and disappeared back into the hinterlands of South Dakota, with Zap and me, who were hardly speaking, waving good-bye.

For the next three days Zap, Sean, and I lived together in a kind of somber melancholy. Sean read the real estate ads in the *Times* every morning, assuring me he'd take the first place he found. He left for work at nine. I went to the office at about ten. Zap wandered around Manhattan, trying to decide what he wanted to do with himself until the University of Illinois agreed to let him return to medical school in January. By the time we saw one another in the evenings, we were exhausted and no one really talked about anything.

But on Saturday morning, several days after Jennie had gone back to the farm, I woke up early and went into the kitchen, thinking I'd make a nice breakfast and surprise Zap and Sean. I opened the vegetable crisper and found a rotten tomato. It had been sliced the week before and left unwrapped in the refrigerator. It was smushy, with a black and white mold growing around its top, and it seemed at the moment, that rotten, vile thing, to encompass the cosmos as I held it in my hand. I knew it was my brother's tomato. I knew he'd used it to make sandwiches the week before, used it as part of his seduction, his havoc, that red tomato. An awful, diseased tomato.

He can't do anything right. He wastes his life. He sleeps with married women he can't have and who don't really want him. He obsesses about things he doesn't even care about and neglects the things he should care about. He can't finish anything he's started. He can't wrap a goddamn tomato in Saran Wrap. It was at that instant that Zap had the misfortune of walking into the kitchen, smiling. "Hi," he said. "Want me to make us some breakfast?"

His smile evaporated when I held the tomato, shaking it at him, as if I'd just found heroin or a copy of *Screw* in the vegetable crisper. "Sure, why don't you make omelettes with this. Look at it, look what you've done. What's the matter with you anyway?"

He squinted, as if the light were very bright. I was shouting at him. "Couldn't you cover it up? Do you know how these things can smell?" So this is what it is to grow old, I thought. You get angry at all the things that don't matter because you can't get angry at the things that do. You scream about tomatoes. "You're just wasting your whole goddamn life. Well, I'm sick of it."

He was furious and I watched as his face turned red and rotten before my eyes. "Yeah, and what're you doing? Years with some uptight attorney who dumps you for some skinny drip. Nobody ever liked him in the first place, except maybe Mom. And now you're with a real man and you don't even notice him, but you notice some crappy tomato. So what if I tried to have a little fling and get Jennie out of my system? At least I'm trying to get on with my life."

"At least I'm honest. At least I don't go around messing up other people's lives. At least I finish the things I start."

"Do you know who you remind me of . . ."

I knew I reminded him of our father. I shut up.

Zap closed his lips tight, pursed them together as I'd seen him do with only one other person in our lives. He closed himself off to me, the way I'd seen him close himself off to our father when he screamed at him. Then he opened his eyes and I saw a strange and distant look, one that was oddly familiar to me, and I saw my brother as I'd seen him in my first childhood memory, staring at me from across our playpen, trying to put words together, and I was sure at that moment in that kitchen, holding a rotten tomato, that he was thinking now the same thing he'd been thinking back then and that if I could translate that infantile expression from across a rubber padded playpen or a grownup's kitchen into words, I'd come up with something that resembled, "What the hell am I doing here with her?"

By noon he'd packed his things and said he was ready to leave. He was going to take a Greyhound back to Chicago, back to Illinois Med, where he'd return for the last time to medical school and would emerge a few years later a pediatrician engaged to a physical therapist. Before he left, I made him some sandwiches. Tomatoes were significantly missing. I insisted on going with him to the Port Authority, but before he walked out the door, he tossed the set of keys he'd had made at the Home Safe Locksmith to Sean. "Here," he said, "you keep them. You might need them. Take care of my sister for me."

Sean shook his hand. "She really doesn't need much taking care of." He clutched the keys in his hand.

We stood in line at the Port Authority and Zap shifted uneasily on his feet. It was clear he wanted to get away from me. I felt as if we were going off to school together for the first time. He wanted to buy some doughnuts, so I told him I'd hold his place in line and waited while he bought a bag of whole wheat and coconut-covered doughnuts. While he was gone, they opened the door and the bus driver began checking tickets. Maybe I should go and let him stay, I thought. I put his knapsack on my back and made my way to the door. Who would I sit next to? The thin priest ahead of me? The thick black woman with too many bags behind me? As I reached the gate, he arrived. Zap took his knapsack off my back and handed the driver his ticket. He climbed on board, flung his pack onto the overhead rack, then slipped off the bus to say good-bye.

"Well, I'm off now." People pushed past us to get on the bus.

"You should have flown. I would have paid for it."

"This is all right. I need the time to clear my head." In his jeans and army jacket he looked as much like Zapata as he ever had. "Look," he said, "no hard feelings, O.K.? I'm sorry about all of this. I can be so damn impulsive."

"Will you let me know where to find you?"

He kissed me on the forehead. "I'm always just around the corner." Then Zap climbed back on the bus, wedged into a window seat beside the large black woman, who'd talk to him about Jehovah all the way across the Midwest, and headed toward some destiny he thought awaited him, leaving me to fend for myself in this foreign land.

That night I walked through the apartment while Sean slept, searching, it seemed, for Zap. I thought to myself how if he were here, I'd crawl into his bed, the way I'd done before our parents separated us. I'd say I couldn't sleep because there was a wolf in the room and he'd make a space, move his leg over slightly.

But we were grownups and I knew it could never be the same. I could never again crawl into his bed and say, "Move over; there's a wolf in my room." And I knew that Zap was right now somewhere in the middle of the state of Pennsylvania, wide-eyed, nose pressed to the cold glass, seeing nothing outside, and thinking the same thing.

10

THE DEJECTED or enraged lover can't slam the door in
Manhattan anymore and say, "I'm leaving." It takes
months to find a place to go to. Mark never would have left me
as easily as he did if he hadn't had Lila's apartment to go to.
And I knew Sean had spoken with much bravado when he said
he'd find a place for himself in twenty-four hours after I told
him Mark was still on my mind. He'd have been lucky to find
even a sublet in that many weeks.

I agreed to let Sean use the keys my brother had turned
over to him, as long as he kept looking for his own place and
paid half the rent for the time he stayed with me. He had begun
working full time on the set in Astoria and could easily pay me
half. What I liked about having Sean in my apartment was that
he felt temporary. Mark had always felt permanent and for
seven years I had liked the sense of permanency, the way I liked
carved marble. But Sean sat around in the morning, sipping
coffee and reading the real estate section of the *Times* or follow-

ing up leads on sublets from the *Voice* before he'd take off for the set. And I knew that anyone who sat around reading the real estate ads had to be temporary.

When I told my mother that Sean was going to live with me until he found a place of his own, she said it was fine with her, but I could never tell my father. "He's seventy-five," she said. "He couldn't take it." I think it was my mother who couldn't take it, but there was something to fear in my father's wrath. In his office, for example, I'd seen him yelling many times at whoever made the latest error. He was an exacting and precise man and never yelled at an employee if an error cost less than a thousand dollars. But at home he didn't exercise economic constraints and his temper could be sudden, irrational, and volcanic.

On the phone my mother concocted elaborate strategies in order to protect my father from the fact that Sean was going to live with me for a while. "Why can't we just tell him?" I asked. She had just told me what hours of the day Sean should not answer the phone.

"No, no, he wouldn't understand at his age. It would kill him." My mother gasped as I pondered whether or not I was going to kill my father.

"How do you know he couldn't take it?"

"He was an old man before you were born. Nice women didn't do that sort of thing, especially not women who are still married!"

"Mark's living with someone . . ."

"He's a man."

"Mother, that's a double standard. I refuse to accept that."

"Darling, I just want to protect him, that's all."

I knew I had fallen into the wastebin of lost children. I was suddenly no better than Renee, who went wild in the streets of San Francisco, not to mention suburban Chicago. I was no better than my brother, who had managed to keep himself one step above being a juvenile delinquent. "What am I doing wrong?" I asked my mother, knowing that I was doing everything wrong.

She spoke soothingly. "You and I know you aren't doing anything wrong, but he won't. And you know we're planning to visit you in a few weeks. It would be such a blow. He had such high expectations."

"He hasn't done so badly on paper. Renee is married to a dentist and does have three legitimate children, and Zap is on his way back to medical school."

"We all know that, dear, but just don't tell him, O.K.?"

A few weeks later Sean, forgetting he wasn't supposed to answer the phone late at night, picked it up. "Oh, excuse me," my father said, "I must have the wrong number."

"You want to talk to your daughter, Mr. Mills?"

"Yes, I do. Who are you?"

"My name is Sean Bryant and I'm living here for the time being."

"Oh," my father said. That was the sum total of his reaction to my living with Sean.

My father was building a housing complex near Hartford, so a few weeks later my parents stopped in New York when my father had a meeting in Hartford. They stayed in town two nights and Sean joined us for dinner on the second night. The dinner he ate with us had the relaxed atmosphere of a job interview. To begin with there was a shooting on Canal Street and police cars streamed up West Broadway as we strolled toward the restaurant Sean had selected. My father, who in the past year had grown rather heavy, chased along West Broadway after the police. "Do you believe that?" he said to us after the police cars disappeared around the bend. "A shooting."

"Dad, this really is a nice part of town. See, look at the galleries. It was just a fluke."

But he was obsessed with the shooting. How far away had it been? Was the killer still at large? Had anyone been robbed? Fatally injured?

"Oo," Mom said. "Look at the pretty shops. I just love those antique blouses."

"SoHo is filled with antique clothing stores, Mrs. Mills," Sean offered. "After dinner we can shop, if you like." My mother smiled a somewhat retarded smile at Sean. She didn't really want to window shop. It was her tactic to talk about some banal detail of daily life to get my father's mind away from his favorite subject — man's impending doom.

"We should've eaten near the hotel," Dad went on. "Plenty of good restaurants right around there. I've eaten in some terrific restaurants in this city. Years ago, but I bet they're still wonderful. The Four Seasons, Le Pavillon."

"I remember when I came to New York in 1935," Mom interrupted. "Or was it 1934? That was when I had a date with that darling doctor who worked at . . . what's the hospital near the Bowery?"

"Lots of good hospitals in this city," Dad went on. "If you're going to get sick, I say this is the city to do it in."

"Bowery Savings?" Mom looked questioningly. "Is that a hospital?" We told her it was a bank. "Oh, I don't remember, but he was a resident somewhere."

"Did you say you were here on business, Mr. Mills?" Sean tried to land on a subject that would interest my father enough to take his mind off the police chase.

"Well, we're just signing contracts right now on some new housing complexes we're doing the engineering for." He stuck his head around the corner to make sure the killer wasn't coming. "I hear your crime rate is way up in this city." He used "your" as if we were somehow responsible. Maybe he thought it had something to do with Sean's beard; he'd been unable to hide his disapproval of it when they met.

"We have our problems here," Sean said. "How's Chicago? Do you do much building there?"

Their voices drifted off and I walked with my mother. She

and I are built alike. We're both tall and slim, though I have
my father's dark eyes and auburn hair. When we walk together, we always drift into stride. She was still back in 1935 or
1934.

My father and Sean had reached the little French restaurant, where you had to bring your own wine. "I'm going for
wine," Sean said.

"How do we get a cab out of here later?" my father asked.
"Maybe we should call one now."

"It's not difficult to get a cab, Mr. Mills," Sean said, not
sounding terribly reassuring.

While we waited at the table for Sean to come back, my
parents assessed him. "Seems like a nice boy," my father said.

"He's thirty-four, Dad."

"Fought in Vietnam, huh?"

"No, he was a radio announcer."

"Very cute," Mom said. "Reminds me of that actor . . .
what's his name? Sam Watertower. Is he Jewish?" My mother
kept a long list of famous Jews: Fagin, Marx, Christopher
Columbus (why else did he leave Spain in 1492?), Lenin, Hitler,
Paul Newman, Lauren Bacall, Spinoza, Christ, Clifford Irving,
Leonardo da Vinci, Kafka, Gershwin, St. Paul, Disraeli, Dinah
Shore, Sandy Koufax, Freud, Sammy Davis, Harry Houdini,
and Levi Strauss, the tailor.

"I don't think he's Jewish, Mom." I thought for a moment,
then felt the need to add "Mark wasn't either."

Sean returned with two bottles of wine and a bottle of
champagne. "Thought we'd celebrate your father's business
deal."

"Oh, who's going to drink all that stuff?" Dad said. "One
bottle's all we need. Don't waste your money."

It was downhill from there. Dad's soup was cold and Mom's
drinking water was hot. Dad said the floor of the restaurant
was sinking. The fish, they were certain, was frozen, not fresh,

as the waiter had assured them, and neither could believe the prices. Dad sent back every course but dessert, and Mom just picked at her breast of chicken with three kinds of mustard, saying it was "all right. Just a little tasteless, that's all."

"Don't order the trout," Dad said. "Too many bones. Get stuck in your throat and kill you."

"Dad, they won't kill you."

"You'd be surprised. You'd be surprised, the stories of people gagging to death in restaurants because of fish bones. I know a doctor who performed a tracheotomy on the dining room table with a kitchen knife on his own little boy. You'd be amazed."

Sean was a little confused. I could see that. He had wanted to make a nice impression but he did not know what to discuss. Mortal accidents, old loves, the destruction of the world, were the only suitable subjects he could come up with.

"So what do you think of the economy these days, Mr. Mills?"

"The economy? I want to enjoy my dinner, son."

"Debbie tells us you're an actor. That must be exciting," Mom said.

I reached into a pouch of my purse to powder my nose and started to pull out my blue diaphragm case. It felt like my compact, and I wasn't looking down. Fortunately, Sean noticed what I was doing; he reached across and pushed my hand back into my purse, under the pretext of holding it. He smiled at me. "Actually I work as an assistant director, right now. I was working in front of the camera but what I really want to do is direct. Of course, everyone wants to direct. Hollywood is filled with people who just want to be directors . . ."

My heart pounded. What if, my God, what if I'd taken out my diaphragm and powdered my nose? Maybe they wouldn't have noticed. Maybe they would have gone right on talking about doom and destruction. But this is terrible, I thought. I am sitting in a French restaurant with my parents, my lover, and my diaphragm case. My mother said it would kill him. I pictured my father, seeing me powder my nose with my diaphragm, then choking on his veal scalloppini. I examined the knives and wondered if I'd be able to perform the tracheotomy.

"It's just horrible," Dad cut in. "I read the other day that sixteen people have killed themselves because of the Russian roulette scene in that film *The Deer Hunter.*"

"That's who you remind me of," Mom said. "What's his name."

"Can you imagine?"

"Please, Howard, don't get all upset. You'll spoil your dinner. He hates violence. He gets embarrassed at sex. I think the last film we went to together was *The Sound of Music.*" My father stared sadly at the tablecloth. "You can't go anywhere with him."

My parents had never had what you'd call the ideal marriage. Actually I believed everything was all right until November 1963, when my mother sobbed as President Kennedy was buried. As the nation mourned, she declared it was the end of America and she wanted to see the country before we went completely to pot. My father wouldn't go with her and he refused to let her go alone. So, instead, she packed a small suitcase for herself and moved from their bedroom into the guest room. She laid out all of her make-up on the dressing table to let everyone know how long she planned to stay. By day our father acted as if everything were normal, but at night, when he thought we were asleep, my father, Howard Mills, such a pragmatic and exacting civil engineer, tiptoed down the hall and pleaded with my mother to come back to bed.

Zap, Renee, and I were amazed at how tenacious she was. How she could open the door to the guest room just a crack, enough to tell him how utterly absurd he was, how utterly bored she was with him, complaints over the details of daily living when the world around them was falling apart. She resisted his pleas and entreaties until at last she broke his spirit and made him give her what she wanted. Marge Mills would have made a terrific horse trainer.

In fact, she had a scheme. One day after sleeping by herself for almost a year, she told him she'd come back to bed if he'd give her a thousand dollars with which to take a trip across the country. He gave her the money and she bought a two-hundred-dollar Greyhound "America the Beautiful" bus pass, the kind that lets you get on and off wherever you want. The rest of the money she put into traveler's checks. She got as far as San Francisco. In San Francisco, she balked and, in a moment of weakness, called home. My father hopped the next plane and brought her home, thus ending the closest thing to adventure she'd ever know.

The summer my mother took off for San Francisco was the summer when it all fell apart for me, or when it all began for me, depending on which way you look at it. It was the summer I caught my brother and Jennie in the drafting room. It was the summer Renee left her underpanties on a neighbor's rosebush and the summer I watched my father languish for love. If my mother wanted adventure and never found it, my father wanted love and never got it. My father, I feel certain, in the depths of his ill-tempered soul, is a passionate man. I've always believed that behind the explosions, the rage, the need to send food back in restaurants, to chase after shootings, lurks a man trying to keep the lid on things. I am afraid I take after him.

When we left the restaurant, my father said, "Can we drop you off somewhere, son?"

Sean didn't know what to say, but I cut in. "Why don't we all go back to my place and have a drink?" My father didn't want to because he had meetings all the next day, but Mom convinced him there were cabs on Columbus Avenue. The subject of where Sean lived or should be dropped was discreetly forgotten. Once we were uptown, Sean and Dad went to mix drinks. Mom and I sat on the sofa in the living room, waiting for them. "So," Mom began, patting my hand, "we've hardly had a chance to talk. Sean's very nice. Your brother likes him. But I guess you're still up in the air about Mark."

"Oh, I'm not up in the air. I mean, I saw him twice recently, but I don't want to get back together."

Her eyes lit up when I said I'd seen him twice. "Well, you'll see. You know, a marriage, that's not something you should give up lightly."

I was getting annoyed. "Who gave it up lightly? I didn't leave. I wasn't unfaithful. I was here waiting for him to come home at night. You make it sound as if I'm the one who walked away."

"You don't have to get all upset about it. I just made a simple statement. I can make a simple statement, can't I? I'm upset, too, you know, that you broke up. We've hardly discussed it, but I felt just terrible."

I felt a little as if I were being sabotaged. "What am I supposed to do? Go take him back from the woman he lives with?"

My mother stood up. "I wonder what's taking them so long?" She started walking away. "Should we go and see?"

What was taking so long was that my father had cut his finger trying to get the electric can opener to open a can of tomato juice. "What's taking so long?" I asked cheerfully.

"I cut myself on this goddamn can opener. I don't know why you don't buy the kind we have."

I looked at my father's finger and at the opener. "You probably used it wrong."

"Used it wrong? I haven't been around for three quarters of a century without knowing how to open a can. Tell her, Marge. Believe me, I know how to open a can."

"I'll finish the drinks," Mom said.

"Naw, forget the drinks. It's too late. Let's go." We wrapped my father's finger in a bandage and went for their coats. My father sat for a moment in his overcoat with his thumb held up in the air. Then they got up to leave. "Can we drop you somewhere, son?" Dad said again. Sean declined. "Oh," my father said, thus coming to grips with the fact that Sean really did stay with me.

After they left, Sean more or less collapsed on the sofa. "You were terrific," I told him.

"My God, that's amazing. Are they always like that?"

"Oh, not always." My parents were often like that when they were upset about something. Right now they were upset that Sean was not the man I married.

The month of October was idyllic, only I didn't know it at the time. Sean stayed with me and the two of us set up house. We knew it was temporary, so we moved into domesticity with comfort and ease. What was wonderful about October was that Sean wanted to see Manhattan the way a tourist sees Manhattan. He wanted to go to every museum, every gallery. He wanted to buy chestnuts in the park and stop at F.A.O. Usually we went out alone, just the two of us. He'd pick me up at the office in the evenings with the *Times* and the *Voice* under his arm and pretend he'd been looking for an apartment. I knew he was looking for films he wanted to see. His work schedule was erratic that month, so he had plenty of time to find things for us to do.

One morning Sean went with me up to that section of the Bronx known as Fort Apache. The Arthur Hansom film he was working on, called *Minor Setbacks,* took place in Bedford-Stuy. It was the story of two Italian boys who grow up in the slums. One leaves, goes into advertising, and marries a wealthy but dumb girl from Manhattan. The other stays behind and marries the former girlfriend — a bright, sensitive woman — of his friend.

Sean wanted to take a look at some slums, so I invited him to come to work with me. We went to the site of a new commercial revitalization project, and together we walked through bombed-out, rat-infested, barely standing shells of tenements.

We stood in a pile of rubble and I told Sean my plan. I wanted to take five of the buildings in that square-mile radius, completely renovate them, turn them into commercial and office space and single-unit dwellings. The plan was to encourage young, single professionals to move uptown. I pointed to a parking lot that I wanted to turn into a playground. I pointed to a factory building, gutted by fire, that I wanted to make into artists' studios. And then there were five other dwellings that I planned to renovate for low-income family dwellings. "You see," I explained, "what I'm trying to do is break down the one-dimensional quality of these neighborhoods. I want an economic mix to bring up the standards of the neighborhood in general, without raising rents . . . Oh, it's all very complicated but I think it can work. It's a new concept in urban design, that's all. The City Council thinks I'm mad."

Sean began to laugh. "Young professionals living up here?"

"Well, that's part of it. It would help the housing crunch, diversify communities without raising rents. The important thing is to keep rents stabilized. I've worked it all out . . ."

He put his arm around me. "You know what I think?"

"Is it going to upset me?"

He shook his head. "I don't think so. I think I'm falling in love with you."

I rolled my eyes and walked ahead of him through a pile of beer cans. "Don't," I said. "I'm not ready."

"Don't worry," he said from behind me. "I'm not either."

Sometimes we'd walk in the evenings through Little Italy or SoHo, and Sean would talk to me about his life. He'd skipped his senior year of high school and gone to Yale when he was seventeen. Before he left for New Haven, he fell in love with a girl. The only writing he did his first year at Yale was to that girl back home. He was kicked out of Yale and drafted. His parents, good Irish-Americans, told him he had to fight, but the army was more merciful. They knew a performer when they saw one. For fifteen months Sean worked as a communications expert in Vietnam. He kept writing to the girl while she was falling in love with someone else.

When he got back home Yale gave him one more chance, and he graduated with a degree in drama. "I swear, the only drama I've ever had in my life has been on the stage or in front of a camera. I'm a very boring person." In Vietnam he never saw the war. He only heard it and heard about it. "But once I saw a tiger," he told me one night as we walked around Washington Square. "I swear to God. I'd gone into the jungle by helicopter to interview some soldiers. I was fifty miles from where there was any action but I was scared out of my mind. Usually they had this guy from *Time* who went into the bush to report, but he had a cold. I was scared shitless. After I talked to the soldiers, I walked back to the helicopter through this thick bush. All of a sudden, I see this pair of green eyes staring at me and I know it's a goddamn tiger. So I just stare at it and it goes away. But that was the scariest thing that ever happened to me in my whole life."

The night Sean told me he'd seen a tiger in the jungle, he told me he'd found an apartment in the West Village. For some reason, those two facts had the same impact on me. They filled me with fear and disbelief.

I think I was particularly surprised he'd found an apartment because we'd spent the day strolling through a cold autumn Manhattan, arm in arm, in our pullovers, stopping for cappuccino to escape the cold. It surprised me because we had gone back to my place after he told me about the tiger, gotten into bed, and made love better than we'd ever made love. I think in part we made love so well because I hadn't been thinking about Mark or Lila for a while. I'd hardly been thinking about hurting them, and the rage that had been in me for so long was subsiding. It was really the first night, that night after he told me about the tiger, that our lovemaking wasn't one-sided. And afterward, I lay in his arms, glad as if this was where I really wanted to be.

That was when he said, "I found an apartment and I'll probably move out on Monday."

"You did?" I sat up. "I didn't know you were still looking. I thought you'd stopped looking a long time ago. I thought you'd just stay here while you finish the film."

He cleared his throat. "Didn't you want me to get a place of my own? Isn't that what I've been doing all these mornings, trying to find an apartment?"

I found myself whispering, to my own amazement, "Don't take it."

"I've already signed the lease."

I know enough about contracts from years of living with an attorney to know they can be broken with some financial loss and I knew that a man who graduated from Yale knew this as well. I got out of bed, went over to the sofa, and sulked. "You can break it."

Sean stumbled out of bed and sat down next to me. "I don't understand you. What do you think I've been doing for the past six weeks? I told you I wouldn't stay here past finding somewhere else to live. I've got a one-year sublet and I don't want to lose it. And besides, you're still married, which doesn't matter that much, but you're still in love with the man you're married to. Any fool can see that. So what if I take the apartment? It's not going to change anything. We'll still be together." He wrapped his arms around me. "It'll hardly change a thing."

It changed everything, though the change would be slow in coming. I helped him take his things down to the one-room studio that had been sublet to him by a homosexual couple. I sat in the kitchen, where Sean was taking things out of boxes.

"I don't get it," I said. "You just come and stay a couple of months and now you're going away. You can't walk into someone's life, then walk out."

Sean sat down on the kitchen table. "Deborah, I don't understand you. Do you always drive men crazy? I'm not walking out of your life. To the contrary, I am moving downtown because we'd agreed I'd do that, but we can still see each other just as much as you want."

"It's a long subway ride. I'll never see you."

"I'll come uptown. Besides, I'm taking you to dinner tonight. It's our anniversary."

"It is?"

"Yes, we met five months ago. I thought we'd celebrate."

That evening we went to dinner at Kelly's and then to a place called Ralph's on Grove Street to listen to music. Ralph's is a tavern with decorations on the walls commemorating holidays. Tinsel from Christmas, turkeys from Thanksgiving, New Year's balloons, shamrocks, Easter bunnies. We arrived early and ordered our first round. Joe Barry, the black man with the slicked-back hair who played a fairly good blues during the week, was already at the piano, and slowly the bar was beginning to fill up.

I was in a nostalgic mood and wanted to hear "As Time Goes By," but I was too embarrassed to make such a request. Sean got up and whispered something into the ear of the bartender, Steve. "Oh, yeah?" Steve said. "How long?"

Sean held up five fingers.

A few moments later Joe played "As Time Goes By" and Steve came over with a free round. "Anyone who's been together five years deserves a free round."

"You told him we'd been together five years?" I asked Sean. He shook his head. He'd just said "five" but hadn't specified the measure of time. As Joe sang "It's still the same old story," Sean wrapped his arm around me. He sang into my ear and licked my earlobe with his tongue. I curled up close beside him. The tinsel that stretched across the room sparkled. Joe Barry's slicked-back hair sparkled. The Easter bunny glistened in the mirror on the opposite wall. Steve's starry earring sparkled. Steve's white teeth smiled at us. Joe Barry had the bar toast our fifth anniversary. "Let's hear it for them, folks. They're together five years and look at them. Still going strong."

I snuggled closer to Sean. The bar was now full of New Yorkers who paid tremendous rents and scratched out their livings, who opened a can of soup at night and ate alone. They all looked at us, smiling, filled with envy. The single people wished they were in love the way we were; the married people wondered how we'd done it.

Sean pulled me closer to him and whispered in my ear, "Act like you're crazy about me." But at that moment I didn't have to act. The meaning of life, so simple and clear, was suddenly obvious to me and I was happy. I was crazy about him. I knew what it was to be completely happy.

The next day we broke up. It was a cold Sunday in New York and we'd spent the night at his place on a mattress on the floor. In the morning Sean decided he had to do some laundry, so we took all his clothes over to Suds-'n-Duds, and while I was separating whites from colors, he struck up a conversation with the woman folding sheets next to him. "Didn't you just move in?" she asked.

"Oh, yeah. I thought I saw you in the building." She had beautiful corn-blond hair and was the kind of woman it might be difficult not to notice, but it bothered me suddenly that he had noticed her, since he'd moved in only the day before.

"I just got here from the Coast myself." She was an actress, doing something at Circle Repertory. "You'll have to come down for a drink some night. I live on Six."

"Oh, I must be just above you then."

"Oh, yeah." She giggled. "Do you have your mattress on the floor?"

After she left, Sean noticed I was a little too engrossed in the magazine section. "Hey" — he nudged me — "what's up?"

"Nothing," I said, feigning indifference.

He sat down beside me in one of those little green plastic chairs. "You in your spin cycle again?"

"You could have introduced me."

"Introduced you?"

"To that woman."

"I don't know that woman. I really didn't think about it."

I put down the magazine. "Look, if you want to see other people, it's O.K. I understand. You aren't under any commitment to me. You can do whatever you want. But I just don't want any surprises. Just let me know, all right?"

"You're nuts," he groaned. The wash was ready for the dryer and Sean took it and flung it in. He took the magazine section and started to read about Ronald Reagan's acting career. I hate it when someone takes my section of the paper, but I didn't want to argue about that. I settled into Arts and Leisure. Sean put down his article. "I am not planning on dating anyone else. I will tell you if and when I want to do that."

"Why don't you just tell me now? I'd rather know right now and get it over with."

We folded the laundry in silence and headed across Sixth Avenue. "I'm sorry if I was rude," he said as we approached his building, "but I swear I just didn't think to introduce you to her. I just met her myself."

"Well, you've found a place of your own. Now you can do whatever you want. I don't care who you see. It doesn't matter to me." I was shouting.

We reached his building and I handed him the wash I was carrying. "I'm going home."

"O.K., so go home. Get on the subway and go and spend the rest of the day by yourself. Go home and sulk and think about everybody who has wronged you."

With that he got in the elevator, pushed the button. I watched him go up. I watched the lights above the elevator as they blinked, like the lights on the switchboard in my father's office, those distant stars, saying things I'd never understand.

Somehow we patched things up, and the next weekend we flew to Nantucket because Sean wanted to get away. Winter was setting in and the island was almost deserted, except for islanders. He said it was the best time to go. We stayed at the Coffin House, whose name left a chill in me. During the day we put on parkas and bicycled down empty roads toward empty beaches. We walked on the cobbled streets and toured the whaling museum, which was about to close for the season. Sean had never been to a whaling museum and he liked it. He liked the history of harpooners, the classifications of whales. He liked the huge skeleton of a sperm whale that hovered over our heads. He liked the stories of the sea and he liked learning that the cobbles on Main Street had been ballast in the ships returning from England after they'd dropped off their cargo of oil from the bellies of the great whales. We went down to Cisco Beach, where the lookout used to be in the days when you could still see the largest mammals in schools on their way out to sea.

On the cold beach Sean shouted, "Thar she blows," but we both looked out across the ocean and we saw nothing at all. The only sound after he shouted was that of the endless, rolling sea. That night we ate cheeseburgers and shoestringers at the Brotherhood and drank hot buttered rum. After dinner we walked the cobbled streets, thinking we heard footsteps behind us. Sean told me that it is said that in November, after the tourists leave, the ghosts of old whalers, lost at sea, feel it is safe for them to come home and that sometimes you can hear them pacing, as they wait for their friends and their ships to come back.

Our room at the Coffin House had a fireplace in it, so I decided to make a fire. Sean sat down in one of the large reading chairs with a copy of *Moby Dick* he'd bought that afternoon. After I got a small fire going, Sean looked up. "That's nice," he said, reaching for a poker. "If you push the logs together a little bit more" — gently he prodded the logs — "you get a better fire." He closed the empty spaces and the fire blazed.

We had been reading for a few minutes in front of the fire, each of us in a large armchair on either side of the mantel, when Sean said, "Hey, listen to this passage." He leaned closer to me and read to me from *Moby Dick:*

> . . . We safely arrived in Nantucket. Take out your map and look at it . . . a mere hillock, and elbow of sand; all beach, without a background . . . Some gamesome wights will tell you that they have to plant weeds there, they don't grow naturally; that they import Canada thistles . . . that pieces of wood in Nantucket are carried about like bits of the true cross in Rome; that people there plant toadstools before their houses, to get under the shade in summer time . . . that they wear quicksand shoes, something like Laplander show-shoes; that they are so shut up, belted about, every way inclosed . . . that to their very chairs and tables small clams will some-times be found adhering, as to the backs of sand turtles. But these extravaganzas only show that Nantucket is no Illinois.

"So what." I glanced up at him from a map of cranberry bogs I was examining. "It's obvious Melville had never been to Illinois."

Sean looked puzzled. "Illinois? Who cares about Illinois? I think it's a beautiful passage."

"I care about Illinois. There are amazing things in Illinois. I love the Midwest." I tried very hard to think of images as magical about my home state as Melville had found about

Nantucket. It is true that Lake Michigan has none of the dangerous threat that the Atlantic has, that meat cutters don't evoke the romance and glamour of the long-gone whalers, that the flowing prairies have none of the mystery of the cranberry bogs, that the streets are asphalt, not cobbles from the ballast of ships, that travelers don't book months in advance to go to Peoria.

So why did I feel the need to argue with him? Why couldn't I just say, "You're right. Illinois is boring." Instead I had to say "And what about Abraham Lincoln and Frank Lloyd Wright and Ernest Hemingway? What about the Museum of Science and Industry? The Art Institute . . ."

"Good night," Sean said, getting up, closing his book, and crawling into one side of the big feather bed. "I just thought it was an interesting passage. I wasn't trying to make a federal case."

"I think you were. I think you were attacking my home state. I think . . ."

What did I think? And what was I doing? A kind of gloom came over me. A gloom that hadn't come over me in a while. An inexplicable urge to thrash out and destroy whatever it was that came near me. I got into my side of the bed and turned out the light. In the darkness near the french windows, I saw the shadow of panthers, which came to me in the night the way Sean's tiger came to me. I saw the dark, sleek body of the woman who'd taken my husband away. I felt her as a moving presence in the room at the Coffin House. She was what stood between me and the world. Lila means night, and she came over me as the darkness came over me. She was a cat that hadn't been declawed. And she was Illinois. Even the letters of her name — the *i*, the two *l*'s — reminded me of Illinois.

If childhood had become synonymous with gloom, if what had been familiar to me was now some dark, obscure foreign place, it was because of her. If some great wall had been constructed, keeping me away from the rest of existence, keeping me away from Sean, it was a wall I'd constructed to contain my hatred of her. The light from the fire cast shadows on the wall, animal-like shapes, and it was as if she were right with us, taunting me. Sean reached across and touched my breast but I pulled away. "Please don't touch me. I don't want to be touched," I said.

Outside the waves crashed. I could imagine whitecaps, cold frigid water. Oh, God, I was cold. I was suddenly very cold. Sean perched his elbow above me, like some wave about to break over me. What fool comes to Nantucket at the end of November, I thought to myself. Just a few dead whalers, I knew was the answer. Sean spoke to me with the flat voice the first mate uses when he thinks his captain has gone mad. "Pray tell, what is the matter?"

I didn't want to start over. I didn't want to try again. It hadn't been all bad. That's what was the matter. It wasn't all bad. Zap could walk away from Jennie because they'd never really shared anything, but Mark and I had had good times — those late-night suppers, sipping wine. Early-morning hikes in Montana. The time I broke my arm in Mexico and Mark told the doctor, "Now listen, this arm is very important to me." And that priest in Jerusalem who told us Christ was betrayed by a kiss and a kiss isn't for betrayal. Mark had agreed solemnly. A kiss isn't for betrayal.

I wished it had all been bad, except it wasn't.

I snuggled against Sean. "I'm tired. Let's just go to sleep."

When I woke in the middle of the night, the fire was out and I was colder than I could ever imagine being cold. I shivered and looked around. The doors leading to the widow's walk were ajar. I threw on my parka and went to close the doors. But just as I was about to close them, I saw a figure, cloaked in some kind of a shawl, gazing in the direction of the sea. It was a dark, shapeless form and it seemed to be grieving for something it had lost. I zipped up my parka and the figure turned.

I went and stood beside Sean, who had taken a quilt off the bed. He was standing, looking out, where I imagined widows had stood, waiting for their men who would never return, women who'd lost the only ones who really mattered to them, blank stares on their faces, unwilling to come away from the sea, a breed of women that didn't exist any longer.

I put my arm on his shoulder. "Bad dream?"

He shook his head. "I haven't been asleep."

"What have you been doing?"

He shook his head again. "Watching you sleep. I've been wanting to wake you."

I tugged on the blanket. "Can I get in?" He opened his arms and let me slip under the quilt with him. He wore a thermal top and sweat pants. As I slipped under the blanket, I felt him go tense, as if he didn't really want me near him at all. He was shaking very hard from the cold. "Why did you just push me away before you fell asleep?"

"I had some things on my mind."

He was shaking very hard. "Like what?"

"Well, I was thinking about Lila and Mark."

Sean wouldn't look at me. "Look, Deborah, I really care about you, but I don't think I want to go on with this. I mean, it's not very much fun for me."

It was odd, because when I crawled under the blanket with him, I knew he had in some way stopped wanting me. I found myself suddenly feeling panicky. "Listen," I said, "I think I could love you. Maybe I do love you. I know I care about you. I just need more time . . ."

He shook harder. "I think you don't know what you want and I'm not sure I want to wait around to find out."

Who can really grasp the fine mechanism of wanting another person? But it seems some of us are destined to want others when they don't really want us any longer. And then there are those who expend enormous amounts of energy in making ourselves loved, only to lose interest the minute we are close to achieving our goal. I always thought I could be counted among those who wanted the people who wanted me. But at that moment on the widow's walk, looking into a freezing sea, I wasn't so sure, because I was aware for the first time that perhaps I really wanted him and for the first time he really didn't want me.

We stood together, teeth chattering, and I realized I probably could fall in love with him if I could just get rid of my rage. But here on this island of lore, this island that had been the scene of Melville's dream of a great chase, his dream of revenge, my own fury came surging back at me. I knew times were different from when men had ventured forth on whatever romantic adventures awaited them while their women waited with one eye out to sea. I knew that once I had fallen in love with innocence and faith, and from now on I would set out in fear and mistrust. I knew that I was now in pursuit of the object of my own anger, blinded by that anger, and that I lived with the same passion and doubt that had driven Ahab after a white whale. And I knew that in a sense you had to be a little like Ahab to have your white whale in the first place.

I persuaded Sean to come back to bed, and we made love gently until we drifted to sleep. Perhaps things would have been all right between us if he hadn't dropped me off at my apartment the next night, when we returned to the city, instead of spending the night with me. "Look," he said when the cab pulled up, "I'm very tired and I have an early shoot in the morning. Why don't you stay here and I'll see you tomorrow night?"

I argued that I'd go up with him to his place and stay there, but he was adamant. "I need some time alone; that's all."

When I walked inside, a strange terror overcame me, a kind of terror I'd never really experienced before. The terror of the person who is alone, the terror of the single person. It took me a moment to understand that my shortness of breath wasn't from climbing the stairs. It was from being alone. I phoned Sally but she wasn't home. I tried other friends and talked to their answering machines.

And so, in an impulsive moment I've since lived to regret, I called Mark, not so much because I wanted to talk to him as because I wanted to know he was still out there. As I dialed Lila's unpublished number he'd given me at the Echo Inn, I knew I'd hang up when she answered and that would be that. But when Mark answered, I said hello. When he told me Lila was out of town, I asked if he would come over.

Mark never loved me more than when I was flat out with the flu, and he could tell on the phone that somehow I was desperate. It still amazes me how I can plan routes and paths for millions of people, how I can organize their lives in ways they never dreamed, and still make such a maze and muddle out of my own.

11

MARK CLAIMS his problems began when he reached puberty and his parents moved from his secure, tree-lined corner in Brooklyn to a crossroads in the Bronx where Cummings Avenue intersected Seaman Road. How, he used to say, could a young boy in his family grow up normal with such street signs glaring him in the face? He lived on a lewd corner and pornography was embedded in his soul. At night Mark touched himself as he stared down at the street signs, flickering in the green neon light, foreboding years of self-abuse and a licentious longing for women.

I never intended to sleep with Mark that night. Actually I'm not sure what I intended. Perhaps simply getting him to come over was a victory for myself over Lila. But it was clear when I opened the door that Mark had come over with the intention of sleeping with me.

I thought of all the nights and weeks and months when I would have given anything to have Mark standing at my door in a flannel shirt, clutching a bottle of wine. But now at that moment I didn't really care very much. "Hi." He kissed me on the cheek. "You look taller."

"Don't be ridiculous."

"Maybe it's the shoes." Mark had always loved the fact I was tall. "But I'm sure you're taller."

"So, how've you been?"

"Oh, you know, busy. Let me open this."

He walked into the kitchen and went right to the spot on the peg board where the corkscrew hung. My heart sank. He still knew where everything was. "We've got a new case in the office. Some mad subway slasher. A disgusting guy. I have to defend him, but I hope they send him up the river for good." He had very smoothly inserted the corkscrew into the cork and now he was extracting it from the bottle. "So how goes the South Bronx?"

"Oh, you know. I keep waiting for funding. I'm thinking of going back to school in historic preservation."

Mark reached for the wine glasses and poured me a glass. "You don't have to go back to school. You could just start working in historic preservation. Oh, I guess you could use an M.A. in architecture."

"Cheers." We clinked glasses. "Mark, I didn't really call you to discuss my career."

He walked with me back into the living room. "So why did you call? Did that guy jilt you or something?"

"Oh, no. We're seeing each other. We're just seeing less of each other. He was living here for a while but now he has his own place."

"Oh, he was living here . . ." Mark's voice trailed off.

It was strange, having him back in the apartment. I didn't quite know what to do with him. I felt as if we should go and check into a motel somewhere. "So how are things with you?"

"Oh, O.K. Lila's in California, finalizing her divorce, I think. We're getting along all right. I don't know. She can be moody."

"So can you."

"Yeah, you're right. Things are O.K."

"You look tired. Are you still taking all those vitamins?" I don't know really why I asked him that, but I found myself struggling for anything to say to him at all.

Mark must have felt at a loss as well, because he answered the question in some detail. He was still taking his multiples and a lot of C's, but he'd quit taking the stress formula and all those E's. "Why?" He ran his hand over his cheek. "Do I look older?"

"Oh, no, not older. Just tired."

"You look pretty good. Your cheeks are rosy."

"We spent the weekend in Nantucket."

"Nantucket." He sat back, surprised. "Who goes there now? It's cold."

"Oh, my friend wanted to get away. He's working very hard on a film and he wanted to go there, so we went."

"Seemed like a nice person. I liked his manner." Mark spoke quickly and I knew he was jealous.

"He's been very nice to me; it's just that . . ."

"What?" He knew me well enough to know I was about to talk about more serious subjects.

"I'm just not over it yet. It's taken me a long time to get over what happened with us."

"And, are you over it?"

I paused and thought for a minute. If I wasn't over it, I was almost over it. I'd been fairly certain on the widow's walk in Nantucket, as I held Sean's trembling shoulders, that I was more over it than I'd ever been. The mere fact that I could see Mark at all meant that I was well along in the process of getting over him. "I'm getting over it."

I knew that somehow I was in control of him, that I could have whatever I wanted from him. For the first time in years with Mark, I had the upper hand. When he kissed me, I kissed him back. He took my hands, curled them in his hands, and kissed me. It was clear to me then that he'd spend the night, that we'd make love, probably for the last time, and that I'd be free to go on. That I'd somehow have the last word. I knew I could make love with him, not so much because I wanted to as because I wanted to see how it felt, the way a doctor pokes an old wound just so that you can let him know you no longer feel a thing.

Mark flicked out the light and kissed me again. His breath smelled of Binaca. He reached under my shirt and undid my bra. I reached under his shirt and felt his fur. He was covered with thick, black fur and in the dark his one continuous eyebrow with the arching points made him look devilish. He took off my shirt and dropped it in front of the sofa. I took off his shirt and dropped it on a chair. He put my bra near his shirt. He kicked off his shoes, and his feet still smelled as if they entered into some chemical reaction with his socks.

He led me toward the bedroom and we dropped the rest of our clothes on the way. When I passed the phone in the hallway, I quietly removed it from the hook, certain that my mother would have some telepathic vision in Illinois and phone to make sure I was all right.

Sean probably started trying to call me at around eleven. He called for an hour but the line was busy. Then he asked the operator to see if I was talking. The operator said there was trouble on the line. He lay on his back, thinking. He had an early shoot in the morning but there was something that made him feel he had to get into a cab and come uptown. What if something had happened? He grabbed the keys to my apartment and caught a taxi heading up Sixth Avenue.

"Sixty-eighth and Broadway, fast," Sean told the driver, who, sensitive to intrigue and desperation, stepped on it. On the way up, he alternated between visions of me, disconsolate, having swallowed Valium with whiskey as a chaser to calm myself down, to me filled with desire and the recognition that we were right for one another.

I heard the doorbell ring, but the kids on my block often ring the bell and run away. I figured whoever it was would ring again if it was important. I certainly was not expecting company. When I didn't buzz him in, Sean made a snap decision.

In his hand, he was clasping the keys to my apartment, which Zap, with the words "Take care of my sister for me," had tossed to him the day I threw Zap out. Sean felt it was his duty to let himself in and go upstairs to see if anything was the matter. He knocked gently when he reached my door, and when I didn't answer, he let himself in.

In the light from the hallway, it was easy to see the pile of clothing trailing across the living room floor — the blouse I'd been wearing next to a pair of men's shoes, my bra draped across a man's flannel shirt. He hesitated for a minute, unsure of what he really wanted to do. Then he shut the door quietly behind him, without my ever suspecting that he'd been there at all.

I woke early, feeling lightheaded, while Mark slept on, curled in a circle, looking vaguely like a defused bomb. I brought him some coffee. "Why'd you get up so early?" He glanced at the clock.

"Oh, you know, early bird catches the worm."

"Oh, yeah." He reached across the bed for me. "I've got a nice little worm for you to catch."

It amazed me how at another point I would have found that line seductive, but at this moment it had the opposite effect: I was repelled. I got up and walked toward the shower.

"Hey," Mark called, "where're you going?"

"I've gotta get ready for work," I called back from the bathroom.

I was enjoying my shower when Mark came and got in with

me. He grabbed the bar of soap and began rubbing me. I surprised both of us when I turned to him and said, "This is my shower. This is my apartment and my shower and you're a guest, so act like one." In a huff he grabbed a towel and walked back into the bedroom. I washed my hair and conditioned it at my leisure. I rinsed for a long time. When I went back into the bedroom, Mark was sitting on the bed, wrapped in a towel, looking like a lost sheik. He looked up at me, miserably. "What's the matter with you?"

I shrugged. For the first time in months nothing was wrong with me.

"Deborah . . . I think I still love you."

I felt incredibly victorious as I replied, "Mark, I'm afraid you're a little late."

When we left the apartment, we shook hands on the street as if we'd met at a singles bar the night before. I walked away from him, knowing he was watching me as I walked toward Times Square, toward the great mural of the man chainsmoking, ready to give Sean a real chance.

When I arrived at work, the secretary handed me a note saying Sean couldn't meet me for dinner that night but he'd phone later to explain. I tried to reach him at home but remembered he had an early shoot, which was why he hadn't wanted me with him the night before. I sat down to work but there was a nervousness in my stomach, and as the day wore on and Sean didn't call, I found that nervousness turning into distress. I wanted to go out to lunch but I was afraid I'd miss his call, so all afternoon I sat at my desk.

I did color work because coloring didn't require much thinking. At three, Sally called and asked me to have dinner with her that night. I said yes, but I didn't really want to see anyone. At around five Sean phoned. He said he'd been running around all day and hadn't had a chance to call. He had to work late that evening, and the next night some friends were arriving from California. "Well, I'm free tomorrow," I said.

"Oh, it's just a group of Hollywood people. You'd be bored stiff."

There was a silence for a moment. "Is anything wrong?" I asked him.

"No, why? I've just got a lot to do."

I knew something had happened, but the worst I could imagine was that he'd tried to phone and found my line off the hook. "Look, can we meet for a drink tomorrow night before you go to dinner?"

Sean was quiet. "If you want to meet us for dinner," he said at last, "we're meeting at Hisae's on Astor Place at seven."

Sally and I went to a Korean restaurant around the corner from our building. She wrote long articles for *Women's Wear* on fashion coordinators while secretly doing research on the history of the labor movement in the garment district for her doctoral dissertation at NYU. Sally used to live with a research scientist who joined a monastic order in upstate New York and shaved his head. She chain-smoked Carltons until our boulgooki arrived. "Look"— she took a drag — "who knows what makes men tick? I go interview gorgeous women, right, and all through the interview they tell me how they can't get a man to love them. They've got the world at their feet, but love, that's what they can't get."

I waved smoke out of my face. "You really should quit." Sally extinguished her sixth Carlton. "I'm not trying to 'get' someone to love me. I'm just trying to lead a decent life."

"Oh, yeah." She waved her hand, clearing smoke away from me. "I tried that too. Forget it. We're children of the sixties."

Over dessert, Sally said to me, "Why don't you give him a call tonight? You know how men get moody when they're falling in love."

Convinced that Sean was falling in love, and not out of love, with me — though the two states sometimes seem remarkably similar — I tried phoning him when I got home. At one in the morning, I gave up. At seven, I called again and this time woke him up. "Listen," he mumbled, "I went to bed very late. I don't have to go to work until the afternoon. I'll call you at eleven." I went to the office, and at nine minutes past eleven I phoned him. "I was just going to call you," he said.

"Well, I don't know that, do I?"

"I said eleven."

"It's after eleven."

He sighed. "It's only a few minutes. I was going to call you. I just got up."

"But I don't know that. I can't know that for sure. You didn't call me when you said you would. You're always on time. You canceled dinner last night. You've never done that before. You always call me when we aren't together at night . . . did you phone me Sunday and you couldn't get through? Is that the problem? Just tell me what's the matter, will you please? Look, this is going to sound crazy, but will you do something for me?"

"What?"

"Will you hang up and call me right back so I can know you would have called me? That sounds crazy, doesn't it? But if we just hang up and you phone me back, then it'll be as if you called and we can start this discussion over again."

"Debbie, that's crazy."

I said I knew it was crazy, but would he do it anyway.

When the phone rang two minutes later, Sean said, "Is this better?"

"Much better. So, did you try and get through to me Sunday night?"

He lowered his voice. "Something like that."

"I took it off the hook."

He sighed. "I know. Look, let's talk tonight, all right?"

Sean was right about my being bored at dinner. We ate with five of his friends from Los Angeles who knew hundreds of people in common, all of whom had had unbelievable things happen to them since Sean came back east. Someone named Mitzi had gotten a huge part in a pilot but then the funding fell through. Victor got married and, no one could believe it, to a white girl. Sean seemed more surprised by the "girl" than by the "white." When I let my knee press against him, he moved his leg away. The only person who talked to me all evening was an actress named Roxanne. When I told her I worked in urban renewal, she said, "Oh, you'll like L.A., then. They need a lot of urban renewal out there."

"L.A.?" I asked.

"Oh," she murmured, "aren't you going . . ."

Sean cut in. "I'm going to Los Angeles after the first of the year to cut the film and start another."

"Oh," I said.

The rest of the meal faded into a kind of haze for me. I drifted into the silence most people think comes from lethargy after eating and watched them chatter away as if they were speaking Kurdish. My high school language entrance exam had been in Kurdish. They gave us fifty words like *exger* or *irdas* and told you they meant horse or leader. The words didn't look anything like words we'd ever seen before, so it was hard to memorize them. It wasn't until years after that exam that I learned Kurds were real people with terrible problems of their own. Even Sean seemed to disappear as I drifted . . .

When we got back to my place, Sean rubbed his brow, then his hands. He seemed very tense.

"When did you find out you were going to L.A.?"

"Just yesterday. Nothing is very definite as yet."

"Is that what was the matter?"

He shook his head. He rose and began to pace. "I came over here Sunday night." And he told me the whole story of the cab ride after trying to phone, ringing the doorbell, the pile of clothes. "I never should have."

It was a while before I moved. I felt so stupid, not having connected the ringing doorbell with Sean. I waited to see if he would go on and was relieved when he did. There really wasn't much I could say. "I came over because I wanted you to know how much I cared. It was really a dumb thing to do . . ." He touched my hand. "Listen, you have a right to do whatever you want. I realize now that I've been putting pressure on you. I mean, you're just getting over a marriage. I had no business using the key and coming in like that. I got what I deserved, but I've had to do some rethinking."

"Don't you care who I was with? Don't you care what happened?" I interrupted.

"I think you can skip the details."

"I called Mark when I got home. I was so mad that you just dropped me off. I saw how I'd been pushing you away for so long, but then when I came to you, you just didn't want me. I had to see him. It was the only way I could see how I felt. And I felt that I want to be with you. I'd like to give it a try."

Sean shook his head. "I think we should just be friends."

"You don't understand. I don't even know him anymore. I don't even like him anymore."

He sat back down. "Deborah, I'm not being judgmental. I'm really not. I'm sorry. I was wrong, putting pressure on you. You have a right to do whatever you want. And we have no agreements, so you weren't breaking any agreement."

"All right," I said. "Let's agree not to see other people."

But Sean had reached the opposite conclusion. "No, I think we should agree to see other people."

"But I don't want to see other people. I wanted to see Mark the other night and I saw him. But I don't think you should judge me for it."

Sean raised a finger and pointed at me. "I'm not judging

you. I'm just telling you, I've been through stuff like this before. I've had this kind of thing happen to me before." His face was all contorted with rage. "This isn't the first time I've made a dumb mistake and walked in when I wasn't invited." I recalled Sandy's words to me, how he went away when he was hurt. "And I just can't give it another try right now." He got up and walked across the room. Leaning against the bookcase, he went on. "You don't understand. You could have had anything from me you wanted. I would have waited for you to work things out. If you'd just leveled with me." He pointed his hand at me again. "If you'd just . . ." He tightened a fist and struck it into the bookcase. The books shook in alphabetical order and Sean grimaced with pain.

"So why can't I level with you now? Why can't I just say now that I'd like to give us a try?"

Sean looked at his hand and massaged the fingers he'd just smashed. "Because," he said softly, "it's too late. I'm not the kind of person who can go back."

We decided we needed time to think and that we wouldn't see one another for a week. Though we spoke almost every day on the phone, I found I couldn't stop thinking about Sean. At night I slept fitfully, imagining him with other women. In the morning I'd boil three-minute eggs and stare at them. They'd become breasts, smooth and bouncing, bubbling breasts, the kind Sean had suckled the night before. I knew it was a vision. Morning after morning I'd eat my eggs hardboiled.

At work in the middle of meetings, while Bill Wicker droned on about supports, openings, jackhammers, and studs, I thought of Sean's peachlike body, his slender fingers, his sturdy arms. While the architects revealed models for low-income units, and planners rerouted traffic, I pictured Sean and me with Eurailpasses on swift trains through the Alps, making love on the upper berth. On the subway I missed my stops. One morning, certain Sean had sought solace elsewhere the night before, I almost missed my stop and had to dash off the train. As the doors closed behind me, I realized I'd left my entire South Bronx development project in a briefcase on the train. "Stop the train," I shouted as it pulled out. I ran to the token booth. "Please, I left my work on the train." As I began to describe the light tan briefcase with the brown handles, a small crowd formed. An elderly man shook his head. "Poor thing," he said, and people pointed at me. Soon I looked to see that they were pointing at the briefcase I held in my hand, the one I'd just been describing to the token taker, who was phoning ahead to halt the train.

I had fantasies of Sean walking right into my office. I'd be in the middle of reviewing working drawings for traffic islands with the landscape architect, and he'd come stand in the doorway. "Deborah," he'd say, "I've got to speak with you." I'd raise my hand — "I'll only be a minute, dear"— but he'd shake his head. "This can't wait."

After not seeing one another for a week, we met for coffee on a Monday evening. I had a speech prepared but forgot it the moment I saw him. "I made a mistake. I'm sorry," I said. "I missed you all week."

He held my hand. "Deborah, you didn't make a mistake. I don't think you should feel that way at all. You have some things to deal with and I guess I do, too."

We ordered cappuccino and pastry. "I've decided to tell Mark to file."

"I think that's a good idea."

"I want to see you."

He shook his head. "I don't know," he said. "I have to think about this . . ."

Even though Sean wasn't the kind of man to go back, he agreed to give us another try. On Christmas we drank Irish whiskey and went ice skating at Wollman Rink, and on New Year's Eve we went to a party given by a cousin of mine in New Rochelle. The guests were mostly dentists and importers of rare objects. Sean seemed to be having a good time with the sister of my cousin's wife, an ex-hippie who ran a pottery mill in New Hampshire. After talking to him for about fifteen minutes, she said, "You know, you've changed a lot since last year. You're easier to talk to and I like the beard."

"I've never seen you before," Sean replied.

She looked at him from all angles. "But aren't you . . ."

"No," he said flatly, and I dragged him away to meet a dentist who puts caps on famous actors' teeth. He'd done Doris Day. "She thought I was Mark," Sean complained. "I don't even look like Mark."

"And you certainly don't act like him, so forget it."

"But doesn't your family know? I mean, shouldn't she know?"

"I'm not even related to her. She lives in a commune up north."

"But shouldn't she know? Shouldn't someone have told her?"

My cousin, Chuck, caught me by the arm and said he wanted me to meet some people. I left Sean with the dentist, who was telling him how he did Lana Turner. Chuck introduced me to two importers, one who stood on the bow of ships and watched native boys dive for pearls and another who trudged through the streets of Tokyo in search of something that sounded about as mysterious and plausible as the Maltese falcon. I glanced over and saw Sean with his mouth open wide while the dentist pointed to certain teeth.

One of the importers said, "Tokyo's just impossible. Do you know they number their houses according to when they were built?" Someone handed us a platter of caviar. Chuck, the tall, Russian-looking redhead on my father's side, had married the daughter of a caviar king. "That's amazing," I said.

Ilene, Chuck's wife, "the caviar princess," as Chuck liked to call her, tapped me on the shoulder. "Ah," she whispered, "your friend . . ." She pointed to the punch bowl. Chuck had put seven kinds of hard liquor into the punch. Then she pointed toward the backyard.

I went to the window and, peering out, I saw Sean, in his jacket and tie, rolling what looked like the bottom section of a snowman down the hill toward the ravine. I sighed, excused myself, and grabbed my coat. When I reached him, I saw he was making not a snowman but a snow fort, and he had begun a small arsenal of snowballs for himself. "Hey" — I caught him by the arm — "what are you doing?"

"Fighting the enemy." He sounded as if he meant it.

I tugged on his arm. "Come on, put your coat on. You'll catch cold."

"Who gives a fuck." I tried to persuade him to drive back with me to Times Square and watch the ball drop. He tried to convince me that there were gooks behind the shrubs and he was going to fight them with little snowballs. He sank down to his knees in the snow. "Those people think Asia is pearls and caviar." He pounded the snow with his fist. "It isn't."

I drove home while Sean slept in the back. He would never remember the car ride home. The last thing he'd remember about New Year's Eve was the dentist looking at his teeth. As I drove, I listened to the radio, playing hits from the early seventies — mesmerizing space-age and hard-rock songs I found indistinguishable from one another. It was the music I'd heard at the party with Bobby Jones, a night I preferred not to think about. I switched stations until I found something more familiar, the Beatles, Martha and the Vandellas, music I'd grown up with. The early part of the decade seemed a blur. All I remembered was Mark. The disc jockey reminded us, in case we'd already forgotten, what had happened in the last few years. Nixon had resigned, the war in Vietnam had ended, oil prices were soaring, inflation was out of control. The night the war in Vietnam ended, Mark was asleep on the sofa and the bells began ringing. He opened his eyes and looked at me.

"Is it Christmas?"

"No, dear," I replied. "Christmas was last month. The war just ended."

And now at midnight of a new year I was driving my drunken, jealous boyfriend home on Riverside Drive, on the brink of a new era, when nothing was going to be clear-cut anymore, and certainly not love.

Sean was sick with the flu for a week and I let him stay with me. He left Kleenex all over the place, squinched-up mucky balls of it, which he wanted me to pick up. He wouldn't bathe or brush his teeth and he sent me to the store at all hours for orange juice and magazines. He called me Andrea and refused to say who Andrea was. When he felt better, he grabbed me in the middle of the night and kissed me passionately while the January winds whirled outside.

Then I was sick for a week. Sean stuck by me, but it was clear he didn't like taking care of me as much as he liked being taken care of. He felt restless being in a room with a sick person. One night he put the word "xerox" down on the Scrabble board and I challenged it. He lost and then said he didn't want to play anymore. "What's the matter?"

He sat at the edge of the bed. "I'm going to L.A. in two weeks. Just for a month or so, but I might move out there." He ran his hand over the covers. "Do you love me?"

I patted his hand. "I care about you a lot. I don't know." I grew sad. I knew that deep down inside me something had changed. I wanted Sean. I probably even loved him, but I knew I could do without him. I knew I could do without anything, if I had to.

As I reached up to touch his cheek, he grabbed my hand. "Come with me for a week or so. Maybe you'd like it."

I thought of all those miles of freeway, all those traffic jams. I kissed him lightly on the cheek. "Thanks, but I hate L.A."

12

I T WAS a jumbo jet filled with librarians going to a convention and they all wore yellow badges with their names on them. Because we were late leaving for the airport, we couldn't get those secluded seats by the window and had to sit, instead, with six librarians to our right. After "snacks" of ham sandwiches with little pickles, Sean complained that we should have blown the money and gone first class. I complained that we should have flown Pan Am for $99.

The stewardess announced they were going to show forty-five minutes of "60 Minutes." The librarians laughed, especially Jane and Harry Hanover, who sat next to us. She read *Ulysses* while he talked to the baby. Sean turned to them and said, "I guess they must be leaving out the segment on the plane crash." Jane stiffened and said, "That wasn't very funny."

"So what are they leaving out?" He turned to me. Then he shook his head. "I must be getting in a West Coast frame of mind." Sean had meetings with the producers of *Minor Set-*

backs and he also wanted to start looking for new work. For a week before he left, he flossed his teeth twice a day. I could tell he wanted to make a good impression. When the forty-five minutes of "60 Minutes" came on, Sean asked the stewardess for a blanket. "It's hot on this plane," she said. But she brought us a blanket, which Sean put over us both. He reached his hand under my skirt. Jane and Harry looked over, shook their heads, and went back to their baby and their books.

It had taken some convincing to get me to agree to come with him, but in the end I wanted to. I was sure I'd never see him again if I didn't come with him, that L.A. would sweep him away in its glamour and smog. Sean seemed happy as we drove along Olympic Boulevard, our Chinese cab driver chattering away about something neither of us could understand. When we got stuck in traffic, Sean's knee idled at about eighty miles an hour. "What'll we do tomorrow?" I asked, trying to get his mind off the bottleneck.

"I have meetings."

"Oh, I know you have meetings, but after the meetings?"

He shrugged. "I don't know what time I'll be done. I can't make plans for the next few days."

He was preoccupied, and when he was preoccupied he couldn't make plans. I slipped my arm through his. "So we won't make plans," I said.

"People in L.A. make me crazy. You know, they have no attention span." He stared out the window as he spoke. "I wonder if prices have gone up here like they have in New York. I hope it's not that expensive. Hey" — he tapped the driver — "are things expensive these days?"

"Sky-high," the driver replied in an Chinese accent.

"I don't know," Sean went on. "We'll find stuff to do. What do you feel like doing?"

The last time I was in L.A., Mark and I had just been married and I was attending a conference on urban design.

"I don't know what I want to do. Let's eat Chinese food somewhere."

"All right, we'll see. I can't make plans."

Our hotel room was all different shades of plaid. There was a yellow and red plaid bedspread and an orange plaid rug. The curtains were black and red check. I glanced down on the street from the window and there wasn't a soul anywhere and here I was in this abandoned city in a plaid room. "I hate this room," I said to Sean.

"What do you mean? It's just a hotel."

"I don't like the way it's decorated. I don't like where it's located."

"Debbie, Four Tracks Films are putting us up here for three nights. That's all. I didn't pick it."

"But do you like the room?"

He shrugged. "To tell you the truth, I'm a little indifferent to it."

We were doomed from the start. A man who was right for me wouldn't want to stay in a plaid hotel with a vibrating bed. Mark once told me California was a place where serious people turn into boiled potatoes in hot tubs. Mark would never have let us stay in a room with a bed that vibrated for a quarter. And suddenly I found myself thinking about Mark.

How long does it take to get over someone, I asked myself, even as I picked up the phone to dial. And why, once you think it's over, does it come creeping back — the face, the hands, the eyes? Why, when I was with a man who was about as straightforward as the Manhattan Yellow Pages, who kept a little book so that he could write down everything that happened to him, who wrote down every photograph he took so he could keep a record, who ate as many chocolate chip cookies as suited him, why did I let Mark come creeping back and spoil it? So I sought refuge in even deeper ghosts. I assured Sean that it was essential that I place a call to my family at that exact moment. "I just want to let them know where I am."

My father accepted the charges. "What's wrong?" he asked.

"Nothing's wrong, Dad. I just wanted to say hi."

"It's two in the morning here. It must be three a.m. where you are."

I heard my mother's groggy voice. "Why's she calling at this hour? What's wrong?"

"I'm in California," I said. "I forgot which way the time changed. You're on Central Standard Time, right?"

"I think so," my father grumbled.

"Oh, and we're on Pacific Standard." I tried to explain the time changes to myself.

"You're going to be on Rocky Mountain Time if you don't get off soon," Sean whispered.

"How's the weather, Dad?"

"The weather? It's the middle of the night. What kind of weather did you have when you left New York?"

"Oh, snow flurries. It's clear and cool in L.A."

"Well, New York should have sunshine tomorrow. We had sunshine today. What're you doing there?"

"Visiting friends. Why don't you go back to sleep?"

Sean pulled the covers up to his shoulder. "You check into a hotel with your lover and call your parents. I've seen everything now."

"Deborah."

"Hi, Mom."

"Hold on," she said. "I want to take this call in the kitchen."

"Mom, please don't get up. I'm fine. I wanted to say hello."

"Come on, Marge, get off the phone. The boys are picking me up at nine."

"Nothing's wrong, dear, right?" I told her nothing was wrong, except that I'd thought they were two hours behind, not ahead.

When I hung up, Sean stared at me. "Was that necessary?"

"I wanted to let them know where I am."

"I'd love to know where you are."

My universe had begun in a small town and in a sense all I'd done was extend myself like the spokes of a wheel from the spot, but in truth I'd never left home. For the world of my childhood was the world of order. If you had work to do, you did it. If you married someone, you stayed with him. Projects that failed, marriages that didn't work out, children that turned bad. These things only occurred to those who had suffered a failure of vision. Even natural disasters happened only to people who didn't think carefully about where they'd live. Earthquakes, unemployment, divorce, such things could never happen to me.

So here I was, drifting off to sleep with a man who was not the man I'd picked to spend my life with, having jeopardized my already shaky position at the New York Center of Urban Advancement by coming to this plaid hotel room, resting just a few feet from the San Andreas fault.

The next morning I met the devil. I'd set off early with my map of Los Angeles, heading toward the Chinese Theater to look at the immortalized footprints of America's immortals, and was just a few blocks away when a rather fat, round man passed me on the street. "Hey," he called as he caught up with me, "I don't believe it. You're a dead ringer for Ava Gardner."

"Oh, yeah?" I was deeply flattered.

"Oh, definitely around the eyes, especially the eyes. Just need to lose a few pounds, change your hair." He brushed the hair away from my face and handed me his card. "I look for look-alikes. That's my job. You know Johnny Travolta? Well, I found his look-alike and that guy's making millions working for Wrangler."

"I can make money?"

"Lots. More money than you make right now. You a secretary? Whatta ya make? Fifteen, twenty? You can make that in a month. See that drug store? They found Lana Turner in that drug store."

"I met the dentist who did her teeth."

"See, she was just buying Kleenex or something. So maybe I'll discover you right here."

Discover me, I thought. Dress me in mink. The little round man looked at me and it took me a few minutes to realize he was the devil. I don't say such a thing lightly, but he really was the devil. Even today I am sure of it. I looked at him carefully. He had a peculiar physical trait I'd never seen before. He had long black hairs growing down from his pointed earlobes. Not hairs that bristled out of his ears, but hairs that grew down from the lobes themselves. "I'm telling you," he went on. "You're just a dead ringer for Ava Gardner. Course, we're not looking for Ava Gardner types, but if we were, you'd be it, kiddo."

"You mean I'm an anachronism?"

"Naw." He shook his head. "You're very pretty." He caught me by the arm. I stared at the long hair, then turned quickly and started to walk away. "Wait, come back. Will you have dinner with me? Will you have drinks?"

"He was the devil?" Sean said as we dressed to go to dinner that night in Venice to meet friends of his.

"He looked like the devil. I think it was a warning. I don't think you should take a job in Los Angeles."

He kissed me. "I think you look like Marilyn Monroe. Hey, you wanta skip dinner and just fool around?" He tried to pull me onto the bed.

"Hey, it's your friends we're meeting. You made the date." He'd met me at the hotel that evening with a bouquet of spring flowers and a big smile. I knew something was wrong.

"Remember Roxanne? She's going to be there."

We drove our rented car, compliments of Four Tracks

Films, down to Venice and looked for the restaurant, the Jetty Sunset. We missed the sunset but got a table near the water. The restaurant was all done in bleached wood and hanging plants. The salad bar, with its red beets, its squash yellow, its spinach green, its twelve kinds of herb dressings, its bacon, egg, and chickpeas, looked more like decoration than food. All the clientele wore jeans and T-shirts and drank gin and tonics, flavored with fresh mint sprigs, with the well-rehearsed casualness that had become the cliché of California. Our waitress, who had thick braids, came over and introduced herself. "Hi, my name's Karen and I'm going to take care of you. For starters we've got our great salad bar and there's a terrific roast beef special." I watched the ocean lap just outside the window some fifty feet away and I was gripped with the insecure feeling that prefabricated housing and insecure relations can give.

Roxanne had had a ghastly day with some producer who wanted her to dye her hair red, and Jill, her friend, didn't talk much because she'd missed a call-back. She worked at Kroch's in Beverly Hills and said if she didn't make it as an actress, she thought she could make it as a writer. All she wanted to do was express herself, but she couldn't say why she was so upset that evening. Jill's boyfriend, Sam, did back-up for Earth, Wind and Fire. He was black and said he could never get a cab when he went to New York. "That city's fucked, man." Art, Roxanne's "man," produced musical events and said he'd rather work with Diana Ross over Stevie Wonder any day.

Sean sat stone-faced throughout the meal and I knew something had happened in one of his meetings that day. After dinner, we all walked along the pier, but Sean and I walked ahead, arm in arm. He told me very quietly that Arthur Hansom wanted him to co-author his next script with him and was grooming him to direct. "They made me an offer I couldn't refuse."

"Oh, I'm really happy for you." I really was happy for him.

He went on. "They definitely want me based here." He let his hand rest on my shoulder.

"Starting when?"

"Probably next month. I don't know what I should do."

"Well, you should take it. That's what you should do."

A tall, skinny girl on white roller skates, with golden hair and a skimpy halter top, skated past us, hurling an electric Frisbee into the air. She had those smooth, dumb features and wonderful camel-like legs and I wondered if she was the kind of woman Sean would start sleeping with when he moved west. Overhead I saw a giant balloon, a red and blue balloon that seemed to come out of nowhere. I saw it turn so that the light off the pier illuminated the sign it was trailing, which read, "Eat my Conch — Ricki's Fish Place."

Two days later Art and Roxanne and Sean and myself were driving along the Pacific Coast Highway en route to San Francisco. "I thought we were going to make this trip alone," I'd said to Sean as we began packing our things and leaving the plaid hotel room. He had told me just as we were getting ready to go that they were coming with us. "I thought the whole purpose was so we'd have a few days to ourselves."

"Look, they just wanted a ride to San Francisco. I couldn't say no. Besides, I hardly get to see them."

"You're hardly going to get to see me pretty soon."

He slammed the suitcase shut. "Debbie, you just can't have it all. You have your own life, your own friends, your own work. I'm going to be working out here again soon. They just asked for a ride, so we're giving them a ride."

"When did they ask you?"

"Yesterday."

I decided not to go with them. "So why did you wait to tell me now? Because you knew what I'd say. That I thought we'd planned to have that time to ourselves."

"I'm not the one who pushed you away our first night in L.A. I'm not the one who pushed you away in Nantucket and a million other times. I want us to have time to ourselves, but we don't have to have twenty-four hours a day to ourselves."

I wondered if there was a flight back to New York that afternoon. "You know, I don't really believe you. I don't think you want us to be alone at all. I think you want us to have lots of people around. I think you're afraid of something. It seems to me that the minute I start caring about you, you find ways to disappear."

He threw some things into his shaving kit. "Did it ever occur to you that I just gave up, that I ran out of patience? That enough was enough? You didn't even want me until I stopped wanting you. I think that's more accurate. It took me four months to get your attention and that was when I'd pretty much had it."

I threw my arms up. So he thought I didn't start caring about him until he stopped trying to be with me, and I thought he stopped trying to be with me the minute I started caring. Sean slumped into the yellow plaid armchair and put his feet on the red and yellow plaid bedspread. "All I'm saying" — he sounded very exasperated — "is that things are complicated. You were just getting over Mark when we met, and I was out of work. Now I've got a lot of work and you're pretty much over Mark, or so it seems. Things are just turned around . . . come here." I sat down on his lap. "I really care about you. More than you know. Let's just not make any big decisions about the future, about what's going to happen. Let's just take things as they come."

Roxanne got very carsick on the winding roads. At first she was fine and she thought the scenery was gorgeous. "I should get out more often. Drive around. See the country." Art was more blasé. He'd made this trip dozens of times and just went along because she wanted to. Roxanne claimed producers were more blasé than actresses in general. Art thought that it

was a difference between men and women. They'd lived together for two years, which was some kind of a record for both
of them.

"How long have you guys been at it?" Art asked. Roxanne
jabbed him in the ribs.

"Just since last summer," Sean said. "God, look at those
cliffs, those waves."

"Feel like driving the car into them?" Art laughed.

"No more of that kind of stuff for me."

"You drive cars off cliffs?" I asked, incredulous.

"Not very often, really. I was the worst stuntman they ever
had at Twentieth Century."

That was when Roxanne really began to get carsick. "Oh,
God," she said; "falling off cliffs."

We stopped at a restaurant on the road so that Roxanne
could put something into her stomach. We ordered tea and
rolls. Sean went to the bathroom and he was gone for a long
time. Art was the first one to hear the banging. "He must have
locked himself in the bathroom."

The waiter had to kick the door very hard to open it. When
Sean finally got out, he pretended nothing had happened, but
Roxanne started to laugh and so did I. Then Sean laughed and
for a few moments we all laughed. It was the last time we'd all
be laughing together.

When we got back in the car, Sean asked me to take out the
map. "What do you need a map for?" I asked. "Aren't we just
going in a straight line?"

He frowned, reached across the glove compartment, and
pulled out all the maps, along with everything else that was in
the glove compartment of the rented car. "I want the map."

"O.K.," I said. "I'll get you the goddamn map. I just don't
know why you need one when you're driving between two
points."

A mist was rising and Roxanne groaned from the back seat.
"Oh, God, what if we get stuck in the fog?" Sean said it was just

a mist and he'd checked with the U.S. Naval weather station and had been assured that U.S. 1 was clear for the day. He studied the map and I glanced over his shoulder. "Deb, would you let me handle this?"

We were driving in sunshine and suddenly we were in a cloud and we couldn't see in front of us. It was as if the road just ended. The redwoods, the Panoramic Highway, Stinson Beach, the mating whales, the cliffs, the coastline of America were all hidden in fog and left to the imagination. Roxanne stared straight ahead, taking deep breaths. I moved closer to Sean, hoping he wouldn't drive the car over the cliff this time. I put my head on his shoulder and reached for his hand, just as he reached for the gearshift. "Don't do that," he said. The car swerved and for an instant I had a glimpse of the very edge of the country. "Can't you relax?" he said. "Can't you take it easy?"

"Would you guys quit acting like New Yorkers?" Art said. "That's it, baby, breathe deep."

"I don't feel very well," Roxanne said. She was a little green.

"I'll relax if you'll relax," I said to Sean.

"I'm just trying to drive," he replied.

In a little while he'd leave me. I knew the end when I saw it. We'd been miserable from the start. We'd been miserable in New Jersey, at Times Square, in the plaid hotel room. We fought over a map. We were miserable because I didn't want him until he didn't want me, or vice versa.

I'd made my mistakes in love. The first time I ever tried to use a diaphragm, it flipped out of my hands and fell into the toilet. Maybe I should have given up then. Where was the guidepost to tell me what to do? My parents had met on a blind date and my father agreed to marry my mother because a Gypsy had told him to. My father, a confirmed bachelor in his late thirties, had gone to see a Gypsy because his Gentile girlfriend asked him to. She wanted to know if they'd marry.

The Gypsy said no, but she told my father he'd change jobs, return to his home town in Illinois, meet a woman, and marry her. So he went home, met my mother, and married her. So where is the wonder of love? Perhaps it's mostly fate, circumstance, and learning to live with our mistakes.

I curled up next to the window and looked into pea soup. Sean patted my arm but I curled closer to the window. You have the right to remain silent, you have the right to one phone call. When Mark and I fought, he read me my rights. Mark once said I exhibited the personality traits of a hostage. Nervousness and a tendency to overreact. I'd been raised like a hostage, a prisoner of my own family. Go ahead, I said to myself, move to California. See if I care.

There is something unnerving about the state of California. Thomas Mann said it was the only place on earth where man could not live. He wasn't referring to the fact that it could crack off and become an island at any time. Rather, he must have somehow sensed that this was all temporary, brutish, without discipline. Those oversized trees, that not so pacific ocean crashing against its rocky shore, hundreds of feet below, as we took the hairpin turns, with Roxanne, sick as she was, saying over and over again, "Gorgeous, gorgeous." In the fog there wasn't much to see, but Roxanne was determined to make the experience a positive one. "Boy, you can sure get into a rut. You know, you live here all your life and you never know how beautiful it is. You can get into a rut."

It was somewhere along that great, obscured highway that I sank into a rut of impenetrable silence. Men were destined to leave me. I knew that now. Everyone has his or her fate and this would be mine.

Sean suddenly pulled off the highway and parked the car. He got out and beckoned for me to do the same. He put his arm around me and walked me to a spot that indicated we'd have a view if we weren't in dense fog. "Would you please tell me what is going on?"

"I don't like the people we're traveling with."

He sighed. "Is that true?"

"No, not really. They're all right." Art and Roxanne looked at us, shaking their heads from the car. They had, after all, made it through two years and I think we must have made them feel they'd been through twenty-two. "I don't know what it is. Everything is all wrong."

"Is it Mark? Are you thinking about him again?"

I shook my head. "I'm thinking about you. I'm thinking about the fact that you're moving west, that I don't know where you'll be next. I was doing all right until you came along. I was fine on my own. But you made me decide what kind of ice cream I wanted. You started spending time with me and asking me to travel with you. And now you're just going to leave . . ."

"They have cities in California, don't they?"

"I just can't pick up and move like that. It isn't so easy."

He put his hands in the pocket of his jeans. "Remember I told you once that if I touch a table, I want to feel the wood, and if I touch a lamp, I want to feel the heat of the lamp. And with a woman, or any person, I want that person to be there. Well, you're just such a jumble of things. And I'm having trouble making my way through it all. I'm not a complicated person, Deborah, and I don't think I'm difficult to get along with." He paused. "I just don't know if we can be lovers anymore. There are too many obstacles now."

Roxanne and Art watched us from the car. They looked incredibly bored. "But I think I'm in love with you," I managed to say.

"I really care about you, Debbie. I really do and probably I love you too. I know there was a time when I would have done almost anything to be with you, and I'm still your friend but this just isn't working."

"Is it because you came in that night when I was with Mark?"

He shook his head. "It's because you aren't ready for anything and I can't make you trust me if you don't trust anybody."

"But you said we wouldn't talk about the future . . ."

He took a deep breath. "All right. We won't. We'll take it as it comes."

"We won't make any decisions, right? We'll just see what happens." He nodded and looked away distractedly, eyes fixed below on the valley. It was at that moment that the fog chose to part, and for an instant I saw, rising out of the clouds, the bridges, the buildings, the skyline, the bay of San Francisco, a city I'd never seen before, which looked to me from where we stood like some Shangri-la, more like someone's dream of a city than a real place at all.

We crossed the rust-red Golden Gate Bridge, holding hands, and dropped Art and Roxanne off at his sister's place, agreeing to meet them for drinks at lunchtime the next day at Seal Point. Sean and I checked into the Union Square and decided to walk around the city. We went to Chinatown and I bought him some slippers and wind chimes. We walked down the crookedest street in the world and over to the marina. At the marina two sea lions poked their heads out of the water as they swam and dived for fish from the fishing boats. It was already getting dark, but I could see their sleek bodies, shimmering in the gaslight of the harbor, their noses as they peered from the water. I watched as they swam diagonally from one another, bodies almost grazing but not quite, passing one another in smooth, graceful passes, and then they were gone.

I wondered where they went at night. Zap told me once that scientists went eight miles down into the ocean in a special pressurized cabin. I didn't know how deep you could go, but Zap said the ocean just seemed to go deeper and deeper. He told me how they'd found little bubbling volcanoes, giant sea worms, flowers, and strangely beautiful anemones that converted darkness into food, but disintegrated when you brought them up into the light.

We went to a noisy Chinese restaurant for dim-sin. "Shall we keep driving north?" I asked him after we sat down. I wanted to plan the rest of our trip.

"I can't think about that now. Let's order something." But he couldn't get the waiter's attention. When he finally got the waiter, who was already annoyed with him for his impatience, Sean wanted explanations and recommendations, which the waiter didn't feel like giving. The dim-sin wasn't as varied as he'd hoped it would be. The Chinese beer was warm. "God, and this used to be a good place."

"Let's just have a nice dinner," I offered, holding his hand.

"How can you have a nice dinner in a lousy restaurant?"

I'd lived too many years with my father to believe Sean was upset about the restaurant. "Do you want to talk about something?" I asked him as we were finishing our first course.

He nodded, looking a little relieved. "Let's just get the bill and go for a walk," he said. We walked, mostly in silence, down to the piers. We walked with Sean staring at his feet, at my hand, staring at the sky. Finally he said, "Deb, I tried, I really did, but I can't go on. I'm sorry. You were right. I never got over that night I walked in and saw your clothes lying on the floor. I don't know what to say. I really can't get it out of my head. And I can't live with it."

The water was very dark and in the fog, which hadn't lifted, it looked eerie, as if you could glide across it. "You know I was having a hard time."

"Look, I want some distance. I want some time apart."

I begged him as I'd rarely begged anyone for anything in my life. "Please," I said, "don't do this. Not now. Please. I just wanted three nice days with you. That's all I want. Please, please." I started kissing him, on the mouth, the neck, on the hands. "Please," I begged, "let's walk back to the hotel. Let's go to bed. Please."

He put an arm tightly around me and we walked back to the hotel. We brushed past the desk clerk and on up into the room. When we got upstairs, I kissed him again. "I'm going to make love to you," I said. He sat down on the edge of the bed and I pushed him back. I knelt by his feet and undid his shoes. I pulled off his socks. I unbuttoned his pants, his shirt. And when he was naked, I let my tongue roll down along his neck to his nipples and I sucked on his nipples as he closed his eyes. I pressed my hips against him and rubbed my belly against his penis.

Then I reached down with my hand and took a firm grip on him. With my tongue, I rolled down his chest, down his belly, my head moving in swirling motions, and then I put him in my mouth and I sucked on him. A drop of sperm came to the top of his penis and I wiped it in a circle with my finger. I ran my mouth up and down and he gripped my head with his hands.

When he came he pulled me up to him and kissed me. "Lie down," he said. He had me sit upright against some pillows and he began to move his tongue in long, drawn-out strokes. And then he dipped his finger inside and, while his tongue flicked, his finger turned slowly. And just when I was ready, he pulled back and stuck a pillow under my hips.

He had me arched high, and slowly, steadily he made love to me. Then when I was so wet I could hardly feel him any longer, he rolled over and pulled me on top of him. "This is how I want you," he told me.

"I don't know if I can," I said.

"Try." His hands reached up for my breasts. He massaged my nipples and then, when he saw I was getting excited again, he reached a hand down and massaged me. "I've got plenty of time," he said. I tightened my muscles, rested my hands on the headboard, and moved on top of him, moving faster and faster, until I felt myself starting to come. "I'm coming," I said. And he reached up for me. "I know," he said, "so am I."

I rolled over and rested on the pillow and Sean put his head on my belly. It took me a few moments to realize that the vibrations in his body were not the aftershocks of sex but rather sobs. I rubbed his head. "What on earth is the matter?"

"Why didn't you want me," he cried, "when I wanted you?"

When I woke in the morning, he was packing. "What are you doing?"

"I'm leaving. I'm going back to Los Angeles. This is just not working out for me."

I tried to be rational, certain I could talk him out of it. "But we're supposed to meet your friends at Seal Point for drinks." For some reason I was sure he might want to leave me but wouldn't want to be rude.

"You go in my place."

I shot out of bed. "Go in your place? I didn't ask for this. I didn't ask you to follow me all over town. I mean, you don't just walk out on someone. What's the matter with you?"

"Debbie, I love you. I think I really do. Something is just not right for us. I wish I'd met you later." He picked up his bag, walked to the door, and suddenly he was gone.

I grabbed a robe, threw it on, and dashed into the hall. "Please don't go. Don't leave me. I can't stand being alone. I can't take it now."

He went with me back into the room. "I'm not sure I can make you see this, but I have problems of my own. Problems that have nothing to do with you. I need some time to think it out as well, but I'm not abandoning you."

"I beg your pardon, but you're leaving me in a hotel room in a strange city in the fog. If that's not abandonment, what is?"

I knew I'd turned away from Sean when he really wanted me. And now I was condemned to want him the most when he wanted me the least. It was all so incredibly stupid. It seemed as if I'd never lived one moment, breathed one breath, without wanting a man, some man, to put his hand on my head and give me life. I have sought explanations and revenge. I could have killed my husband when I learned he'd betrayed me.

I've tried to make, out of this amorphous mess of life we're given, something that bordered on sense, something within my grasp. But in the end I have loved only gentle failures like my brother, successful tyrants like my father, smart women who were bundles of doubt and fear. I have journeyed between weakness and strength, kindness and power, and I know that it is not easy to be a woman and it is not easy to be a man and all we can really do is the best we can.

"I think you're right," I said to him at last. "I guess I need some time too." He kissed me and said we'd see one another again. That some distance would do us good. But I sensed we wouldn't see one another again.

I called Art and Roxanne and told them what had happened, and they insisted I come over and spend the day with them. "No, I think I'll just try to get a flight out." I sat on the edge of the bed, numb. When Sean had closed the door behind him, I'd held my breath, thinking he'd open it again before I fainted, but he hadn't opened it again and I'd started to cry.

"Come on," Roxanne said. "Just come over. Get out of there."

The disconsolate desk clerk at our hotel seemed immune to my frenzy as, teary-eyed, I asked him to call me a cab. In the taxi over to Art's sister's place, I asked the driver what the weather would be the next day, when I planned to leave. "It's going to snow," he said.

"Snow?"

"Yeah, a real blizzard."

"That's what the radio said?"

"Lady, you didn't ask me what the radio said. You asked me what the weather would be. Why do people always take cabbies for granted? What am I supposed to do? Listen to the radio all day long, give everybody the weather?"

When I arrived, Art handed me a glass of warm ginger ale. "Tough break, kid," he said. The weather outside was still terrible and they didn't want to go anywhere. They thought a game of Class Struggle would cheer me up. I was the worker. Art was a farmer and Roxanne was a capitalist. The purpose of the game was to prepare for struggle in a capitalist society. "I don't think I'm in the mood, Art," I said, but he said it would take my mind off things. I drew a "Prepare to Negotiate" card and fought back the tears. Art could merge and wanted to merge with me, but I had a plea bargain and could work out a deal with industry if I wanted to wait, which I wanted to do, but then I learned the class struggle was progressing and I had to move immediately to a confrontation square.

I finally convinced Roxanne we should go to Seal Point, but Art was more difficult. "We aren't going to be able to see a damn thing," he argued. "This fog can drive you nuts."

"Well, we're going to go nuts sitting inside all day," Roxanne argued back.

In the car, she squeezed my hand. "You seem to be all right, honey. He probably did the right thing. You know, I think he cares about you a lot. Maybe more than he's cared about anyone in a long time. Sometimes it's just a matter of timing."

"We weren't getting along very well. Oh, it's a long story."

Roxanne nodded compassionately. "It always is."

Seal Point was fogged in, the way that guy I met at Jennie's the night I met Sean said it always was, so we decided to have a drink in the bar. The bar was crowded and completely engulfed in fog. "What kind of a place is this?" I was incredulous.

"Fog, smog, muggers. Every place has its problems," Art said philosophically. Then he sang a few bars of "California, Here I Come."

"It's all timing," Roxanne said, unaware of her non sequitur.

We ordered Irish coffees, and after finishing one, Art began to sing "I Left My Heart in San Francisco." He completed about one measure before Roxanne told him to shut up.

I wanted at least to try to catch a glimpse of the seals, and Roxanne said she'd come with me. Art said, "You're crazy. You aren't going to see any seals out there today." But he joined us reluctantly. We snapped up our down vests and headed out.

There were only a few other tourists there, climbing around in the fog across mud and stones, disappointed that they could not see the famous, gentle creatures. The truth was we could see nothing, but we heard their distant barking and the ocean as it lapped the shore. At first I climbed, with Roxanne right behind me, Art pulling up the rear, but after a while I climbed down. The incline was muddy and slippery and my feet were unsure as I moved across the boulders, away from them in the fog.

Suddenly I was aware that I stood alone on the rocks with all of America at my back and nothing I could see ahead of me. The seals barked, obscured by the fog, from their place somewhere at sea, not very far away really, but as inaccessible as some promise unspoken, some hope unfulfilled. I felt like the first person to come to the edge of the continent, the first person to comprehend how infinite possibility is shattered by human limitations.

I was lost, utterly lost. Some bad things had happened to me, the way some bad things happen in most people's lives, but at that very moment I had no one but myself to blame. Somewhere behind me I heard Roxanne calling my name, and I did not miss the ring of desperation in her voice. She knew how easy it would be right then for me to slip, to go off the edge, down the embankment. No one would hear me. No one would see me. And life just seemed so incredibly stupid to me as I stood on that precarious point.

Roxanne caught up with me and grabbed my arm, afraid to let go, it seemed. "Hey," she said, "where've you been?"

"Well, where do you think? I've been right here. Why?"

"Oh, you know, we were just looking for you, that's all. It's kind of creepy out here right now."

For some reason, I hadn't noticed it was creepy. I was almost beginning to enjoy the fog, to enjoy not being able to see above me or beyond. It was like being in one of those sensory deprivation tanks, where you see dream images shoot through your mind and then a wonderful calm comes over you. It was a womb to me, this fog with the ocean below, and then Roxanne intruded with her hand on my arm. "Come on," she said, coaxing me. I tried to convince her that I wanted to stand out there by myself for a while, but the girl who'd gotten sick on the winding curves was suddenly very firm with me. "No," she said, "Art's waiting; let's go."

When I got back to the hotel, I asked the desk clerk if my husband had phoned. I'm not sure why I felt the need to say husband, but it didn't matter because you couldn't fool this desk clerk. He'd seen this happen a dozen times before. He shook his head without looking up from his copy of *Lui*. But as soon as I walked into the room, the phone rang. "Thank God," I said.

But it was Roxanne. "You going to be all right?"

"Oh, sure, I'm going to be fine."

"Honest Injun? You left in a bit of a hurry."

"I promise I'm going to be fine."

When I hung up, I knew I wasn't going to be fine. I put on my coat and walked outside. The desk clerk looked up, bored with my comings and goings, sighed, and went back to his magazine as I strolled out into the cold San Francisco night. I walked through Union Square, up the hill, until I stood at the base of the crookedest street in the world. It was a confused, impossible street and I thought how it wasn't good to make people take such tortuous routes. If it wasn't a landmark, it wouldn't be a street at all.

All my life I've wanted order. Straight roads, honest love,

even keel. And yet it's never been that simple when my emotions are involved. I walked on, down to the marina, to the bay, to the spot where Sean and I had watched the graceful seals almost touch but not quite, then disappear into the dark sea. I found a spot on the pier and stared into the black water, or at least what I could see of it through the fog.

Life's banal repetitions were not lost on me. It was to San Francisco that my mother had come in a Greyhound bus over fifteen years ago, when domesticity proved to be less than what she'd thought it would be and she still had thoughts of a world out there, bigger than marriage, bigger than family or sex and its holding powers. But the truth is, if you're moving east to west, which is the way America got discovered by the people who recorded its history, San Francisco is at the end of the line. You can't go any farther, so if you're a pioneer, this is where you stop. As far as landscapes went, for my mother and myself, there was no place left to go.

My mother had once stood more or less on this same spot and we'd both gazed into the waters at the same moment in our lives, and here we'd made our choices. She had returned home, to domesticity, and I was still in the process of deciding. Out of the fog, I glimpsed the Golden Gate Bridge, its cables and towers only partly revealed. At an early age I'd learned that you need tension to connect two points and my father's dream of bridging the Bering Strait was an impossibility. Some bridges, my father taught me long ago, would never be built.

I had to talk to someone. Someone who understood what I wanted. Someone who knew me perhaps better than anyone else. I looked into the bay one more time and knew I didn't want to drown. I wanted to place a phone call.

I went back to the hotel and got the Illinois operator. It took a while, but Zap had a listed phone number in Champaign. This time, well aware of the time difference, I placed a call and to my surprise he answered. "Hi," I said.

"What's wrong?"

"Nothing's wrong. I just wanted to say hello."

"Bullshit." He didn't sound annoyed.

"How do you know something is wrong?"

"Deborah, is the sky blue? Are you my sister? It's three a.m. I know you're in California. I know something is wrong because we haven't spoken in weeks and because your voice is about to crack."

So I explained to him that Sean had gone back to L.A., that we'd agreed it was for the best, that I thought it was because he'd found me with Mark that night, among a million other reasons. I told him there was a thick fog all around me and I couldn't see a thing. I told him I thought I'd fallen in love with Sean after all and that life at best was the most fragile of enterprises. "I don't think I'm going to make it." I was crying now, sobbing into the phone at my brother.

"You're going to make it."

"How do you know?" I cried.

"Because you called me."

"I'm lost, I'm alone here, and I don't know how to get out of the fog."

Zap said there were lots of ways out of the fog and he gave me explicit instructions. He said I should take a cab to the airport first thing in the morning and wait for a plane to New York. Eventually, he assured me, a plane would have to leave. He said I should go home and go back to work.

During the night I vacillated. I wanted to go west, across the fifty-six miles of Bering Strait, back to Russia, the nation of my embittered and persecuted ancestors, back into the land where Anna Karenina, rejected by love and society, had hurled herself onto the tracks of the oncoming train. But I picked another means of transport and took TWA to the East, at my brother's suggestion.

13

THE FIRST MONTH was terrible. After Mark left me, I'd wake up in the middle of the night, trembling with anger and rage. Shaking as if something had terrified me as I slept. But with Sean it was different. This time I couldn't find the name for what it was I felt. This time I didn't wake, shaking and trembling. This time I slept. I slept long, deep, endless hours of untroubled sleep and woke more exhausted than before. The fatigue perplexed me. I lay in bed for hours like a beached whale and thought how this time I really had only myself to blame. Sometimes I blamed Lila for making me mistrust so deeply, but mostly I blamed myself.

It was Sally who figured out what it was that was making me so tired, that barely let me get through the day, then buried me in bed hours before anyone in Manhattan would ever dream of going to bed. She invited me to dinner one night. "You look like you have permanent jet lag," she said when she opened the door. Sally made us green tortellini with funghi sauce, salad, and an Italian marinated chicken that was delicious. I could barely lift the fork.

"It's not like the last time," I mumbled as I tried to eat. "The last time I was furious. Now I'm just sleepy." It had been more than a month since I got back from California, and I still dragged around. Sally listened to me patiently through dinner and into dessert. She didn't protest when I hardly sampled her gourmet meal.

After dinner she lit one of the two dozen or so Carltons she'd smoke in the course of the evening. She ran her fingers through her frizzy black mop. "You know," she said after a while, "I felt like that once. After my dad died. It wasn't like anything I'd ever felt before. I was just exhausted. Maybe what you're feeling is grief."

It was having a word to label what I felt that enabled me to start feeling better. I was feeling a sense of loss as awful and festering as a child feels when it finds its puppy squashed flat as a manhole cover right before its eyes. How do you behave when you've lost something? A pen, your keys, a ring whose value is only sentimental? The first thing you are is disoriented. You look in all directions. Then there's a rush to figure out where you may have left what you've lost. But retracing your steps doesn't help. It's gone, and you have to learn to live without it. Having the word for the emotion that ails you is like having the diagnosis for the disease. Only then can you begin to treat it. Once I understood I was grieving for something I'd lost, I began, slowly, to return to the world.

One Saturday I fell asleep in the middle of the afternoon, and when I woke, I decided the apartment looked dark, even though it was still daylight. It looked very dark to me. It occurred to me that the apartment had always been dark and that what I needed, what had suddenly become essential to me, was to purchase a new lamp. For five years I had lived in that living room with the same light, but on that dreary afternoon I had to go and buy a lamp.

I put on a rain slicker and headed toward Seventy-second Street. I wasn't thinking about Sean; I was thinking about my new lamp. The store on Seventy-second Street had lamps that hung from the ceiling like sparklers and fireworks. It had lamps that looked as if they should live at the bottom of the sea. Twisted green tentacles, pink globs floating inside glass. It had regular old lamps, some with little Cupids at the base, some with elephants; a camel wore a lampshade as a hat; a rickshaw driver had a bulb for a head and a lampshade hat. It had regular old desk lamps, Tensors, night lights, Lightoliers, lamps for serious people, lamps for drawing tables, lamps for seduction, Donald Duck lamps, goose lamps, lots of lamps. Over the Muzak, Debbie Boone sang, "You light up my life," and you could tell from the brainwashed pallor of the salesmen that this was the only song they heard all day.

But I wasn't brainwashed yet. I'd simply entered this world of light, waterfalls of light, animals of light, giant squids of light. "Well, sweetheart, what can I do for you?" a bright-eyed salesman with a round belly asked.

"I want to buy a lamp."

He chuckled. "You've come to the right place." He began showing me lamps, but I knew what I wanted and spotted it right away. A five-foot-high Oriental bamboo lamp with a straight, plain shade stood out among all the tentacles and the geese with marked serenity. "I want that one," I said.

When I handed the salesman my check and driver's license, he looked at me, stunned. "Come on, you can't be over twenty-two. I thought you were handing me your college I.D."

"I'll never see thirty again."

"I don't believe it." He scrutinized me under all that light. "How do you do it? Special diet? Exercise?"

"It's all mental," I said, pointing to my head.

I walked along Columbus Avenue carrying my lamp. People paused to admire it. I passed the flower man on the corner of Seventieth. "Hey," he called to me, "can I see that lamp? That's a real beauty. Where'd you get it?" I told him. "In that junky store? You got the best thing in the place." We talked for a minute and he told me it was a good time to buy birds of paradise. "They're just coming into season." I walked a little farther and an old woman, walking her three Yorkies, stopped and said, "What a lovely lamp!"

Everybody likes my lamp, I thought as I brought it into the house. As I dragged out the lamp it was replacing, one of those modern, space-age silver things Mark had picked out, I thought to myself that you don't buy a lamp if the world looks grim. You don't buy a new lamp if you aren't planning on looking around.

The New York Center for Urban Advancement covers two floors of the newly renovated building that houses it. The architects, the planners, and engineers work side by side in large rooms with drawing boards. Only a few of us whose work is of a more private, contemplative nature have private rooms. I am one, and Frank Atkins, the landscape architect, is another. Frank was someone we'd stolen from Skidmore and he took a cut in salary but said he had to have privacy.

I never paid much attention to the men I worked with because I was married to Mark and then I was with Sean. But after I bought the bamboo lamp, I began to find excuses to go into Frank's office. He was more than happy to show me how to take a brick-filled playground that doubled for a garbage dump and turn it into a little rock garden. I brought in some working drawings for a group of renovated, burned-out fifty-unit dwellings whose roofs, once our contractors put them back on, I intended to turn into sunbathing and picnic areas. I asked Frank to help me with shade, and he said, "Sure, how about over dinner?"

Frank looked a little like a tree. He had green eyes and dark skin, dark hair. There was a coarseness about him. "I never really got used to living in the city," he told me as we ate seaweed in a nearby Japanese place. "I'm a country boy at heart. I guess that's why I went into landscape."

We had a lot in common. The next night we went to dinner and a Broadway play. During the play, he held my hand. His palms were a little sweaty. We saw *Loose Ends,* a play about the people of the sixties who suddenly found themselves in the seventies. "Boy," he said afterward, "I can really identify with that. We experienced life differently because of the sixties. We saw a revolution. We had a feeling of commitment."

Frank wanted us to go to Joe Allen's after the show and I said, "All right, but I want us to split it, O.K.?"

He clasped my hand. "But I like taking you out. You aren't under any obligation . . ."

"Oh, I wasn't implying that."

In the restaurant Frank pointed to the posters on the wall. "Do you know that those posters are from all the shows that flopped?" Yes, I knew that. *Mata Hari,* with Bette Davis. *Home Sweet Homer,* a musical version of the *Odyssey,* with Yul Brynner, *Dude,* by the people who brought you *Hair.* Sean and I had once sat at dinner and laughed over those flops. Over all the flops. I cursed the love that lingered, and made a decision, as the seafood combos arrived, to have a nice, simple, friendly relationship with Frank.

After dinner, we went back to my place and he thrust his tongue into my mouth. When we completed that first, breathless embrace, he said, "I wish I'd met you months ago. I've been having a hard time."

"So have I," I heard myself say.

The next afternoon, Frank was completing a rendering when I stopped by his office. "Hi," I said, leaning against the doorway, waiting to be asked in. "You sure left early this morning."

"I wanted to get an early start. Didn't wake you, did I?"

I shook my head. "You going to be working late? I thought maybe we could go out for a drink."

He was coloring a lawn a deep shade of green. "Oh, that'd

be great, Deb, but I really want to complete these drawings."

"You don't even want to grab a bite . . ."

"Naw, I'm going to work straight through." I was aware of the molding of the doorway as it pressed against my spine. I tapped it to see if I could identify the wood by its sound. Oak, spruce, pine. A cheap wood, no doubt.

For the rest of the week, I didn't approach him. Once he came into my office with half a tuna fish sandwich he couldn't finish. I knew I'd broken the cardinal rule: you should never date someone where you work. But on Friday he asked me to go out with him for a drink. We had the drink at Harry O's. Then we went to see *Mean Streets* and *The Wild Bunch* at the Quad. Then we had dinner at Scribbles in SoHo. I told myself I wouldn't sleep with him, no matter what, but when it came time to go home, he asked if we couldn't go back to my place. I thought it was a little odd, since his apartment was just around the corner, but we went uptown.

On the way, he told me he thought I was really a great person. "Oh, I think you're great too," I told him. "In fact, I'd love to see more of you."

He said it could be arranged, except for this one little problem. "You see, I've got this lady. She lives part of the time in New Jersey and part of the time with me. But when she's in Jersey, we can get together."

"Uh-huh." I didn't feel so good. I'd eaten boiled chicken, and maybe it didn't agree with me. Or maybe it was *Mean Streets*. Or maybe it was Frank. But in my old age I was growing pragmatic. I didn't want to think about Sean. I didn't want to get involved with Frank or with anyone else. But I didn't want to be alone. I decided to expand my horizons.

I met George at La Fortuna. He was eating a cannoli and had powdered sugar all over his face. I laughed, then looked down into my cappuccino. "Not easy to eat these things," he said. "Wanta join me?"

George Goldman taught sociology at Fordham and lived in the neighborhood. "I come here all the time. Best cannoli in the city."

"I like to work here in the evenings sometimes," I said.

"Oh, me too," George agreed.

We started meeting at La Fortuna at night. He brought papers to grade. I brought my maps and sketchbooks. I was seriously thinking about returning to school in design, a fantasy I hadn't had in a few years. It was easy to sit across from George and draw. George was very serious. His watery gray eyes, like pools of brackish water, his reddish beard, his wire rims, they all contributed to the sense of seriousness he exuded. "Do you know," he said once, looking around at all the homosexual couples, "why there aren't any S-and-M bars for men and women?" I couldn't figure it out. "Because men and women don't need them. It's built right into the relationship." He started to laugh, and I thought, Good, a serious man with a sense of humor.

With a little coffee in him, George was very talkative. He could talk and he could listen. He liked to talk about problems, especially mine. "Why didn't your marriage work?" he asked me the second night we met at La Fortuna. "You know, marriage is very tricky stuff. I wrote my thesis on it."

He reminded me of Mark in some ways. Mildly neurasthenic. Long, slender hands that moved all the time. Fine features. I wouldn't go to bed with him. I didn't want that. For the moment having someone to meet in the evenings at a local coffee house was fine with me. "My marriage? Why didn't my marriage work? Oh, you know. It was just one of those things that was sixty percent right and forty percent wrong. I mean, we had tons in common, but Mark was sort of . . ."

"Insensitive?"

I smiled. "Yes, he was insensitive. He was very smart. A good lover, but basically, deep down, I think he wasn't . . ." I searched for the right word describing what Mark was not, which I knew was something Sean was. "Mark wasn't kind."

"You still love him, don't you?"

"No, I don't love him." I could now say that and mean it.

"Yes, you do. I can tell. I've done research in this area." I shook my head. "It's written all over your face." I looked at my reflection in the glass. "I bet you haven't been with anyone since you and your husband split." I told him I'd been with lots of men, which was only mildly the truth. "Women," he said sardonically, shaking his head.

George didn't walk me home that night because he had an exam to write for the next day, but Lila did. That is, she walked about twenty yards behind me. I saw her at the deli and newspaper store on Columbus and she watched me as I walked by. At least I think it was Lila. She wore a fuzzy, pink angora hat, the kind I'm sure Mark would have hated, and she was reading a copy of the *SoHo News*.

I think she signaled to me as I walked past her, but I looked away. Maybe she didn't signal me. Maybe I just wanted her to. I remember how Sean used to tell me I should just go up to her and tell her what I thought of her. But instead I picked up my pace. I knew she was behind me but I didn't want her to catch up. I didn't want to talk to her. As I crossed Columbus, I saw her reflection in the window of a store. The pink angora hat, the thin spindly legs. I wondered what she wanted. I wondered if she knew I'd spent a night with Mark. As I walked, I decided I should turn around and talk to her. I shouldn't be afraid to confront her.

But when I turned, I saw she was gone, if she'd ever been there at all.

It was comfortable, meeting George in the evenings at La Fortuna. It was easy, and after a while I suggested we go to my place for a nightcap. Usually he wanted to go home. He always had exams to prepare, lectures to write. But one night he accepted. He fidgeted and was nervous inside my apartment. "And this is where you lived? When you were married?"

"George, listen, that was a long time ago. I'm over my marriage. I've had another serious relationship since my marriage ended." George downed his Scotch as quickly as he could and said he'd meet me the next night at La Fortuna. For a few weeks we met there regularly and from time to time I suggested going to a film, a lecture. He always had some reason why he couldn't go, and finally it struck me. I couldn't get him out of the café.

One night I asked him to dinner. I managed to pin him down to a Friday and he could find no reason not to come. I was preparing a fish casserole with sour cream sauce when the phone rang. "Oh, Deb, listen, something's come up. Have you gone to lots of trouble?" It turned out he had to teach a class for a sick friend that night, but I told him the food would keep until Saturday.

George arrived in jeans and a green turtleneck, without any wine. He poured himself several double Scotches and managed to get drunk enough to sit still for dinner. I put on Charlie Parker and lit some candles. After dinner, he said, "Boy, I love that music. Come on over here, baby, and sit by me."

Half an hour later, George sat naked on the rug with his hands hiding his face, pressing his palms to his brain as if it were a grenade about to explode. "Look," I said, "it's all right; it really is."

"You don't understand. This has never happened before."

"So then it probably won't happen again. I wouldn't worry about it." I was putting my clothes back on.

"It's because you're so intense. I can't take all that intensity."

"George, it's really all right. Let's get some sleep."

He shook his head. "I couldn't possibly sleep here."

He went home, promising to call. I waited three nights. Then I went to La Fortuna. George wasn't there, but Lila was. That is, she stood outside in a raincoat, wearing that same pink angora hat, and she stared in. It suddenly occurred to me that

she was looking for Mark. Just as I realized that, she saw me.
My heart pounded as the two of us made eye contact for the
first time since I'd learned she was sleeping with my husband.
But then she got a startled look in her face, and before I knew it,
she was gone again.

I buzzed Sally when I got in and we sat down to have a
drink. "So," she said, "how's it going? You look better."

I shook my head. "I'm better, I think."

She looked at me, puzzled. "You're not better?"

"The woman Mark lives with is following me."

"Are you sure?"

I shrugged. "I'm not sure. I may be going nuts. That's
another possibility."

"And Sean?"

I sighed. "Nothing. I think about him all the time."

"Maybe you should call him. And call her while you're at
it."

"I know I should. Everyone says I should . . . So tell me,
what's new?"

"Roger called me." Roger is a man Sally used to live with.
"He's going out with my sister. Isn't that incredible? He's left
the monastery and is dating my sister. So I called her and
asked what she thought she was doing. She asked me, 'Do you
mind?' I said damn straight I mind. So she told Roger she
wouldn't see him anymore. So now he calls me and wants to
see me. The slime."

Whenever I wanted to feel better about my life, I knew I
could always talk with Sally.

A few weeks later I met a man named Samuel on a
crosstown bus and he asked me out. He was doing his residency
in sports medicine at New York Hospital. We started talking
because there was an old woman sitting across from us,
dressed like a baby in bonnet and diaper, nursing from a bottle.
"You meet all kinds," he said to me. Samuel took me to dinner
a few nights later at the Saloon, where the waiters serve you on

roller skates. He ordered a caesar salad and asked the waiter to hold the anchovies. The waiter thought it was one of the funniest things he'd heard in weeks. "And man," he said, "you hear some pretty funny things in this job."

After dinner Samuel invited me up for a drink. He lived at Lincoln Towers in a studio and he had a huge poster of an orangutan over his bed. He had a large Snoopy doll with a stethoscope around its neck. Samuel told me his specialty was going to be the Achilles' heel, and we spent the rest of the evening looking at the x rays of famous athletes' mutilated tendons. As he walked me toward Broadway, a mouse ran across the sidewalk. "Aren't you going to scream?" he asked me. "I thought girls always scream when they see mice."

I decided to stop at La Fortuna before going home to see if George was around. I just wanted someone to talk to. I walked in and he was sitting alone. "Hi," he said, "I was hoping you'd call."

"I thought you were going to call," I replied.

"Well, I was hoping you'd call to apologize."

I wrinkled my eyebrows. "Apologize for what?"

George stiffened. "Well, I think we both agree it was your fault. I mean, you were acting like a very threatening woman the other night."

I'm not sure why I hadn't noticed before that he was crazy, but I considered myself fortunate to have gotten away unscathed. "George, all I did was invite you to dinner."

"Well, you were very pushy."

So I apologized. Not so much to George as to myself. I said, Please forgive me. I'm sorry for what I've done. I canceled my cappuccino and assured George I'd see him around. I walked out. It was almost the end of March and I'd spend the spring, the summer, alone. I'd never spent those seasons alone before. I walked on Columbus past florists and pet stores, past all the zillions of mediocre restaurants. I walked past all the possibilities of human creatures eating together. Men and women,

women and women, men eating together, women and men, gay people, straight people, people who had their kids on weekends, people who'd never have kids, kids with other kids, old people, tired people, miserable people, people who had it all, people who'd never appreciated what they'd had.

I walked among them like an invisible alien. I felt the pavement, hard and resistant beneath my feet. Something terrible was missing. There was some empty pit inside. It had a name. It wasn't home and it wasn't Mark. It wasn't having a lover. What I missed was simply a friend. A pay phone stared at me. I found a dime and called. A woman answered. "Is Sean there?" I asked, not really caring very much what her relationship with him was.

"No, who's this?"

"An old friend. Do you expect him?"

"Not really. He's away. Who's calling?"

I told her there was no message and I hung up. If he was with someone else, I didn't want to bother him. I hadn't been too much help to him when we were together. Maybe I really did love him, I thought as I wandered home. Maybe when you really love someone, it's very subtle and doesn't hit you over the head. Whatever it was, it would be a long time before anyone else meant to me what he did.

When Jennie called to tell me she had to get away from Tom, I told her Lila was following me. Neither of us really believed the other. She said Tom had not been the same since she'd spent time with Zap, and I told her that when I went to certain places in my neighborhood, Lila was there. Jennie had begun her class in microbiology, and we decided that the next time her class met, she'd spend the night with me.

If she hadn't waved, I'm not sure I would have recognized her. She wore a long skirt, boots, and she dragged a canvas bag. When we sat down to eat, I noticed she'd bitten her nails down to the quick. "So," she said, "tell me."

I didn't really want to talk about myself. I wanted to hear about her, but in the end I understood that I needed to talk about Sean. "I guess if I talk about Lila, I'd better talk about Sean. You don't know about it, do you? We went to California."

Jennie interrupted. "We saw him recently. He told us some of what happened. At least he told me. I'm not sure he and Tom are talking very much."

"Did he say anything? About me?"

"Yes." She paused. "He asked about you. I think he's very upset about what happened. I also think he got hurt, somehow."

I wanted to know all the details. "So how did he look? Is he the same?"

She laughed. "Well, he's shaved his beard. And I think he's gotten chubby."

I wanted her to tell me more. "But what did he say about me?"

She hesitated. "It was difficult to talk with him. He . . . he wasn't alone."

"Oh." I tried to appear nonchalant. "Who was he with?"

"Oh, I think it was just a friend. In fact, I think he's recovering. He told me he'd had some bad months."

Suddenly I felt very fat. "Jen, do I look fat? Have I gained weight?"

She laughed. "You look terrific. Are you kidding?"

"But am I still attractive? I feel so ugly."

Jennie held my hands in hers. "What happened with you two?"

I shrugged. "Well, I think the straw that broke the camel's back was he walked in on me and Mark."

"Oh." She widened her eyes.

I described to her the basic logistics of that night. "It wasn't the greatest. The problem is, well, I was slow to come to my senses. Too slow."

"Maybe it'll just take him a while to come around."

"I want to see him."

She shook her head. "You know what I'll never understand about you? Why don't you just call the people you want to talk to on the phone?"

I sighed. "I did call him. A woman answered."

"So what? That doesn't necessarily mean anything." She thought for a moment. "He's not here now anyway. He went back to L.A. But I don't see why you can't contact him."

I maneuvered the conversation to get her to talk about herself and Tom. "Please, tell me what's happening with you."

"Oh," she said, "where should we start? He leaves for work at six, comes back at ten o'clock at night. Never talks to the kids, never talks to me. I've tried to get him some help. I phoned a local shrink and made an appointment, but he wouldn't go." We had left the restaurant and were walking back to my place. "The only thing he ever asks me is what really happened with Zap. He's driving me crazy. I'm ready to leave for good."

The next night Tom called. "Hello, Debbie," he said to me rather stiffly. "Is my wife around?" His voice had a very cold, mechanical ring to it. I was on the phone in the kitchen and shouted for Jennie to pick up in the bedroom, which is what she did.

When Jennie got on, I was about to hang up when I heard Tom say, "Zap's there, isn't he? You lied to me again."

"Tom, you are going to drive one of us completely nuts."

"Tom," I cut in, "it's just me and Jennie. I'm getting off now."

"No," Tom said, "don't get off. I know you're both lying to me. I know he's there."

"Tom, would you please stop it." Jennie spoke with a great deal of control. "You're drunk and you don't know what you're doing. I think you need help."

"You're right, Jen, I probably do need help, but it's probably too late for that. But I have something for you. Something you're going to remember all your life." From somewhere in the state of New Jersey, there was the sharp, amazingly clear blast of what I knew was a gun going off.

For an instant there was silence. I think Jennie and I had both screamed, but after that there was silence. Then Jennie began to talk, slowly, softly. "Tom . . . I am not having an affair, but you are going to have to get some help. Tom, I want you to tell me you're all right."

And then I heard a very soft voice say, "I'm not all right."

Jennie sighed. "Good. I mean, it's not good, but it's good you haven't hurt yourself. Now, listen, can you just sit there? I'm going to get in the car and drive home and I'll be there in two hours. Can you wait two hours?"

"I can wait two fucking hours. I'm drunk as a skunk."

"I know you are. I can tell by your voice. Now you just sit still."

"I'm going with you," I said.

We got in the car and drove quickly. "Maybe he'll get help now. Idiot. If he doesn't get help, I'm not staying with him, that's for sure." It amazed me that I hadn't understood how much he meant to her until just then, as we headed back to the farm.

When we pulled up to the house, it was all dark, except for one light coming from the den. Inside the den, Tom sat alone in an armchair, a gun lying on the desk, staring into space. Jennie rushed in. "Are you all right?"

"I'm all right." He nodded numbly.

"What the hell were you trying to prove?" She folded her arms across her chest.

"I think I was trying to get your attention."

Jennie shouted back at him. "Well, why don't you find a more constructive way to get my attention?"

I didn't really want to participate in this, so I walked back to the living room and sat on the sofa. It was dark as I looked around. I stared at the spot where I'd first seen Sean, standing in the corner, Coke glass in hand, looking bored with us all.

Tom's voice rose from the den. "I never was good enough for you. You always wanted someone better. My family wasn't good enough for your family. My grades weren't good enough for your family."

I wandered through the darkened house. I didn't want to listen to their fight, really. I walked down the corridor to where I'd slept. The bedroom was orderly, the bed neatly made. There was no trace of us here. I went back into the living room, hoping I'd see Sean really standing in the corner, sipping his Coke. I guess Roxanne was right; I guess it all is a question of timing. I looked into the dark corner again where I'd first seen Sean. This time I saw a form, moving, and I saw eyes, bright, glistening eyes, staring at me. Actually I saw two pair of eyes, and I walked closer to the corner. "Hello," I said, "who's there?"

I was moving closer to where the eyes stared at me. I heard muffled sounds, tiny voices whispering. When the light was switched on behind me, I spotted two children in their pajamas, huddled in the corner.

"What're you doing up?" Jennie said. She walked across the living room. "Huh, what're you doing here?" At first I thought she was angry but then I saw she wasn't. She hugged them and made them come out and meet me. "Melissa, Cory, this is Deborah Mills. She is my old friend. I told you about her." Melissa, who was perhaps eight and very ladylike, stepped forward and shook my hand. Cory gripped a blanket and nodded his sleepy head. He had dark, soft eyes and couldn't have been more than six.

Tom walked into the room. "Why aren't they in bed?" He did sound angry but then he noticed me. "Debbie . . . I didn't know you were here."

"Oh, I just came along for the ride." He looked embarrassed. "It's really all right," I told him.

Jennie said she was going to take the kids to bed, but Cory

started to cry. "You must've scared the daylights out of them," Jennie said. "You're going to get some help."

Tom nodded. "I said I would." He spoke softly.

Melissa gave me a kiss good night and Cory hid his face in his mother's shoulder as Jennie took them upstairs. Tom looked at me, a blank expression on his face. "I don't know what to do," he muttered. "We'll get some help."

Jennie came downstairs a few minutes later. "They went right back to sleep. I told them you had to shoot to scare a dog away."

"I didn't even know I'd woken them."

Jennie turned to me. "Can you stay the night? I can drive you to the bus in the morning."

"I have to work tomorrow."

"I'll get you there in time."

Tom slumped down on the sofa. "You're as bad as I am," he said to me. "You didn't know a good man when you saw one. He was a terrific man. You just pushed him away. One of the best."

"Shut up," Jennie said to him.

"It's all right, Jen. He's probably right." But then I thought that if Sean was a good man for me, I'd probably see him again.

In the morning I got up for the early bus, which would get me into the city before nine. "Are you sure? Can't you stay?" Jennie kept asking.

I shook my head. Cory, Melissa, and Aretha Franklin all piled into the station wagon. I kissed Tom good-bye and Jennie drove me to the bus stop. "So," I said to her as we waited for my bus, "what're you going to do?"

Jennie looked at the station wagon, full of kids and the drooling black dog. "I don't know what else I can do. I'm going to give it another try. It's never easy, I guess . . ." Her voice trailed off. She paused and turned to me. "Have you thought about what you're going to do?"

I thought about it for an instant as my bus pulled up. "I think I'm going to look for Sean."

14

M Y ENCOUNTER with Lila occurred at the same time that my SAP project was terminated. I'm not certain which event surprised me more. I had, after all, been designing and writing specifications for a slum renovation project for the past several years. Mr. Wicker came into my office carrying a bottle of rum one night as I worked late, and for once his hair was out of place. He put down two glasses. "No, thanks," I said. "I have miles to go."

"You know," he began, "I admire your work more than anyone else's work here, I think. It's not only your design work. It's your reports. They read like poems, epics really. The way you talk about the neighborhoods, the people who live in those neighborhoods."

I was expecting a raise from the way he talked, but instead he told me that the City Council had terminated funding for my project, my unit, and, by extension, me. Mr. Wicker offered to buy me dinner but I told him I still had work to do. Whether the South Bronx Area Development Project would be built or not, I could finish it on the drawing boards. He said I should take my time. He was giving me a month's notice and hoped that soon he'd find a new project for me. I told him I'd been thinking of going back to school in design anyway, so perhaps the timing was right.

Even in the heavy spring rain, I could see it was Lila standing across the street at the bus shelter. She did sometimes work at the courthouse, so it wasn't impossible that she'd be standing there in front of my building. But somehow I felt certain she was waiting for me.

When I walked outside, she looked up, and for a moment she didn't show any sign of recognition. But then she waved. Actually, it was more a beckoning than a wave, and I simply turned and walked away, heading toward the subway. "Debbie," she called, "please wait." I saw her cross the street in the rain. I kept walking. "Debbie," she called, "please."

But I really had nothing to say to her and no interest in talking to her. If she wanted to ask about when we were getting divorced, she could talk to Mark. And there wasn't anything else for her to discuss with me. I walked for a block or two, but then I remembered Sean's advice to me. Why didn't I just tell her how I felt? But I didn't want to tell her. I didn't want to give her the satisfaction. I walked on until she caught up with me. "Debbie, please, I have to talk to you." She touched my arm. The only thing that kept me from smashing her in the jaw was a strange and evolving sense that you don't follow your lover's soon-to-be ex-wife down dreary Manhattan streets in a March rain unless you are desperate enough to think that someone else may provide you with answers you can't find for yourself.

For some reason, which in retrospect looks ludicrous to me, I tried to act as if meeting her were the most natural thing in the world. "Hi, Lila," I said when she finally caught up with me. "How are you?"

She wore a brown raincoat that matched her hair. "Oh, look." She fumbled for words. "Are you going anywhere now?"

"No, as a matter of fact, I've just been fired from my job."

"Oh, I'm sorry. That's terrible, isn't it?"

I shrugged. I wasn't going to give her an inch. I have played many parts, but the martyr at that moment suited me best.

"Do you have a few minutes? Could we stop somewhere and have drinks? Or maybe eat something?" I didn't say anything. She sighed. "I'd like to talk to you."

"I don't think there's really anything to talk about, do you?" I could not contain myself any longer. "I mean, a year and a half later, a year and a half after my husband tells me he's involved with you, you decide you want to talk. Do you have any idea how long that is, how much time has elapsed? Well, you're a little late. There isn't anything to talk about."

She looked up at me. "Believe me, I understand how you feel . . ."

"Oh, you do? And how do you understand that? Do you know we come from the same home town? We went to the same high school? Do you know that you've never once had the nerve to come and say to me you were sorry? Do you know that I lived in dread and fear of running into you, like that night down in the Village? I don't know what to say to you. I wouldn't know how to greet you. How do you greet the woman you've known since solid geometry class, who broke up your marriage? I mean, I used to get on the 104 and say to myself, What'll I do if I run into Lila? What'll I say? 'Have you seen any of the old gang?'"

For some reason, she was still listening, her head bowed, and I just went on. "All you had to do, just once, was come to me and say, 'I'm sorry it worked out this way. I didn't plan it.' So what if I would have gotten angry, and screamed? You know what? I'll tell you something that you may or may not believe. There's no one in this world I have held a grudge against, no one in this world who's enraged me, the way you have. So I'll go to my grave with that grudge. And I hate it. I hate the grudge more than I hate you. It takes a lot of energy to hate someone, to stay angry at someone. And I've spent months thinking about how to get back at you, because not only did you ruin my marriage, but you managed to get in the way of the next relationship as well . . . I'm sick of hating you, I'm sick of being afraid of running into you. So let's drop it. I don't have anything to say except if you'd been a halfway decent person, if you'd come to me months ago and told me you were wild about Mark and couldn't help yourself, I wouldn't have been walking around with this open wound . . . It's just something I'll never be able to forgive."

I waited, my hands poised as if I could go for the throat. And then I heard the words come out of her mouth. "I'm sorry. I really am sorry . . ."

"I appreciate your saying that and I'm sure it wasn't easy for you to say that. But it's just a little late. You see, I don't really care anymore. It's this stupid thing about life. We always get the thing we would have given anything to have when we don't need it anymore. Anyway, I'm sure you haven't been following me around for the past few weeks to say you were sorry."

She rubbed her eyes as if she had a sinus headache. "The first time I ran into you it was an accident. But this time, well, I was waiting for you. I called your switchboard and they said you were leaving."

I couldn't believe her. "Why didn't you just call me? Why didn't you just get on the phone like a normal person and say you wanted to talk?"

"Why didn't you just call me all these months and tell me to drop dead?" She was raising her voice. "Do you know how many times I picked up the phone to talk to you? Do you think I've felt good about what happened? I didn't start seeing Mark until he told me you were going to split. Every time I asked if I should talk with you, he said there wasn't anything to talk about."

I shouted back at her. "Do you need a man to make up your

mind for you? You can't figure out the right thing to do by yourself?"

She shook her head. "Please. There's a little Italian restaurant nearby. Couldn't we just go over and sit down?"

I was undecided. I was also curious about what she had to say, so I told her I'd go with her. We both ordered linguini with clam sauce and a bottle of white wine. Lila wore a dark suit with a red and white polka dot shirt. With her hair pulled back and in that suit, she looked like a flight attendant.

She ate her linguini daintily with a fork, twisting it into a spoon, and she managed to eat without so much as a slurp. By contrast, I just burrowed a hole and dug in, sucking in the strands I couldn't manage to twist onto my fork. "God," I said, "how do you eat it like that? I make such a mess when I eat pasta."

In the middle of that admiration, she dropped her fork and covered her eyes with her hands. "Oh, my God," she moaned. "I'm so miserable."

That came as a surprise. I thought it was guilt that had driven her to talk to me, but now I saw that she was as tormented and distraught about him as I'd ever been. "Is he acting that way again?" I asked softly.

She didn't need encouragement. "He says it's his caseload. Then he says it's you, then it's me. He goes into these funks. He'll stop talking for hours at a time. And then all he'll talk about is . . ."

"The Supreme Court decisions of the week." I filled in the blank, and she nodded. This was no panther in heat, no queen of the Nile, none of the impossible things I'd imagined her to be. She had not beguiled Mark with incredible tales and Kamasutra-studied sex. She was just another person with all kinds of person-related problems, a Brownie from my own Brownie troop, a woman I'd learned to hate and now, suddenly, to pity.

"Yes." She looked at me, puzzled, as if she'd just found me

sitting in her living room. "And sometimes he'll be walking across the living room and I'll ask him something and he'll just, well, stop."

"You mean freeze, right? He's in the middle of doing something and suddenly he stops like a statue. That just means he's thinking. Lila, when you started seeing him, he was terrific in bed, right? A great lover. And then once you start to care, once you want to spend time with him, it all stops. He's very busy. He never comes to bed at night."

She nodded numbly. "I left a man who really wanted me. I mean, Robert wasn't glamorous or dashing, but he was a good man, and now I don't know what to do. I don't know what I was hoping for, talking to you. It's just that things were so . . ."

"Passionate," I said.

"Passionate when we started and now I just don't know. I know he spent a night with you. He told me. I was crushed. I couldn't believe it, and you know what he said? He said, 'Why not?' It was legal. You're still his wife. And then he wanted to see you. He got crazy about it. He couldn't stop thinking about you. The minute you rejected him, he went nuts."

"And so now he doesn't talk. He won't tell you anything. You feel like he's lying. He wants more space."

"Yes, he does all of that." She looked terribly defeated.

I'd finished eating all I was going to eat at that meal. "Lila, I don't know what to say. I know that when he left me, I didn't know how I'd go on, and now I'm doing just fine. I know I'll find a new job. I'm just not worried about things. You'll be all right, I'm sure."

I started to put on my coat to leave. "Would you just tell me one more thing?" She seemed to be pleading with me. "I know he spent a night with you, but do you think he'd do it again?"

"He was faithful to me for a long time. At least I think he was. Now, I don't know. I don't think I'd trust him again."

Lila nodded. I got up to leave. "Anything else?" She shook

her head. I picked up the bill but she snatched it away. "Please, Lila, let's not fight over the bill. Let's just split it, all right?"

She thought for a moment. Then she said, "All right."

I buttoned my coat. "I hope it works out, whatever you want to work out." The woman who had once seemed invincible now looked weak and small.

I held out my hand and she shook it. "Debbie," she said, "I just want you to know. I really am sorry and I wish I'd come to talk to you sooner."

"That's all you ever had to say to me," I said, and I walked out the door.

A few days before I left the New York Center for Urban Advancement, my father called. "Hi, dear," he said. "How's the weather?" I told him the weather was fine. "Well, let me tell you, we've got a terrific day in Chicago. Clear skies, a warm breeze. You'll get that weather tomorrow." Chicago always gets New York's weather a day before New York, due, I believe, to a prevailing something-or-other. "You should be getting two nice spring days." I looked out at the freezing rain that fell on a gloomy Manhattan. "It's a good thing you don't live in California," he went on. "You'd never know what the weather was going to be, unless your family lived in Waikiki or something."

"What's up, Dad?"

He announced that he'd fainted the other day. Nothing serious, but his blood pressure was a little high. "So your mother and I are going to move down to the Everglades. Well, near the Everglades."

"In the summer?" I asked. But they said they were sick of Chicago winters and arctic winds and they were going to check out now. He said he had a lot to talk to me about, but he just hemmed and hawed at the other end. "Dad, just say it."

"I . . . I understand," he stammered, "that you're looking for work."

I had told Zap not to say anything, but obviously he had. "I'm looking," I replied.

"Well, now Zap asked me to tell you it just sort of came up in conversation. I mean, he didn't make it a point to tell me, but I just mentioned that I was going to make some plans for the office, and Zap said you were looking." It took my father about fifteen minutes of this garbled dialogue to ask me to come and run the office for them. "Not permanently. Just for a little while. The summer, six months. Long enough to get work off the drawing boards. Zap said you were thinking of going back to school. You could put the money away." I was very quiet at the other end. "You can keep looking for work. Leave when you want. Stay here rent free, go to school at night. If something else comes up, you aren't under any obligation."

I thought about it for five more seconds. "No strings?"

"None," he assured me. "It's your show."

"I'll do it," I said.

It took me a little over a month to put my things in order. One of those things was divorcing Mark. When my lawyer got the papers in order, I called Mark, told him I'd sublet my place to a friend of Sally's, was going to Chicago, and that I wanted us to sign. He said he wanted to wait, but he finally agreed to meet me one Saturday morning at Didi's on Amsterdam Avenue.

"So you're going back west," Mark said as he sat down. I told him it was just for a little while. He looked around him uncomfortably. Didi's was filled with homosexual couples having brunch and complaining in loud voices about the latest failure of the New York courts to legalize sodomy; it was, I had to admit, a strange place to sign divorce papers. Mark stared at me rather grimly, the same way he'd once stared at me in a library years ago when I fell in love with him, with that same look of inexplicable sadness which now wasn't quite so inexplicable.

I handed him the papers. "Why don't we get this out of the way and have lunch?"

He looked at me, stunned. "Debbie, this isn't so easy for me, you know. It's not my idea to do this now. I think we should wait. We've been together a long time."

"Mark, I think you should understand something. There's no reason to wait. Nothing is going to change. Besides, I'm in love with someone else." It was the first time I'd been able to really articulate that to myself. I suddenly felt much more clear-headed than I'd been before. I did love Sean. Not in some mad, passionate way, but in the way that lets you want what's best for him.

I was clear-headed, that is, until right there on Amsterdam Avenue, next door to a Chinese laundry and a funeral home, surrounded by homosexual couples, two tears formed in the corner of his eyes and rolled down his cheek, and that was more tears than I'd ever seen come out of him. "Can we go to the apartment?" he said.

Once we got inside the building where we'd lived together, married, I felt terrible, too. "God, I don't know what we should do," I mumbled. "I was so sure."

He wrapped his arms around me. "You should have left me years ago."

"Oh, you were great in bed," I said.

"Was that it?" He laughed.

"We liked the same causes. We had a lot of things in common." Now I really was crying. "I guess I'll always love you."

"Well," he said, once he was certain I was miserable, "I guess we'd better sign these papers if you're going away."

I gave him the coldest stare I knew how to give. "I thought you wanted to wait?"

"Well, I don't know. I guess we should."

My fury at him welled. It had taken me years to stand on a diving board and take the plunge. Like Zap, I was born feet first and have always had a fear of doing anything head first. My mother claims I had to be yanked from the womb. But at this moment I took the pen, and without batting an eye, I signed my name. Mark was stunned. "Oh, I don't know, Deborah. Maybe we should talk."

"You," I said as perfunctorily as I could as I signed the duplicates, "are confused."

When we finished divorcing one another, Mark wanted a beer. "I'm a little tired," I told him. "I have a lot to do." He got up and stood behind me and began rubbing my neck muscles, the space between my shoulder blades. If I were an angel, I know I'd have tired wings. When stress enters my body, it always gets me right between the blades. And Mark knew that spot and went right for it. He massaged it; then he began kissing my neck. If I go to hell, it will be because I could never resist him. But this time, in an amazing act of will, my body wanting, my dignity refusing, I stood up. "No," I said, "not now."

When he got to the door, I asked him how things were with Lila. He said something about how they were "redefining what they wanted from one another."

"I saw her, you know," I said.

He nodded. "She said you were nice to her."

"She seemed distraught." I found to my surprise that I didn't care what their "redefining what they wanted" led to. "I hope things go well." I kissed him on the cheek.

I went to the window after Mark left. I wanted to see what my ex-husband looked like when he was alone. I wanted to see if he did anything strange. Anything to make me regret. What if I'd just made a terrible mistake? What if I were one of those brokers who just sold all his stocks, only to see them skyrocket?

He did do something to make me almost regret. Mark came out of the building and looked at the sky. He held out his hand to see if it was drizzling. That was something he always used to do. He paused for a second on the sidewalk, unsure, it seemed, of where he wanted to go. Then he looked up at me and nodded. He knew I was watching him. "It's all right," that nod seemed to say. I nodded back. He gave me a tiny salute and I saluted him. He turned right and I thought to myself, I wonder where he's going. And then he was gone.

I sat down at my desk, which was right by the window, uncertain myself of what I wanted to do at that moment. Then I took out some stationery and an envelope. I addressed the envelope first and then wrote *Please forward*.

I'd written Sean dozens of letters in my head but I hadn't tried to put any on paper until just then. "Dear Sean," I began. "I've just signed my divorce papers and thought I'd drop you a line." I tore it up. "Dear Sean, I'm not sure if you want to hear from me or not, but . . . I tried to call you once and a woman answered." I tore it up.

Then I wrote the letter I eventually mailed:

Dear Sean,

I'm leaving for Illinois in a few days. The city finally gave up on my SAP project, though I haven't, and they closed my unit. My parents are moving to the Everglades, of all places, because of Dad's blood pressure, and he asked me to take over his office. I don't know what they're going to do down there with all the alligators and flamingos, but they want to give it a try. I've sublet my place and am also going to give the office a try for about six months. I'm also thinking again about my M.A. in architecture. We'll see.

I tried to phone you a couple of times but you weren't in. I wanted to tell you that I'm sorry about so much that happened between us. I wish we had met later, after I'd had more time to recover. But this is by no means to excuse my ridiculous coast-to-coast behavior. It's just that it's taken a while for me to realize how important you are to me, how much I care for you as a friend, a person, a lover. I made a lot of mistakes and I guess this is why I'm writing. I want you to know that you shouldn't take the things that happened between us personally. If I acted the way I did, it's not because you did anything wrong. I just wasn't ready. It's important to me that you understand that.

214

I'm divorced now and I feel relieved. I feel, in fact, a sense of peace. I saw Jennie, by the way. They aren't having an easy time but they seem committed to trying. I suppose having children makes a huge difference. They asked about you and they also told me they'd seen you. I hear you shaved your beard.

I just wanted you to know I'm thinking about you and I hope you're doing well. You must be almost ready to distribute Minor Setbacks, *so I'll look for it. I'm not sure where I'll be staying in Chicago but someone will forward mail from here or you can phone me at Mills Associates. I miss you,*
Love,
Deborah

I waited a day or so and then mailed it, thinking I'd hear from him soon. But it would be months before I'd hear anything.

And so I left the East, not because I didn't like it, but because it had confused me and I had things to unravel. The Midwest, for all its tedious flatness, has never told me a lie, but the East was filled for me with distortions. And so, like the career soldier on a brief furlough from the wars, I headed home.

15

CHICAGO is the chewing gum capital of the world and we Chicagoans cling to one another with a certain banal stick-to-itiveness. They gave me a hero's welcome home. My parents invited everyone who'd known me since before I was born.

Renee and her husband, Eddie, the periodontist, were there with their three children, Wendy, Sam, and Jody. Renee had grown rather chunky, and that once rounded Renoiresque body was on the verge of fatness. Eddie, who'd always been built rather tall and broad-bottomed, with a long, spindly neck, looked more like an ostrich than I'd remembered.

My parents had also invited my great-aunts and great-uncles. My great-uncles, Irv and Al, were twins in their nineties who'd been born in Russia, but all they remembered about it was the mud. My uncle Al, however, remembered the entire industrial revolution from the invention of the incandescent bulb to the airplane, the car, the flush toilet. "You know what killed my uncle Mort?" he said. "The flush toilet. He was ninety-five and he used to run down the stairs to the outhouse all day. Then they put one toilet in the building, so he dies of constipation, waiting in line." Uncle Al also recalled perfectly the Wright brothers' first flight.

What he couldn't remember was my marital status. "So, where's that husband of yours? The lawyer?"

"Oh, he couldn't make it today, Uncle Al."

Uncle Irv told him to shut up and mind his own business.

My parents had invited all my cousins, including two who weren't speaking due to some minor litigation no one could discuss. They invited people who remembered me when I was "this" big and people who were sure I couldn't be a day over twenty. And then there were the Applegartens, the Baumgartens, the Snares, the Shears; there was my parents' canasta club, my father's golf group, the Women's Board of the B'nai Emet Hospital.

It was the end of May and my parents had thrown open their town house in old Rogers Park, and all day Sunday people filed in and out, people I often didn't remember. A nearby deli had made huge trays of smoked fish and finger sandwiches, and I felt somehow, in the face of the jovial people trying to have a good time, that I'd arrived in town just in time for my own funeral. "Look," my mother said to me, "look who's here." She brought over a woman I'd never seen before. The woman looked at me and clasped her hands across her large breasts. "Deborah," she said. "Oh, I remember you when you were this big," and she cupped her hands as if she were holding a loaf of bread. "You were such an itsy-bitsy thing."

My father called me to the phone. "Your brother." Zap called from downstate and said he'd be up to see me soon. He had a new girlfriend named Brenda, who was just "a living doll," according to my father. Zap put Brenda on the phone. She giggled and said, "Gosh, I don't know what to say," and handed the phone back to Zap. "See you in a week or so, O.K.?" I said O.K., as Renee motioned for me to come say good-bye to someone I didn't remember having said hello to.

Before Renee left, she asked me, "Where are you going to stay while you're in the city?" I told her I'd assumed I'd stay with our parents. "What are you?" she said. "A real live masochist? Why don't you stay with us for a few weeks?" I told her I'd think about it.

While Dad drove my great-aunts and uncles back to their nursing homes, Mom put on a tape recording that hypnotized her so that she wouldn't eat. "You are fat, you are disgusting. You will eat only one can of water-packed tuna a week. You will not eat lamb chops. You will not eat more than six ounces of chopped beef . . ."

When Dad got home, Mom turned off her recording. We all put on our robes and settled down to watch "The Rookies." In the middle of the car chase, Dad said, "Marge, have you seen her feet?"

My feet? What was wrong with my feet? I followed my parents' gaze as each grabbed a foot and examined it with some care. "Ooh," Mom said.

"What is it? Warts? Fungus?"

"Calluses," Mom proclaimed. "Just look at those calluses."

"I walk on them," I offered by way of explanation.

"When was the last time you had a pedicure, young lady?" my father asked.

I couldn't remember ever having had a pedicure. So Dad said, "Marge, get her a pedicure this week."

"Not at twenty-five dollars, I won't."

Before I knew what was happening, my parents had procured towels, cuticle scissors, Pretty Feet, a steel scrub brush, nail clippers, and manicuring tools. "I don't know how you can even walk on these feet," my father said. Before I could think to protest, my parents revealed the dark, cracked crevices of my toes, my feet, feet that had always managed to get me where I needed to go, feet that had never been criticized before, examined before, the one part of me that had somehow managed to get away unscathed, now being pumiced over.

They systematically went to work. My mother applied creams and scrubbed calluses. My father worked on the nails, trimming, oiling, snipping away. And so I sat, amazed, a drawn-and-quartered child, almost the same age as a long-playing record, having her feet studied and cleansed by two aging parents who cannot ask or tell anyone about her divorce, who pretend she does not have lovers, and who have resigned themselves to retirement among the 'gators of the Everglades.

"My God!" my mother said. "You've got potatoes growing under these nails. Cauliflower. Look at that, Howard." She displayed some crud she'd discovered under the nail. Howard shook his head, disconsolate. No wonder she got a divorce, no wonder her marriage didn't work out, he was thinking. Whose could, with all that dirt under her toes.

My parents had almost finished with my feet, and they looked forlorn as they shook their heads back and forth. But in an odd way, this made them happy. This made them feel needed. So I let them clean and prim my feet as they'd once done my bottom. With all the skill of an ancient mother, my mother put large dabs of Vaseline between my toes. Then she rested my feet on a towel. "Now," she said to my feet, "don't move." She disappeared somewhere into the kitchen and returned a few moments later with plastic bags and rubber bands. "What're you going to do with those?" I watched with some amazement as they stuffed my feet into the Baggies and closed them with rubber bands.

"So you don't get grease all over the place," my mother said.

That night as I drifted to sleep, my feet still in plastic bags which I'd tear off in the middle of the night, I listened to the distinct voice of my mother's rasping hypnotist. "You are fat, you will eat only . . ."

The next morning I went to a nearby audio shop and bought a set of headphones to go with my mother's tape recorder. She was very pleased to receive them, and like some lobotomized roller skater she drifted through her domestic chores of the day, in a TM-type trance, mumbling from time to time to herself, "I will not eat lamb chops."

Renee, "the revolutionary," as our parents once referred to her, lived in a prefabricated house in a development outside Downers Grove. She and Eddie had taken a lot of care in picking the right place to live. They wanted a neighborhood where the taxes weren't going to go sky-high but where the public schools were as good as the private schools, without busing. "What's the sense of paying school taxes if you can't send your kids to school?" was the extent of Eddie's commitment to political thought.

Renee, however, was active in the PTA, and on Saturdays Eddie was a scoutmaster, which he considered to be his civic duty. "What's the sense of having kids if you don't spend time with them?" was Eddie's theory of child-rearing. You could hardly tell the house was prefabricated. It had been well landscaped, with lots of shrubs and a cherry tree. Any time Eddie thought one of the kids wasn't telling the truth, he'd point outside and say, "Remember about the father of our country and the cherry tree."

Things hadn't always been so sweet and simple for Renee. When she was very young, she was the perfect child. She played the piano beautifully; she made her own clothes; she got straight A's. The catechism of our youth was "Why can't you be more like your older sister?" Zap and I honestly tried. We spent a lot of time trying, until we realized Renee couldn't be like Renee anymore.

"Zap got the looks and I've got the brains," Renee used to say. She stuck me somewhere in the middle of them, both chronologically and spiritually. I was the orange sheep of the family, flamboyant and obvious in my errors, which never reached the blackness of Zap's. While I bungled along after my brother, who somehow managed to stay out of juvenile court on at least three occasions, Renee, who had a reputation short of perfection, was in fact a time bomb ready to go off. The summer when my mother took off for California and Dad went out to bring her home, Renee was supposed to take care of us. While Mom and Dad thought she was cooking our meals and making us keep our curfews, Renee was phoning up for pizzas and abandoning us to our own devices while she let strange boys buy her popcorn and cop a feel in the balcony of the old Alcyon Theater, where she'd once played a piano recital of Chopin preludes.

When our parents returned from California, a concerned neighbor, trying to be helpful, informed them that things had been a bit chaotic at our house while they were away and that one morning they had found a pair of girl's underpants on their rosebush, which Renee claimed as hers. When our parents asked Renee about the incident, there flowed from the lips of the perfect child a stream of curses such as our house had never heard uttered before, hurtling my mother into incontrollable tears and my father into paroxysms of rage. Zap was impressed with her for the first time in his life, and I was stunned.

Mom said she'd been such a terrific kid, and Dad threw her out of the house, a useless gesture, since she was already in her junior year at Stanford and hardly ever home. She told him that "the revolution was coming" and that he'd missed his historic mission and was a failure to his own time. Then she hit the streets of San Francisco as a flower child. She took a flat in the Haight and painted naked men at the San Francisco Institute of Art. She sent us a photo of herself with a diamond in her nose and flowers painted on her cheeks, her frizzy black hair grown wild, like Medusa's head.

Renee wasn't going to paint flowers on her cheeks and draw naked men forever. But our parents didn't understand that. They didn't realize times were changing. Juvenile delinquents were graduating from our high school and becoming serious artists, and our prom queen had a baby out of wedlock in Big Sur. Renee went from the streets of San Francisco to a good job in public relations. She cut her hair to a respectable length and married a periodontist with a good practice in the Loop and began producing children. After three years of barely speaking, Renee and our parents resumed cordial relations, and Mom went to Eddie from time to time for gum work at cost.

After much discussion and several phone calls, everyone agreed it did make sense for me to stay at Renee's while I was in Illinois. My parents were, after all, moving to the Everglades. Downers Grove was an easy, forty-five-minute commute, when the CTA was running, to the Loop. Eddie said it would be "hunky-dory" and "if it's O.K. by her, it's O.K. by me." Well, it was O.K. by Renee, so I moved in. Renee greeted me at the door in an apron. "I could use the help," she said with a laugh, kissing me. When she hugged me, our breasts crushed against one another and I realized it had been a long time since I'd hugged my sister. Eddie was in the living room, helping Sam with his toy train, and they all seemed fairly happy to me. Eddie either knew nothing about her sordid past or, if he did, he didn't care. From the mirror they had above the bed, I suspected he may have participated in it.

For dinner my first night at Renee's she served Campbell's beef consommé with sherry and Pepperidge Farm garlic and herb croutons, instant mashed potatoes with Blue Bonnet margarine, Birds Eye frozen peas and carrots, roast beef with instant thick gravy, salad with Wishbone Italian dressing, heat-and-serve garlic bread already wrapped in foil, and, for dessert, Sara Lee brownies with Cool Whip, and Brim with Sweet 'N Low and Coffee-mate nondairy creamer. And my sister had been a vegetarian at a time when they were shooting vegetarians in this country.

After dinner Eddie said he'd do the dishes "so you girls can catch up on things." Renee helped me get settled in Wendy's room. She moved handfuls of stuffed animals out of the way and helped me put my things away. Wendy, who was four, would stay with Jody, who was eight, while I was with them. "Now, listen," Renee said to me, sounding more like my mother than my sister, "I know you've had a rough year and I know a lot has happened. So I just want to tell you, if you want to talk, that's what we're here for." She was using the royal "we." "Any time you need to say something, don't sit around in your room and mope. Come out and talk to me. Is that clear?"

I told her it was very clear. That night I was given priority in the bathroom. Sam, who was six, waited outside in his army uniform and saluted me as I went in and out. Jody set and unset her hair three times while I got ready for bed and each time asked me how I thought it would come out. She finally went to bed with huge, pink jumbo rollers all over her head. Wendy came into her room on the pretext of looking for a doll or something. She felt displaced. I'd cleared off a space for myself on her desk, and when she came in she asked me why I'd moved her things. "Oh, I just needed some room," I said. "I'll move them back when I'm done."

Wendy had wide black eyes and black hair, and as she walked toward me, her black eyes got wider. She bent over and bit my arm as hard as she could. Like some Indian being taken into the tribe, I didn't flinch. And when she was finished, she stared at me. "Why did you bite me?" I asked.

"Are you going to tell?"

I shrugged. "I don't know."

"My daddy is a dentist and he says I have a perfect bite."

I looked at the red marks on my arm. "Yes, it's very good."

"Are you going to tell?"

I shook my head. "I don't think so. Are you going to bite me again?"

She said she had to think about it and she left the room.

I hadn't forgotten and I couldn't forget Sean. Every day as I rode the CTA to work I thought about him. Every day as I looked at the bleak city of Chicago I wondered why it mattered to me at all, what city I worked in. In bed at night, I thought of him. I thought of making love to him and I wondered where he was, who he was with. I called my apartment in New York one night, and my sublessee, a dancer who was hard to reach, told me I had some bills, a few phone messages, a letter or two, but nothing from Sean. I thought about him more. I wondered if he'd gotten my letter and if he had, had he answered it. Could the letter have gone astray? Or perhaps he didn't even know I was trying to contact him.

I phoned his apartment. The woman who answered said he'd been on location out west working on a new film. I asked her if she had forwarded a letter to him but she didn't remember any letter. She didn't know where he could be reached but she said he would phone in during the week. I asked her to have him give me a call.

At night I went to bed, legs clamped tight together, because I didn't want to think of that first night, when Sean had gotten me to relax. Sometimes Wendy crawled into bed with me if she couldn't sleep, and both of us slept better. In the morning I went to work. My work consisted mostly of winding down building projects my father still had on the drawing boards and only selectively taking on new work. Two nights a week I took a class in architectural drawing at IIT, and I began applying to graduate programs in urban design for the fall.

The office was more or less the same, though the surfaces had changed. The dull gray rug in the entranceway was now a bright burgundy. Overhead spots had replaced the naked bulbs in the corridors. I worked until five-thirty or six most nights. On the nights I had classes I ate downtown. Other nights I got a ride home with Eddie. Eddie liked to talk about his work all the way back to Downers Grove. He told me about the gold crown he'd removed that afternoon, about the case of gingivitis he'd nipped in the bud on its way to becoming pyorrhea alveolaris. He told me the wonders of laughing gas and how once in a while, but not often, he liked to take a whiff.

When I could, I tried to stay in the Loop and take the CTA home later. I began working until seven or so in my father's office. It really had hardly changed at all since I was a girl and had gone in the summers to run the switchboard. Clarice O'Leary, my father's secretary, was still there, except now her hair was blue. Clarice was a good Irish Catholic and a widow, who'd lived apart from her husband twenty-five years prior to his death but who'd never had a moment's thought of infidelity. Clarice had only two points of pride. For some reason she was proud of the fact that she'd married a man descended from the family whose cow started the Chicago fire. And she was proud of the tight control she had over the office. She knew more or less how many sheets of paper were in the supply closet and how many pencils "the boys" went through in the course of a week. And she kept a hawk's eye on me.

"You're using too much tracing paper," she'd say to me. Or, "Don't put on the blueprint machine until you have ten prints to make. It's a waste to get it started, then stop." It made no sense arguing with her that I needed a certain print at a certain time. Clarice had her way. Who wanted to argue with someone with blue hair? I had to beg her to leave in the evening if I wanted to work late. Basically she wanted everyone to leave when she did so that she could lock up and make sure everything was in its proper place. "Clarice," I'd have to say to her, "I'm going to work late tonight, so I'll lock up, all right?" Eventually she'd agree.

That summer, in the evenings, I'd often find myself alone in the back of the drafting room. I can't honestly say I stayed late to work, though there certainly was work to be done. I think I was trying to put my life back together in that room amidst the drawing boards, the stools, the blueprint machine. There is something terrible yet soothing about returning to a place where you once lived. You are one of your own memories. And so, late at night, in the dim light of the twilight as the summer wore on, I thought of walking in and finding my brother, bent over Jennie. I thought how I'd once believed he'd always want to be bent over her and how he'd believed it. But desire can come upon us, then go away. I had wanted Mark more than I'd ever wanted anything and now I didn't want him at all. And I thought about Sean, wherever he was, and how much, to my surprise, I still wanted him.

One night on my way to class I decided I was becoming a creature of habit, always walking up La Salle and down Washington. I decided to alter my route and go past the Picasso statue. It was a hot night in early July and I paused to look at the statue. It was a strange, animal-like so-called woman he'd given to the city, and some people thought it was a big joke.

When I turned to cross Dearborn, I saw on a marquee the name of the film *Minor Setbacks*. It had just opened in the Loop and was playing right across the street. The theater smelled of stale popcorn and cigar smoke. I found a seat but a man started breathing down my neck, so I moved to another seat. The theater was almost empty, so I went near the back where the usher stood, and no one bothered me.

The film wasn't bad really and the story was something like what Sean had told me, but not exactly. The parallel lives of two Italian boys, one who makes it out of the neighborhood and into an ad agency in Manhattan, the other who runs his dad's pizzeria. Somewhere in the middle of the film, the ex-girlfriend of the boy who went away tries to seduce the boy, now a man, from the pizzeria. But he is a man of character. As she leans against the railing of his porch, her blouse half-opened, he understands she is just trying to get back at her former lover. She moves toward him but he pushes her away. "Listen," he says to her, "when I touch wood" — he grabs the railing — "I want to feel the wood, and when I touch cloth" — he touches her shirt — "I want to feel the material, and when I touch a woman, I want to feel that woman. I want that woman to be with me and not with someone else."

The next night I sat through the film twice in that stale popcorn-, cigar-smelling theater, listening to the words Sean had once spoken to me being repeated on the wide screen. Then I cried on the commuter train all the way back to Downers Grove. I cried as I walked from the station to Renee's house. While I cried, I decided to write to Sean directly, care of Four Tracks Films, Incorporated. This time I would receive a reply.

Shortly before they left for the Everglades in the beginning of July, my parents came to Renee's for a barbecue, one of Eddie's infinite varieties. During the summer Eddie had barbecued everything — pork, chicken, T-bones, ribs, shish-kebab, ham, corn, potatoes. Our parents arrived at one-thirty sharp. They are the only people I know who can actually manage to be early but never late. "So," said Mom, bursting into the living room, "who's glad to see Grandma? Sammy, are you happy? Jody? Where's my baby Wendy?"

"Hi, Grams." The kids waved lethargically. Mr. Rogers was on the tube.

"Aren't you going to kiss Grandma?"

The sound of a rattling motor coming up the street made me look out the window. A black and blue Volkswagen bounced to a halt in front of Renee's placid development, and Zap and Brenda got out. My brother looked thinner and he'd trimmed his hair. Brenda was small, only about five feet, and she looked like a miniature person as she walked beside him. They came up the steps laughing over something. Brenda had a camera around her neck and a box of candy in her hand. Zap toted a small pack. They had met, Zap told me over the phone, in anatomy class and shared a cadaver. He was a rather plump and pungent old man with a permanent smile on his face, nicknamed Smiley, which was coincidentally what our mother called our father.

Brenda was the eight millionth woman Zap had brought home, so it was difficult to take the relationship too seriously, but there was something I liked about her right away. Most of Zap's women were passive creatures who stretched out in chairs and moved only when he asked them to or when they somehow sensed a need of his. But Brenda was right in there, and though I'd gotten a funny impression of her on the phone, she wasn't really flaky at all. "Hi," she said, walking into the kitchen. "Are you Renee?"

"God," I replied, "do I look like the mother of three children?"

"I'm the mother of three children," my mother piped up.

"Oh, you must be Debbie. Listen, I'm sorry I was so stupid on the phone . . ."

Zap scooped me into his arms. "How's my favorite little sister?" I reminded him that I was still eleven months older than he. "Hey, guess what?" he whispered into my ear. "I'm going to marry that girl." I told him I'd believe it when I saw it.

We walked out to the backyard, where Dad was sitting at the picnic table and Eddie was getting the barbecue going. "The bees are so big out here," Dad said, "they don't sting you; they bump into you." Zap and I sat down with Dad as he proceeded to tell us how they were going to get to the Everglades. He was very proud of himself. He'd called the Triple-A and gotten all the maps. They had their reservations. "Three days, three nights, straight to Florida. We're staying in Holiday Inns all the way. One in Louisville, one in Atlanta, one in Gainesville. The Holiday Inns are right on the highway. That way we never have to leave the road."

Zap smiled at Brenda, who was snapping pictures of all the kids on their swings. "They've got these cute little country inns down in the South," I mentioned to Dad. "There's this book called *Country Inns in America.* You could stay in those kinds of places too . . ."

"What for? I don't want to stay in country inns. Stay in Holiday Inns and you know just what you're getting. You make one phone call and it's all taken care of."

"Come on," Zap said. "Let's get in Brenda's pictures." Brenda was taking pictures now of everyone with Help, Renee's dog. Why would anyone name a dog Help, Dad always wanted to know. But Renee thought it was funny. She loved it when he ran away and she could walk around the neighborhood, yelling, "Help! Help!" But Dad didn't think it was funny at all. "Just wait until something's wrong and you walk around yelling Help. Remember the little boy who cried wolf."

Eddie put a small steak and a chicken leg on Dad's plate when we sat down for our barbecue, but Dad said it was too much and Eddie took the chicken away. "You know," Mom said, "there are more carcinogens in a barbecued steak than in five packs of cigarettes." Renee frowned, knowing Dad would probably not eat after that comment. He looked at his steak and said it was tough anyway. The cat walked across the picnic table and lay down somewhere between the cole slaw and the potato salad, and when Eddie shooed her away, she knocked over Sam's lemonade.

Otherwise, the barbecue was uneventful until later, when Dad spotted a paper clip and cookie crumbs on the living room floor. "Marge," he called, holding up the paper clip, "look at this." He showed her the paper clip, somehow fallen and tucked into the thick carpeting, waiting there like some mine at the depths of the ocean since World War II to put out the eye of one of his grandchildren. On closer inspection, he found other things. Among them, a needle.

"Oh, dear," Renee, the placid mother, chirped. "Someone must have gotten into the sewing kit."

"Well, your housekeeper doesn't come until Tuesday," Dad said, "so why don't we vacuum?"

"Dad," Renee protested, "you're our guest. I'll vacuum later."

But he already had found the electric broom. "No problem. This little broom will do just fine." My father ran the electric broom in even, linear strokes across the orangish rug while

Mom stood nearby, scanning the carpet, as if they were both archeologists on some dig in a remote land. "Lotsa dirt here," Dad shouted into the kitchen, where we were now doing the dishes. "You better get a new girl. I bet she hasn't done this rug in a year."

Renee shook her head from the kitchen, as if she couldn't understand a word her Polish housekeepers were saying in the other room. Zap gave Brenda a knowing wink. But my reaction was different. I have come home from the wars and someone is exploding cherry bombs in the next room. I have spent months trying to comprehend the mistakes I made in love, and in the next room my parents are bent over a carpet, looking for paper clips.

But isn't this where longing and love began for me? In the dark coupling of this odd couple, brought together by the prediction of Gypsies, now hunched over a Model A Electrolux electric broom, vacuuming the wall-to-wall carpet in an attempt to ward off the death and destruction that lurks everywhere? I watch as the vacuum swallows hair, fur, dust kitties, crumbs, filth, rot, decay, an apple core, a dried cat turd, a semen trace, a hairpin, the deadly needle, sucking all of it into its unsuspecting canal.

As I dry Renee's earthenware china with a clammy dishtowel, it is more than I dare imagine. But somehow we are born, made. It happened, I want to shout to them over the noise of the vacuum. I am certain it happened. I have a brother and a sister and I am flesh and blood. So what was it? The stork leaving a little package at the door? Or maybe, as Zap liked to think, you did it three times and were very lucky. But what if that's not the way it was at all? What if those two people, now bending over the vacuum, trying to figure out how to open the bag because it's clogged, what if they were as filled with desire as the rest of us? What if, deep down, somewhere, they'd been as crazy as we?

My father, trying to change the bag, flicked the wrong

switch, and all the dirt he had just vacuumed fell in a large pile onto his feet. He shouted at us, "Help. Do something." For a moment Renee thought he was calling the dog but then she saw that the vacuum had unloaded itself on our father's feet. "Oh, oh," she said. "Zap, you'd better do something." But the three of us were already laughing out of control. Renee buried her face in a dishcloth and Zap motioned Brenda to take a picture.

"How do you fix this goddamn thing?" Dad called from the other room. Zap somehow managed to get the vacuum back together and Dad tried to get it to work again so that he could vacuum up the pile he'd vacuumed a little while ago. Mom tried to take it from him. "Here," she said. "You'll just hurt your back."

"What's the matter?" he retorted. "You don't think I can vacuum a goddamn rug?"

What if the vacuum turned on them, I wondered. What if it turned around and sucked them up, as if they were dust, hair? Would that free us of the past? And so what if we were free of the past? It wouldn't solve anything; it wouldn't erase the mistakes.

"Dad," I finally said, "why don't you just relax? We'll clean up that mess later."

That was when his face changed. It has perhaps been one of the worst parts of my life to watch my father's face turn from confusion to rage. "Relax, all right, you want me to relax. Nobody wants help around here, it's O.K. by me."

"We just want to have a good time today, all right?"

"Oh, and I'm ruining it, is that it?" I knew I'd said the wrong thing the minute the words were out of my mouth. "It's all my fault, is that it? It's my fault the bag opened on the floor, it's my fault someone left a needle on the floor. Believe me, if someone didn't worry about all those details, you kids wouldn't be in such good shape today."

I was twisting the dishtowel in my hands. "Why don't you take it easy. It's really not such a big deal."

Telling him what he felt was a big deal wasn't such a big deal was about the worst thing you could say. It was like telling a hypochondriac that he has hay fever and not pneumonia. It makes the hypochondriac know, if he thinks about it, that he is acting in an unreasonable way. That was when my father turned on me. He tossed down the electric broom. "All right, if you don't think it's such a big deal, if you have to decide what's important and what's not important for the rest of us, then why don't you take care of things around here? You know how to do everything . . ."

I raised my hands, imploring him. "Why don't you cool it? We're trying to have a nice day."

His face reddened; his eyes were filled with a terrible rage. "And I'm ruining it, right, daughter? I'm the one who always ruins it. Well, don't worry. I won't be around much longer to ruin it for you."

I threw down the dishtowel. "Oh, give me a break, will you?"

Renee and Zap and Brenda had long ago ceased drying the dishes and were staring straight ahead of them. I stood, glaring at my father. Eddie walked in, with Help bounding behind him. "Well, the fire's out." He beamed.

"No, it's not," Renee whispered.

"Dear," our mother cut in, "why don't we just forget it? Let's go outside with the kids while it's still light."

"I'll forget it. I'll forget it, all right." And then, turning to me, "You can do whatever you want, daughter. Go ahead. You can divorce me if you want to."

"I'm not married to you," I shouted back.

"And with your rotten disposition, you're not going to be married to anyone for a long time!" he shouted back at me.

That was when my brother intervened. He walked across

the living room in long strides and stood, his arms folded, in front of our father. Zap raised a finger and pointed it somewhere at our father's chest. "You will never" — he spoke firmly — "you will never yell at her like that again. Do you understand?" Zap stood his ground, finger raised.

And then a strange thing happened. Our father backed down. "All right, all right," he mumbled. And he walked outside.

The fight ended as all our fights end, in front of the television. Mom wanted to watch an ABC News special, but I knew they'd decided to stay a little later in order for us to make our peace. The television was to our family what the confessional was to the Catholic. The place where we were always somehow absolved. During a commercial, everyone left the room, leaving me alone with my father. Before they came back, he said to me, "Doesn't love mean never having to say you're sorry?"

Ah, my father, quoting Erich Segal to me. "O.K.," I said, "so I won't say I'm sorry."

"We're like two turtles, snapping at one another," he went on. "Well, I'm sorry."

"I'm sorry, too."

"Let's go for a walk," he said. It was a warm summer night and we walked out along the street. As we strolled, my father did an unheard-of thing. He started to talk about himself. "Listen," he began, "I want you to listen to what I have to say. I want to tell you about this dream I had the other night. I know a lot has happened to you this year. We haven't talked about it very much, but I know a lot has happened. But I want you to know something: you always have your family. Family is important. And we're here for you. I don't want you to forget that."

I told him I hadn't forgotten. "But I think if you're angry I got divorced, you should yell at me about that. Not about some vacuum cleaner."

He shook his head. "I'm not angry that you got divorced. I'm concerned about you."

I sighed. "You have a funny way of showing it sometimes."

"Listen, I want to tell you this dream. First I have to explain something. Seventy-two years ago my father bought a dry goods store in Nashville. He put every penny he had into that store, which was very stupid, because the bank wouldn't give him a loan to buy dry goods. He didn't leave any capital in the bank and he went bankrupt. But that's not the dream. The dream isn't about being poor or about the dry goods store. It's about the night before we moved to Nashville. That night we went to stay in the house of an aunt and uncle of mine. She was very fat and he was very skinny, like a toothpick. I don't remember where anyone else slept, but that night I had to sleep between my fat aunt and my skinny uncle. Well, my aunt put this comforter over me that must have weighed a ton and I was stuck there, all night, wedged between them with the comforter on top of me, and I thought I'd choke. And so seventy-two years later, I dream about the night before we moved to Nashville when I slept all wedged in with a comforter on top of me."

He paused, looking back at Renee's house, and sighed. "I don't know what the dream means. Maybe it means I feel trapped. Maybe it means I want to be a little boy again. But I'm an old man and if you'd asked me about the night before we moved to Nashville, I wouldn't have remembered it, but now I remember it as if it were just yesterday. I guess that's why I lose my temper. It's all there. My life lives inside of me," my father said. "And everyone I've known and everything I've done, it's all there. I'm an old man now and I know that."

16

THE SUMMER WORE ON in an endless torpor, a kind of
limbo of barbecues, Clarice's memos on office efficiency,
various children asleep in my bed, an alligator in a washbasin
out back. Our parents phoned every Sunday from the
Everglades to tell us about the flock of flamingos they saw,
about the house with the kidney-shaped pool they wanted to
buy. And then one day two packages arrived, containing a baby
orange tree and an alligator, both of which had managed
somehow to make it, alive, to Downers Grove, Illinois, though
the alligator would long outlast the orange tree. The alligator,
in fact, grew at a startling pace and was soon relegated to a
washbasin beside the garage, from which he escaped one August night and was never seen again.

I entered a new state of calm. I went to see *Minor Setbacks*
more times than I'd seen *Casablanca*, until I was finally certain
I was purged and Sean was a mere mistake I'd made on the
rebound. I watched him drift into the past, watched him become a memory, as far away from me as the night my father
slept between his aunt and uncle under a comforter. And when

I was fairly sure I was free and immune, I heard from him.

I walked into the office one morning and Clarice handed me a pile of tedious correspondence, bills, specifications, and a letter from Sean. I opened the letter last. It was postmarked Hollywood and dated a few days before and it was written by hand. He wrote that we had gotten our signals crossed, mostly because of his sublessee, who had not forwarded mail or given him messages and he finally had to tell her to leave. My letter care of Four Tracks had got to him at last. He had been on location in Glacier National Park, working on a new film with Hansom, and was about to co-author Hansom's next film. He had hardly been back to New York at all since we'd separated.

And then came his apology: "I want to tell you how sorry I am about the way I behaved. My reasons for leaving you in San Francisco, well, they're a little complicated, but it boils down to the fact that I was sure you were going to leave me. And I guess there's another reason that is just as important. It wasn't because you spent a night with Mark that I was so hurt. It was because you kept throwing up these walls, these huge barriers, and I just wasn't strong enough to break through. But I want you to know that I think I've understood more than you think I understood. In my way I really care for you and I'm going to try to see you soon."

It was late the next evening when I settled down to write back to him. I'd just written his name on a piece of paper when the phone rang. No one calls Renee's house after eleven. I knew when Renee opened the door in her lime-green gown, pincurlers in her hair, and told me "It's for you" that it was Sean. And then she said, "I think it's that man you don't want to talk to."

"Oh." I reached for my robe. "It's all right. I'll talk to him. I'm sorry if the phone woke you." I knew as I made my way down the landing and heard the wind rustling through the leaves that the season was going to change soon. I knew as I peered outside and saw for the first time the traces of orange and red on the edges of the leaves and the wind churning them up that we were much closer to the end of summer than the middle of it. I tiptoed downstairs, trying to remember what time it was everywhere. In New York, California. Is it daytime in Florida and nighttime in Chicago? Are the flamingos asleep, with their heads tucked under their wings? The whole country felt like this tiny, knowable place, as if my hand grasping the bannister, and my other hand finding its way along the wall, were reaching from coast to coast.

"Debbie, it's me, Sean. I guess I woke everyone."

A strange kind of peace came over me. "They go to bed early," I replied. "I'm back in the corn belt."

"Well, I'm sorry. God, I'm apologizing again."

"Yes, you are." I laughed. Nestling into the corner of a sofa, I listened into the phone. There was the sound of water, like a brook running through the cord. Or the Colorado River rushing past. But I knew it was the static from the Rocky Mountains between us. "You're still in California."

"How did you know?"

I told him I could hear the hum of cameras behind him.

"How are you?"

I curled smaller into the sofa. It was so strange to hear his voice. "I'm fine," I said. "I've missed you."

His voice was soft. "I've missed you too. God, I can't believe how it got screwed up. I had to throw that woman out of my place. She didn't forward your letter. I didn't even know you were trying to reach me."

"I'm cold," I said. The central air conditioning came blasting out of a duct over my head.

"Right now? Get a blanket," he said.

"It's long distance."

"Get a blanket." I went and got a blanket and came back to the phone. We made small talk for a while. Then he said, "I think we should see one another in person. I'm coming to New York in a few weeks and could stop over." When he said that, I suddenly felt as if I couldn't wait five more minutes, let alone a few weeks. I thought of hopping a plane to go to see him, but then I remembered he had left me in a lonely hotel in California and that it was perhaps best to proceed with caution.

We agreed he'd stop over in Chicago and said we'd talk before then. As we were hanging up, he added, "I still really care about you." And I told him I still really cared about him.

When we hung up, I sat alone on the sofa for a long time, thinking about what I really wanted to do. Renee came downstairs and sat beside me in her lime-green gown, looking terribly married, terribly settled, terribly my stout older sister. "I don't know what I want to do," I told her. "I've missed him a lot these past months, but now that I'm going to see him soon, I just don't know. I was starting to feel free again."

She patted my hand. "You don't have to decide anything right now, do you? You can see him and see how you feel."

"Oh, no," I said, "that's much too sensible."

"Come on," she said, "I'll rub your back." I turned around so that she could get to those tense muscles between the blades.

"He can stay in a hotel," I said after a few minutes of reflection. "When he gets here."

"No," she said after a brief pause, "let him stay here."

Renee kissed me good night and went upstairs. I watched her as she walked, watched the maternal sway of her enlarged hips in their lime-green smock. The same sister who had painted flowers on her cheeks and danced in the streets of San Francisco. She paused on the landing and turned around. "You going to be O.K.?" I nodded faintly. "Well, good night then."

I sat alone for a few moments. The feeling was within me that I couldn't wait another minute, that I had to have him with me right then, right that moment, or never again. I thought of that night when Sean had led me back to my apartment to make love for the first time. I thought of the night at Earl and Sandy's when he made love to me under the crazy quilt. I thought of all those nights I'd wanted him and hadn't even known it, and now, when it was far away, when it was out there but out of reach, when it was almost impossible, but not quite impossible. I still wanted it and that must say something about the way we desire.

I had worked a long hard week and was the last one to leave one Friday night. It was hot in the building and the air conditioning had been turned off earlier in the month. We were in the midst of Indian summer, that last burst of heat we get before winter sets in. I flicked off the lights and stared for a moment at the darkened drafting tables, the stools, the very spot where Jennie's back had arched over a drawing board. I thought of all the years spent playing beside the plants, the blueprint machine, the nude snapshots and pinups of girls thumbtacked to the bulletin board, where there was now a Sierra Club calendar. This was where it all began for me, and now in the dim twilight of a Friday evening I suddenly felt rather old, as if everything that was going to happen to me had already happened.

The corridor was hot and airless as I waited for the elevator. I pushed the button in sharp, impatient, staccato punches, even though I had nowhere in particular to go. At last the elevator arrived and the doors opened slowly. There were two or three aging Chicago Bears, gray-haired and paunchy, who probably did PR now for the team but who longed to make those great pass interceptions again. And then there was Sean.

"What are you doing here?" I asked him as he stepped off. I wasn't at all prepared. We did not embrace.

"You didn't get my message? I called this morning before I left. Your secretary, some crazy lady who gave me the third degree, said you were in meetings and she'd give you the message."

I sighed. "That's Clarice. She's taken to deciding what messages I should get and which ones to skip."

"Great secretary." We both stood still in the hot corridor.

"Well, here I am and I'm not going to apologize for it. Do you want me to leave or go to a hotel or something?"

"No, no." I shook my head. "Let's go back in. I'll call Renee and tell her you're here."

We went back into my father's office, but not so much because I had to phone my sister as because I needed time to collect myself. Renee, after all, had plenty of instant mashed potatoes, frozen steaks, and frozen broccoli. She had closets full of clean washcloths. My sister is a woman prepared for an invasion. But I am less well prepared. Ask me if I like surprises and I'll say sure, every kid loves surprises. But then surprise me and I'll be annoyed with the inconvenience.

I had to go back to the quiet safety of the drafting room. I called Renee, who said, "Fine, fine. He called here for you. He said he had to leave for New York suddenly. I thought he'd reach you at work."

I hung up. Sean was wandering around the office. I saw from the way he stood in a corner that he was sad, uncertain. He had flown through three time zones to find that I was totally unprepared to see him. We looked each other up and down. "Well," I said, "Renee says it's fine. You look terrific. Jennie told me you'd shaved your beard."

He ran his hand across his face. "It grew back." He looked at me, critically, I thought. After all, he had just left Hollywood, and here I was in beige slacks, a wrinkled brown shirt, my auburn hair pulled back into a pony tail, red eyes, blotchy skin, sandals, and my feet, I thought shamefully, caked with city dirt.

He stood with a leg raised, resting on a stool, his hand fondling his beard. He gazed out the picture window at the skyline of the city of Chicago. An undifferentiated mass of gray buildings, blue-gray in the twilight, lights flickering on all over the city. It was almost seven o'clock on that early fall night, and Sean was a portrait of disappointment. "I should have called and talked to you directly but I had to dash. This is some kind of a mistake. I can see that now. We just keep getting our signals crossed."

I walked toward him and touched the back of his neck ever so gently. In the kind of single, swooping gesture directors spend many takes perfecting, he swung around, an arm catching me in the small of my back, and turned me at the same time. He pressed me against a drawing board and kissed me with as much tenderness and confidence as one could expect from two terrified people who had not seen one another in a while.

We were in the middle of that embrace when the door to the drafting room opened and Clarice walked in. At first she looked frightened, then enraged. Her blue hair was the color of the evening. "Oh," she said, "I forgot the mail and was on my way home." Her mouth was full of dental packing and she sounded as if it were stuffed with marbles. "So," she said, "this is what you do when you say you're working late." And she left the office in a huff.

The kids were all asleep in their respective beds when we returned to Downers Grove, and Renee had made up the couch in the living room for Sean. They liked him right away, and Eddie got him into a game of Ping-Pong in the basement. Sean, an expert, let Eddie beat the pants off him. Renee had left the broccoli soaking in hot water and it was limp, as if someone had clubbed it to death. She threw on the steaks and whispered in my ear, "Um, he's cute."

After dinner she and Eddie discreetly wandered upstairs, expecting me to bed down with Sean on the sofa. Instead we just sat quietly, holding hands. "So," he said, after a while, "I'm kind of at a loss for words."

I nodded. "Me too. We'll talk tomorrow. There's no rush."

Sean rubbed my hands in his and agreed there was no rush. I kissed him lightly on the cheek. "I think we shouldn't sleep together. I mean, not yet. Not tonight." He kissed me back and told me he thought that was a good idea. "We shouldn't rush into anything," I went on and he kissed me again.

"Get some sleep." Sean gave me a mock order. "I'll see you in the morning."

I woke to the sound of a lawn mower, and then a Frisbee whizzed past my window. It was Saturday, and below me stretched the perfect Midwestern domestic scene. Help, the dog, was chasing Eddie, the dentist, as he mowed the lawn, his big ostrich bottom waddling by, and my nephew, Sam, was playing catch with Sean, who now appeared to me a little like the boy next door.

Sean wanted to see the city of Chicago, so, it being a weekend, I decided to take him around. We spent the morning at the Art Institute, then drove up to the Museum of Science and Industry. We rode down into the coal mine and journeyed in the submarine. We stumbled through Paul Bunyan's house and had our pictures taken in old Chicago. We watched with horror as Mrs. O'Leary's cow, the one Clarice was related to, kicked over the lantern that started the Chicago fire, and were elated when Bell Tel, through the wonders of telecommunication, saved the life of a little boy who'd swallowed a bottle of shoe polish. We looked in awe at the giant doll house of Mrs. Moore and with disgust at the bodies of embryos in bottles.

Then we entered the heart. That huge, pulsating, pumping thing whose auricles and ventricles one could walk through. We stood inside and gaped into the aorta, the vena cava, and listened to the endless, dum-dum, hypnotic beat. I have always loved this giant, pulsating heart. I am, after all, an expert in roads, and the heart is the perfect traffic pattern. I used to sit inside and listen for what seemed like hours as the beat beat and the blood pumped. It was there, inside the left ventricle, that my leg brushed against Sean's thigh and I felt something for him again, something of what I'd felt so many nights ago. Sean put his hand on my shoulder as we both listened. "I guess they must turn it off at night," Sean said.

"Turn what off?"

"The recording. I don't imagine they keep it going all night."

I was suddenly confused as Sean took my hand and led me toward the right ventricle. In my youth I came here with my class at school and we raced through as our impatient, fatigued mothers, envious of our energy, rocked on their sore feet, waiting for us to exhaust ourselves. I'm not certain why it never occurred to me in all those years that they would turn it off, that the steady sure beat was a mere recording, that it did not go on and on, into the long hours, alone in the night, in this museum, amidst submarines and fairy castles and bottled babies. It had never occurred to me that late at night this place was silent as a tomb, because for all those years I had pictured this darkened musem, this entire city, with only one sure thing, the heart that beat on and on, and not some mere recording of a heart that got switched off.

Sean put his arms around me. "Maybe they don't turn it off. Maybe they just let it go all night to keep the guards awake." When he kissed me, he felt me grow tense in his arms. I was afraid and Sean sensed it. "I don't want to put any pressure on you," he said. "It didn't work out the last time."

I kissed him back, even though something made me want to run away. My life had once been simple and clear, and now I just didn't know. Later, as we drove through the city streets, heading back to Downers Grove at dusk, tired and sweaty from a day of sightseeing, I found myself fighting against the past. I had made this trip with another man at another time. I battled back memory the way the lion tamer battles to get the wild beasts back into their cages, when in truth they should be running free in the woods. But my father had given me the answer that night at my sister's barbecue. My life lives within me. Now I knew what he meant.

That evening something changed, and it was understood he would sleep with me. That evening Renee didn't tuck me in and there was no line waiting for the bathroom. Instead, Renee and Eddie politely said good night. Sean and I tossed away the stuffed animals and pushed the twin beds together. He pulled out a joint, which we smoked in my niece's room in Downers Grove, Illinois, and a calm came over both of us. We made love on the bed with ruffles and frills and I fell asleep in his arms.

In the night I dream of a huge, white whale, swimming off the coast. I dream it beaches itself and dies a simple death of old age, no violent harpooner to bring it home, no maniac with a horrid obsession to drain it of its ambergris and oil. He just pulls up to the beach, rolls over, and dies.

I wake to find Sean on top of me, making fierce and desperate love, and to find that I am as fierce and desperate as he. I clutch him to me and bury my face in his arm and we hold one another so tightly, as if anything, a word, a sound, could make it all slip away. We are bathed in sweat, afraid that Renee and Eddie might hear, while they sleep in their smooth bed in lime-green matching night clothes, placidly, side by side.

I want to say something to him but I can't think of anything to say. I feel myself waking to things I'd thought were dormant or gone. I wish, I think as I lie in his arms, disheveled, that I knew what would happen next, the way I used to think I knew. I wish I could be sure. I wish there were no place else to go.

I prop myself up on the pillow so that I can look outside, and wrap my arms around Sean. He curls against me and I feel his beard, his warm breath on my arm. The moon is like silver. As I gaze at the clear Illinois sky, at the flat suburban lawn, I think how this is my place, this is where I'm from. I wish I could say this to Sean, who is asleep now against my arm. I think maybe I will.

About the Author

Mary Morris was born in Chicago and now lives in New York City. In 1979 her widely known short stories were collected and published in *Vanishing Animals and Other Stories*, which won her the American Academy and Institute of Arts and Letters' coveted Rome Prize. Morris has been the recipient of a CAPS award, a Guggenheim fellowship, and a fellowship from the National Endowment for the Arts. She teaches at Princeton University and is at work on a new novel.